LAST ACT OF ALL

Also by Aline Templeton

Death Is My Neighbour

LAST ACT OF ALL

Aline Templeton

St. Martin's Press ⚋ New York

Library of Congress Cataloging-in-Publication Data

Templeton, Aline.
The last act of all / by Aline Templeton.
p. cm.
ISBN 0-312-14303-6
1. Villages—England—Fiction.   I. Title.
PR6070.E49L37   1996
823'.914—dc20   96-779   CIP

First published in Great Britain by
Constable & Company Ltd.

First U.S. Edition: May 1996

10   9   8   7   6   5   4   3   2   1

To
JWR and MMR
with love and gratitude

LAST ACT OF ALL

PART ONE

1

Each time tonight, when her eyelids dropped over burning eyes, she could see the scene again, lit by memory as mercilessly as any performed under television arc-lights. His shoulders, straining the Tattersall checked shirt as he slumped across the figured walnut desk; his hands splayed in stark surprise, and his profile sharp in relief against disordered papers, the visible eye open but glassily unseeing; the back of his head –

Always, at this point, her eyes shot wide open, staring into soundless dark. Heart pumping erratically, she gulped the stale air inside the cell, her only orientation threadlines of light leaking round the edges of the peephole shutter.

The last night. Tomorrow she need not lie in darkness, confined with the hobgoblins of night. Tonight, her mind was stirring, like the Kraken, dislodging from fathomless trenches the ugliness she had buried there.

There was fear; there was rage; there was confusion; there was deathly sorrow. But she, with somewhere still a small core of fierce pride in her skill at acting these emotions, unfelt, had contrived to invert that talent. It had enabled her to banish thought, even when the key was turned in the lock, and she lay down upon the narrow bed. There was only the texture of blankets under her fingers, then oblivion, descending as heavily as a big brass poker with a shiny knob on the end.

But tonight she was feeling something, like the tingle of pins and needles, the forerunner of pain in a frost-bitten limb. Excitement – no; that suggested pleasure or happiness, emotions she had relinquished with the rest, though round the words still hung a faint, recollected fragrance. Fear, perhaps?

She had been very afraid at first, rigid, almost cataleptic in her terror, but gradually a survival strategy was born.

Every minute of every hour of every day was a discrete entity, unconnected to those gone before, or coming after. 'I will measure out my life in coffee spoons.' Her mouth might frame the words, but her mind had to learn not to trace their source.

Minute by minute, she loosened her spirit from the fetters of memory, and the tide of pain and retrospection ebbed, leaving her mind blank as sea-scoured sand.

Even the other women, whom she had feared, became blessedly remote, and they, after initial reaction to her notoriety as the woman who murdered Neville Fielding – 'Badman' Harry Bradman to his numberless fans – lost interest in the quiet, unresponsive robot she had created. This useful artefact she programmed as the perfect prisoner, learning Spanish or doing the most unpleasant kitchen chore with the same obedient indifference.

Tomorrow was an abyss of uncertainty. Tomorrow Edward, her husband, would be waiting for her. She had not thought about him, did not wish to think about him now. Yet thoughts wormed in and writhed about her mind.

Could she bear, tomorrow night, to lie with another body close, breathing, turning, intruding on her space? Could she bear his touch, or would caressing hands burn like a garment of flame?

His letters, which she opened dutifully and passed her eyes across, spoke of love, but it meant nothing now. It was a word, like happiness, from another country. The wench he loved was dead; had she loved him, even then?

She had loved Neville, when they were married, or perhaps she had hated him. There didn't, now, seem to be much difference. Helena had felt both passions, but Helena was insubstantial, like a character in an ill-remembered novel. It would be strange, being Helena again.

Or Mother.

That ultimate, forbidden thought brought her upright, in a spasm of agony. She must not lie here, while the smooth, taut, blank sheet of her mind grew rumpled and soiled.

She got up, not caring that the floor struck icy, February chill to her shrinking bare feet. Up, down, across; six steps, four steps, six steps, three to the bed. She stopped only once, when the shutter on the peephole was momentarily lifted. But no one came in, and like the polar bear going slowly mad on its apron of concrete, she resumed her pacing, four, six, three, six again.

But she was used to confinement. Perhaps her whole life had been a restricting process, forcing her into smaller and smaller spaces, till she was nothing but a tiny wooden doll, coffined at the heart of it.

In the mirk of the February morning, the meagre-faced clock on the gatehouse of the women's prison showed eight o'clock, and as it began a tinny chime the postern in the huge black gate began to open.

The figure that appeared, a carry-all in her hand, was small and slight. Her hair was silver-blonde slipping imperceptibly into grey, unskilfully cut into a longish bob.

As she surveyed the world outside, her gaze was almost blind; a blank, incurious stare from shadowed eyes huge in the pinched peakiness of her face.

She stepped over the deep sill and turned blunderingly to her left. She was wearing a suede jacket and an expensive tweed skirt: good clothes, but the skirt hung in folds as if bought for a larger person, and the drooping jacket was creased by folding.

A Rover, not new, but well-polished and maintained, was parked on the other side of the street. A man was climbing out of it and hurrying towards her, a tall man, but otherwise nondescript; thin-faced, with light brown hair receding at the temples.

He didn't look exactly exciting, and she didn't look exactly excited, stopping short of the step that would have taken her into his arms.

He said, 'Hello, darling, how are you?' then bent forward to kiss her lightly on the cheek.

Sensing her withdrawal, Edward acknowledged withdrawal in himself. She was his wife, his own Helena, of course, but she looked so – so strange, thin and ungainly, with a disturbing emptiness in her eyes, and even – though perhaps he imagined it – with a faint whiff of the prison smell about her. He had experienced this flicker of revulsion before, when he had visited her, but believed he had ignored it.

He relieved her of her bag, then grasped her elbow to escort her across the road. He might almost have been collecting her from the London train.

'Edward. Thank you for meeting me.' Helena turned up the corners of her mouth in a smile, as if someone had instructed her that this was how it was done. He could feel her shaking, her arm fragile as a chicken's bone under his fingers.

The car was warm; he settled her in the passenger seat as solicitously as if she were an invalid, then got in himself.

A small, cold fear was edging itself into his mind. What if the experience had left her permanently unbalanced? How would he, with what he himself would have described as a thoroughly normal English distaste for any kind of untidy emotion, cope with a wife who was not – normal?

There was nothing new about human life presenting problems, and over the centuries useful strategies had been devised for coping with them. You couldn't change the past, so agonizing messily and uncontrollably over the whole thing wouldn't help. Like spent nuclear fuel, it had to be effectively sealed off, dumped and forgotten, if you didn't want to find that the contamination had spread.

Social structures were there to take precisely that sort of strain, to help you keep your life within your control. It might not be feasible to put things back exactly as they had been, but by following the rules, you could avoid violent and unproductive change.

Which made sense. If he smashed one of his Chelsea teacups, he wanted it repaired as perfectly as possible, even if there would always be some hairline cracks. It wouldn't help to start from the pieces and try to make a wholly inadequate milk-jug instead.

But the image made him wince. It was her beauty he ached for, the perfection that had drawn him to her in the first place. Beauty was rare in Radnesfield, which was perhaps why it meant so much to him; he had thought himself the luckiest man in the world when she had agreed to marry him. The way she looked now provoked not admiration, but pity.

And guilt. His responsibility was to protect her; he had failed, and all he could do to compensate was to try to restore now, as nearly as possible, what she had lost.

That he could acknowledge; strictly censored had been any recognition of anger, his own anger that she had, by her actions, implicitly rejected that protection at the outset.

That was behind them now, anyway. What lay ahead – what *must* lie ahead – was the smoothest possible return to everyday life.

So Edward began to talk, easily and superficially, as if Helena had returned after some quite ordinary absence – a holiday, perhaps, or a visit to friends. He talked about the house, about the garden, about the effect of the housing market on his estate agent's business, and like the actress she still was she played to the cues he fed her.

At last, firmly as a horseman with a nervous mare, he brought her round to the first of the hurdles.

'Stephanie should be at home by the time we get there. Darnley Hall agreed to let her come home for the weekend.'

At her daughter's name, he felt her stiffen, and knew, as if he could read her mind, that she was reliving their last meeting, suffering once more the agony of the child's frantic rejection. He carried on, swiftly and smoothly.

'I think there was a hockey match or something, but I got the impression that Stephie wasn't too heartbroken to miss it.'

Her voice was not entirely steady, but at least she replied.

'She was never too keen on hockey. Horses, now . . .'

He laughed. 'Oh, horses!' he said, with a gesture of resignation. A little silence fell.

His next task was more difficult, but it was not one that he could shirk. He had gambled everything on this one bold act, and she had to accept it, she had to agree . . .

He spoke unemphatically, though out of the corner of his eye he was watching for reaction.

'I decided it would be a good idea to have a party for you, darling – just to celebrate having you home again. The day after tomorrow – I've asked everybody I can think of, and we've arranged the catering from Limber. So there's nothing you need do except enjoy yourself, and catch up with all your old friends.'

He sensed that, like the nervous horse, she was going to refuse. Her hands, previously unnaturally still in her lap, began a panicky fluttering of protest, and glancing at her he could see that she had turned pale.

He reached across to imprison one of her hands with a grip that was so urgent as to be painful.

'No, Helena, you mustn't. You've been doing so well. Can't you see, my darling? This is what we *must* do. Get it all over at once, behave normally, and you'll see – no one will ever mention it again. It's over. Finished. Sealed book.'

Sealed book. Those were clearly the words that caught her attention; the philosophy that chimed with her own. Close it. Shut it off. Bury it, so that not even in dreams need she glance at its pages.

'Finished,' she murmured, her eyes closed.

'Finished,' he said, and it was a promise.

There was a long, long silence. He looked at her anxiously once or twice, but said nothing, and eventually she opened her eyes. When she spoke, she sounded almost casual.

'How many people are coming?' she asked, any wife to any husband.

His relief was such that it was difficult to match her dispassionate tone.

'It's hard to say, really – I haven't given them much time to reply. I've asked all the usual village people, and our neighbours nearby – the Morleys, Annabel and James, if his political duties allow, Nick and the Whites and one or two others from the office – you know . . . .'

'And – Lilian?' she said stiffly.

'My dear girl, you should know by now that if you don't ask Lilian and she wants to be there, she'll come anyway.'

He thought that she almost smiled. Certainly, inviting Neville's widow to this sort of coming-out party could have been tactless to an offensive degree. But Lilian being Lilian, she had contented herself with a brief cameo performance of the widow's role, before reverting to one more suited to her disposition.

'Surely she wouldn't want to come?'

There was a trace of panic in her voice, and he soothed her swiftly.

'Oh, she'll certainly behave with perfect sang-froid if she does. She's got nerve enough for anything. And talking of nerve, Chris Dyer's coming.'

His voice darkened at the mention of the television producer, and for the first time Helena turned her head to look at him, though she said nothing.

'He phoned me yesterday, asking about you. I made it clear it was none of his business, but all he said was that he had the hide of a bull rhinoceros and would be coming to see you anyway. So I asked him to the party by way of damage limitation. His lease is up on the cottage, apparently, so he's going to clear it at the same time. So at least we should have seen the last of him after that.'

'Tell your gorgeous Helena I can't wait to see her again,' Dyer had managed to slip in, before Edward sharply replaced the receiver, but Edward did not relay the message.

'Oh look,' he said, changing the subject. 'Radnesfield, nine miles. Not long now.'

With his head turned to look at the signboard, he did not notice the shudder of revulsion which wracked his wife's slight frame.

'Bringing her home today, he is.'

A silence fell as Martha Bateman, making a pretence of consulting her shopping-list, tossed the remark to the other women in the village shop.

She was tall and raw-boned, with a face that could have belonged to any period of history in this part of the Fens, angular, harsh and leathery of complexion, with watchful eyes under hooded lids. She looked as if the lighter experiences of life had passed her by, but her thin-lipped, unpainted mouth suggested that she would not have welcomed them. She dominated her audience without exertion, not only by her membership, both by birth and marriage, of two of the three local families who went back to the days of the Old 'Uns, or by her position as housekeeper at the Red House, but also by the steeliness of character which had long established her the ultimate authority on every question from morals to spring-cleaning. She was graceless, insular, secretive and suspicious by nature, brusquely implacable in her judgements.

In a sense, she was Radnesfield.

Right at the point where, in the Upper Pleistocene period, the primeval ice-sheet had stopped its advance on the east coast of the British Isles, south of the Wash, Radnesfield had its beginnings in a circle of skin tents. Later, there were mud huts: later still, farming homesteads began to crown the ridges of the low, smooth glacial folds.

By the time it had a name, it had been ignored by half a dozen foreign invasions, lived under Roman law and Danelaw while ignorant of either, and brought itself painfully into the age of the wheel, the horse, and the iron ploughshare.

Turning a wet, heavy furrow is a slow business, and they became deliberate of speech and manner, taciturn and stubborn, as set in their ways as impacted mud, their feet planted firm in the solid clay.

Two thousand years later they were little different, fiercely private in an age when cars and the television set threatened the age-old rhythms of village life.

Now there were strangers, 'foreigners', who came into the pub among the close-mouthed countrymen, talking too loudly and too familiarly, until frozen out by annihilating indifference: they were dismissed, afterwards, with a devastating, 'Don't know enough to keep their great old mouth shut.'

It was not considered unkindness. As well ask a badger to relate to a humming-bird, as ask the villagers to appreciate attitudes which were as unreal to them as the images that flickered across their television screens in the darkened parlours.

Confidences were, to them, embarrassing as nakedness, while, paradoxically, gossip wove the fabric of their lives. Gossip was an art form, related and received with a relish betraying its origins: what, after all, did Homer do but spread some unfounded and scurrilous rumours about what Odysseus got up to on a business trip abroad?

It was a game with unspoken rules, where investigation was part of the pleasure. Questioning was as vulgar as obscenity; learning your neighbour's business was a slow, absorbing, lifetime's occupation. Life was people, not ideas.

Ideas were dangerous. 'Fancy ideas' had lost the village many of its young, lured by the brighter lights and prospects of Cambridge or Ipswich or even, unimaginably, further afield. They would never know its comfortable, uncritical acceptance where the easy, half-contemptuous, 'Oh, he's all right,' was all that need be said.

With these desertions, the last days were upon them, when treasured links back to the Old 'Uns would be severed, and the established order, the secrets and certainties of village life, would be blown away upon the winds of change.

Sullenly, the old families – the Batemans, the Edes, the Whittons – drew closer in their indifference to the outside world. They seldom became heated over events beamed into their sitting-rooms with the six o'clock news: their forefathers had greeted Roman decrees and the repeal of the Corn Laws with much the same head-shaking detachment and amused contempt. 'That's their business' took care of most things.

For their own, there was savage loyalty and protection, a formidable defensive alliance. They had been spared the late-twentieth-

14

century invasion of weekenders which had leeched the life from so many other, more picturesque Radnesfields. Those not discouraged by the mean ugliness of its housing stock, mainly post-war, were repelled by its atmosphere. To an outsider, the inhabitants seemed remote and coolly hostile, their interest furtive and spiteful, their unconcern so pointed that it was cruel.

'It's a masterpiece, the way he's taken it,' Radnesfield's personification went on. The air was thick with the avidity of their curiosity, and she was, as she would have put it herself, in her height and glory.

It was nothing new for a member of their community to be returning from a sojourn as a guest of Her Majesty: indeed, the cadet branches of the Ede family spent as much of their time in as out.

It was, however, a new and titillating experience when it was Edward Radley's wife, his family having been for centuries the closest approach to squires that Radnesfield would recognize.

Gratification loosened Mrs Bateman's tongue. 'Very steady, he were. Just quietly, "Now, Martha," he says, "Mrs Radley will be home today. You can move my things into the spare room, because she'll be very tired and will need to rest." '

Eyes widened in enjoyment, voices lowered in pleasurable speculation as to what this titbit might imply. Only Jane Thomas, Martha's schoolmate and old sparring partner, spoke robustly.

'Sounds real thoughtful. She won't feel much like keeping company first days, seems to me.'

'Well, catch my Dave, after all that time.' The girl who spoke had bold dark eyes, and rolled them expressively.

The laughter was ribald, the comments had a mocking edge. Sensitivity was not a village virtue.

Martha Bateman let the talk ripple on, like musical improvisation, only until she chose to gather them, once again, under her direction.

'We all know about your Dave's courting habits,' she said unkindly, and watched the girl flush a dull, uncomfortable red, as if one of the shaming marks of Dave's attentions still disfigured her face.

15

'Anyway,' Mrs Bateman continued, 'that's what he said. And that Stephanie's coming home, isn't she, to see her mother for the first time since she was took away.'

'Wonder how she'll take it.' Mrs Ede, behind the counter, voiced the common thought. 'Weren't too happy at the time, by your account, Martha.'

There was a little silence. They had heard it all then, the child's hysterical refusal to see or speak to her mother, as a result of that most dramatic event in village history.

There was nothing fresh to add, and Martha pursed her lips in annoyance. She had uncharacteristically kept nothing in reserve from that feast of scandal for this later famine.

So she frowned, repressively. 'I wonder at you asking me to demean myself, gossiping. That's their business, isn't it?'

Then briskly, with a change of tempo, she closed the discussion. 'Well, them as lives longest 'll see most. Now Mary, you going to get my order, or keep me standing all day? You're getting slow as that clock of yours. You want to get Willie Comberton to see to it, you do.'

There was laughter as Mrs Ede complied, and Martha Bateman, feeling the grim satisfaction which was her nearest approach to pleasure, read out the next item on her list.

With automatic movements Sandra Daley wiped the draining-board, peeling off the silly rubber gloves with red tinted nails attached that she had once thought so amusing. Wearing them now was an unthinking habit; below them, her hands were rough and her own nails chipped and broken. She didn't bother now, any more than she bothered about her face or her hair, showing its dark roots.

Jack had gone to the front door on his way out to work. He was coming back, so the postman must have called, but she did not turn. She took no interest in the post nowadays, and it was always painful to see how Jack looked at her.

'Something for you.'

So she must turn, had no option but to face his cold distaste.

'You'd best open it.' He thrust it into her hand, since she showed no sign of taking it. 'It's an invitation. We don't get too many of these now, do we?'

He knew something about it already. His light brown eyes observed her without affection, as she accepted the envelope reluctantly, opening it with fingers that had become clumsy.

'Mr and Mrs Edward Radley,' she read slowly, like a child unfamiliar with its letters. Then 'Oh!'

'Yes, "Oh!" ' he mocked her cruelly. 'Should be quite a party, shouldn't it? Make a change to go out – we haven't had too many knees-ups, not since –'

Hard and uncaring, he sounded, yet he could not bring himself to say the words. She began to shake her head, slowly at first, until the movement was almost a shudder.

'No, no. I'm not going, I can't go –'

'Oh yes you bloody can.' In a sudden violent motion he caught her wrist, turning it to the edge of pain. 'You're the one who likes parties, remember – the good-time girl. "Oh Jack, it'll be such fun!" ' His voice was shrill and venomous in mimicry.

She hung her head. 'It was – different, then,' she whispered.

'Maybe it was for you.' He released her arm with jarring force and spun away from her, to stare with unseeing eyes through the window, across the meadow and the spinney towards Radnesfield House. 'Well, as it happens, you've got no choice. Lilian got her invitation yesterday, and she wants to go. But she doesn't want to go alone.'

'Lilian!' she spat the word at him. 'You go with your precious Lilian. You don't need me.'

He faced her again, his mouth twisted into a sneer. 'Need you? God, of course I don't need you. Take a good look at yourself – what sort of use are you? But Lilian wouldn't like it if you stayed at home. It wouldn't really look very good, would it?'

'You can't make me –' she began, with a flash of her old spirit, but faltered under his cold, contemptuous gaze.

'We agreed, didn't we? As you said – when was it now? I'm not sure, but perhaps you could remind me – "We've been through too much to quarrel now." Something like that. A bit of an understatement, really, I thought it was, at the time. And you didn't care what my conditions were, you said, in one of your more grovelling moments.'

'Yes, I know.' Her voice was so full of tears, as to be barely audible. 'But oh, Jack, I never thought it would be this way – '

He wouldn't meet her eyes. 'Should have thought of that before, then, shouldn't you?' he said gruffly. 'And for god's sake do something about yourself. Have you passed a mirror, lately – you're a ratbag. No wonder you disgust me.'

The tears began again, welling up and spilling silently, as she heard the front door slam behind him. He had every right to punish her, but as she stood shaking uncontrollably, she wondered how much more punishment she could take.

It was, as usual, just on twelve o'clock when George Wagstaff came into the farmhouse kitchen.

There was a savoury smell coming from the elderly Aga, and he went over to warm himself, removing a cat and a protesting terrier from the bright rag rug with the toe of his stockinged foot.

Dora, his wife, was busy at the sink. His son Jim had come in ahead of him and was already washed and sitting at the table set for what was the main meal of the day.

'Go and get yourself washed, Dad,' Dora said. 'I'm going to dish up now – that's Sally back from Limber. I can hear the car.'

They were all waiting for him, when George returned to take his place at the head of the table.

'Hear Radley's bringing his missus home this morning,' he said gruffly.

It was, on the face of it, a simple enough remark, but it made his wife look up sharply from the chicken stew.

'Is Stephanie back?' she asked, ladling a heaped spoonful on to his plate.

'Well, a taxi came in earlier, so I reckon that was most likely her coming home from that posh school. Good news for you, eh Jim?'

His sister shot him a sardonic look, as the young man flushed a dusky crimson.

'Have a heart, Dad, she's only a kid. It's the horses that are the attraction, not me.'

'Oh, I can well believe that she prefers the horses, but what about you?' Sally, at eighteen, always had the upper hand in any exchange with her elder brother. 'Mum, not that much for me! You're always trying to feed me as if I were baling hay instead of tapping a word processor.'

'That's no reason not to eat properly. We'll have no slimming nonsense in this house.' Wagstaff's response was automatic, but now that his daughter had attracted his attention, his heavy brows came down.

'And where were you last night anyway, miss? I didn't get you that little car so you could come in at all hours.'

Sally was an attractive girl with her father's fair hair and high colouring, but her jawline was as squarely determined as his, and now she looked mulish.

'Just out,' she said, meeting George glare for glare.

Dora, dark and quiet-mannered like her son, hurried as usual to intervene.

'That's no way to speak to your father, Sally. And you might as well tell us, before we hear it in the village.'

The girl banged her fists on the table. 'Why does anyone live in this place?' she cried in fury, then, 'Oh, all right, if you really want to know. I went out with Len Whitton.'

Jim, who had taken no part in the conversation, winced. His father's colouring, heightened already, became a suffused purple, and his bright blue eyes bulged.

'Len Whitton!' he roared, bringing both huge fists down in exactly the same movement as his daughter's, but shaking the thick pine board so that the terrier, startled, set up a frenzied yapping. 'You've been told before, you're to have no truck with the village lads. And Len Whitton! By god, if you were a bit younger I'd set to and put you over my knee.'

Tears springing to her eyes, Sally pushed away her untouched plate and sprang to her feet.

'You're such a snob!' she cried hotly. 'Oh, it's all right for Jim to fancy Stephanie Fielding, because she's posh and talks proper. But I'll make friends with who I like – I don't care what you say.'

'Len Whitton's bad news, Sal,' Jim said gravely.

She coloured, but went on. 'Len Whitton, Will Ede, Dave Thomas – it's all the same to Dad, whatever they're like. Just because their parents are working class and we're farmers, even if we haven't got our own –'

'That's quite enough, Sally,' said Dora in the tone that had always meant business. 'We're prepared to make some allowances for your tantrums, just the way we did when you were two years old, but

19

you weren't allowed to be plain nasty then, and you needn't think you're going to get away with being nasty now.'

For a second the girl met her mother's eyes rebelliously, then, bursting into tears, whirled round and ran out.

Jim rose. 'I'll go after her, see if I can talk some sense into her.'

His mother, sighing, took his plate over to the Aga to keep warm. George was struggling for control.

'Len Whitton!' he said at last, through clenched teeth. 'If he harms a hair of her head, I'll – I'll kill him!'

Dora gave him a straight look. 'Oh, hasn't there been enough trouble yet for your taste? George, your temper's going to kill you, never mind anyone else.

'Sally's young still. She's not taken with Len, and she'll have done with him soon enough if you don't go forcing her to carry on, out of defiance. Just let things be.'

Wagstaff glowered like one of his own bullocks. 'You wouldn't want to see her marrying into the village, any more than I would.'

She sighed again. 'No, of course I wouldn't.' She sat down once more, looking at her cooling plateful without enthusiasm, then said slowly, 'There's a bit of a funny mood in the village, the last couple of days, George, have you noticed?'

He shot her a look from under furrowed brows, but it wasn't anger she saw there now.

She had seen that look in the eyes of a stable cat, hunted by the farm dogs. Frightened it might be, but it had been ready to sell its life dear.

In that moment she realized, for the first time in her life, what they meant when they said, 'My blood ran cold.'

'Do you know, that woman doesn't even seem to have heard of recycled loo paper?'

Marcia Farrell dumped a packet of luridly pink toilet rolls, along with a small jar of jelly marmalade, on to the vicarage kitchen table.

'And then she said, pointedly, "And will that be *all*, madam?" as if she expected me to pay the fancy prices she charges for the whole of my weekly shop.'

The vicar, wearing a frayed grey wool cardigan over his clerical shirt and collar, was sitting beside the stove which was failing to heat the draughty, stone-flagged vicarage kitchen. His study was even colder, so he had brought through a pile of books in the so far unrealized hope that they might provide fresh inspiration for Sunday's sermon.

'I suppose she doesn't have the advantage the big supermarkets have,' he felt obliged to suggest.

His wife snorted. 'They somehow managed to go to Mallorca last year on their profits. And we don't exactly have the advantage of the salaries other people have. Or even the sort of vicarage that you can heat, or keep clean.' Her eyes raked the shabby, untidy room disparagingly.

Peter Farrell winced. He was morbidly sensitive to the sufferings of his wife, who was not an instinctive home-maker, with the old and inconvenient vicarage. The church had tried unsuccessfully to sell it, handicapped by its unattractive nature and the cost of putting right the defects which made the months of November to March almost intolerable.

He depended so totally on her, on the robustness of her character and her faith, to make up for the shrinking delicacy of his own. It was disheartening that the bishop had not found him a charge where Marcia's interest in women's groups and poverty initiatives would be appreciated, and now he felt selfish for having condemned her to being underused, and worse, resented, purely to indulge his vocation.

It might have been different, if he could convince himself that his was a successful ministry, but in Radnesfield he could never feel that modern Christianity had eradicated another, more ancient creed. And increasingly, of late, he had felt himself powerless against the stealthy advance of evil. He could never tell Marcia, but at times the wings of darkness seemed to brush his own face.

Marcia had put the kettle on and was continuing her saga. 'Then she made a fuss about Nathan, when he knocked over some stupid tins, and you know how sensitive poor little Nat is! I nearly lost my temper, but I was given grace just to smile at her and say, "Suffer the little children, Mrs Ede!" '

Her husband smiled weakly. Oh, he loved his children, of course – that went without saying – but sometimes it did seem to him that suffering was the *mot juste*. Marcia was wonderful with them, simply wonderful, encouraging them to express themselves, and be real individuals, but without her, he would be totally lost. His face grew sombre at the memory of that nightmare day, Marcia broken and sobbing and threatening to walk out on them all. It had been the death of her hope, so callously engendered by that – he swallowed the word, one which vicars shouldn't even think of – by Neville Fielding . . .

Almost as if she had followed his train of thought, Marcia went on, spooning decaffeinated coffee into Oxfam mugs, 'I noticed Edward Radley driving out early, presumably to get Helena. I asked Mrs Ede if she knew if she was getting out this morning, and I'm sure she knew, but all she said was, "I really couldn't say, I'm sure." Very helpful!'

'Well, you know how they hate being questioned –'

'Oh, I know that, all right! You could hardly live in this village for five years without realizing that if you so much as ask them how they are, you get a metaphorical slap in the face. How they expect you to do your job unless they tell you the problems, I don't know.

'Though of course, doing what's right when it's easy isn't really a challenge, is it?'

Then a frown darkened her mechanical smile. 'But I must say, it is hard to be treated as a vulgar gossip, when I'm doing my best to help with your pastoral duties. Because if Helena is coming home, you should go up and see her immediately.'

He became visibly agitated. 'Oh – oh no, surely not! They've asked us to go on Saturday, and at first they'll want some peace and privacy – they won't want me to intrude –'

'Intrude? Peter, how can her priest *intrude*? That's like suggesting that a doctor intrudes at the scene of an accident! This is a spiritual emergency, Peter – she must have a desperate need to lay down that burden of sin and guilt! Seeing her at the party will hardly meet the case, now will it?'

She smiled at him rallyingly, and noticed, with irritation, that he had started that unconscious wringing of his hands again.

'So misguided – so unwise –' he muttered.

'Well, you could say that a party shows a more frivolous attitude than one might hope – it's not one of the more usual manifestations of repentance, is it?'

She laughed, but getting no response, went on, 'Still, being charitable, it may be they see this as a way of putting the whole thing behind her –'

'Behind her!' The words burst from him. 'How can anyone be foolish enough to think that this will put it behind her? It's starting something – it's got everything stirred up again, and you can feel how uneasy people are. So much evil, so many of us drawn to sin! And now it's all coming to the surface, all over again, like some foul, loathsome – '

Stumbling into incoherence, he broke off.

Marcia, pouring boiling water into the mugs, stopped in astonishment, and some dismay. Impervious to atmosphere herself, she considered her husband's sensitivity dangerous, and even a little self-indulgent.

She pursed her lips, then said, with forced cheerfulness, 'Dear me! You are getting yourself into a state. Look, I've just made you a nice cup of coffee –'

He stared at her wildly. 'I'm going across to the church,' he said, and fled.

She looked after him with a sigh. He took refuge in the church more and more often these days, and while naturally she would be the very last to suggest he shouldn't, there were times when it might be more constructive to go out and tackle problems head on. She found herself contemplating, not for the first time, the prospects opening up with the ordination of women.

She looked so *awful*, that was the thing. And that horrendous artificial voice! Stephanie pulled a battered pack of forbidden cigarettes from her overnight bag and lit one.

She had managed to say, 'Hello, mum,' while Edward wittered on, trying to paper over the cracks. Then she had mumbled something about having unpacking to do, and fled.

The puffing was soothing, even if she hadn't mastered inhaling yet, and wasn't sure if she liked it much. She needed to feel laid-back and adult, though, and this helped.

She had almost convinced herself she hated her mother. But she didn't want to hate her. She wanted to run into her arms, and be safe, and loved, and comfortable, like it had been before her mother became what she couldn't believe she was, before that dreadful night when she had stolen the newspaper and read that her mother was pleading guilty. She'd insisted she never wanted to see her again, but nine months, when you are fourteen, is a long time.

It had been wonderful when she was little. Daddy was so much handsomer and more exciting than other fathers, and spoiled her rotten and took her to places where none of her friends had been. He was unpredictable, of course, and when he was cross you felt sick inside, but once he was in a good mood again it was like the sun coming out on a dull day, and he would make Mummy laugh, and they would all be happy together.

Naturally, as you grew up you stopped thinking your parents were so terrific. You wanted to hang out with your own friends, and then, somehow, Daddy changed.

She noticed the change around the time they came to Radnesfield. Sometimes she felt it must have a curse – hateful, ugly, unfriendly little place, where people didn't care about you at all.

And even after Dad divorced Mummy and married loathsome Lilian, she couldn't escape, because Edward dragged Mummy back to marry him.

She didn't really blame Edward. He'd always lived there, after all, and he did his best. It wasn't his fault he wasn't exactly dynamic, and that every so often she got a desperate craving for the excitement Dad always generated, even though she knew now how horrible he had been.

Once she'd read all the papers Em Morley had saved her, she could see Dad had asked for it. But that was different from your mum actually killing him. That was heavy.

Still, at least Edward hadn't insisted on discussing it, and now he was obviously going to stiff-upper-lip the whole thing. As long as Mum would play along, they could make like nothing had happened, and in just over a year, when she had left school, she could start a new life. She would be sixteen, after all – almost an adult.

So perhaps the stranger downstairs with the thin, bird-like body and the oddly-cut hair wasn't so important. Once you were grown-up and independent, you didn't need a mother, like you did when you were newly fifteen, and had only a gaping hole where your mother used to be.

Somehow, Helena got through the achingly long day. At meal-times Stephanie sat avoiding her eyes, replying politely to Edward's small talk and disappearing at the first possible moment.

24

Somehow the robot-Helena, in her bright brittle voice, replied politely too, until at last Edward could say, 'I really think you should have an early night, darling. I'm going to be masterful and make you go to bed.'

Obediently she followed as he picked up her bag from the cloakroom and led the way upstairs.

'By the way,' he said over his shoulder, 'I've told Martha to put my things in the spare room. I want you to get lots of rest, and you know what I'm like – late to bed and early to rise.'

The relief was overwhelming. Despite the prohibitions of her conscious mind, the dread of physical intimacy had been a lurking shadow. An unexpected touch was enough to make her shrink, and it was a measure of her gratitude for the delicacy of his gift of privacy that she reached out, of her own volition, to squeeze his hand, wordlessly.

He was ridiculously pleased, returning the pressure.

'Not for ever, though, darling. We'll be happy together again, won't we?'

She was still too absorbed in self-preservation to be sensitive to others, but the thought did occur to her that his remark might be meant as much to reassure himself, as her.

Helena slept that night heavily and dreamlessly, as if she had been drugged. When at last she woke, the house was silent and it was full daylight.

She picked up her watch, squinting at its hands with eyes still heavy from sleep. Was that really twelve o'clock? Fourteen hours! She hadn't slept like that since she was a teenager.

She had a long, luxurious bath, and by the time she was dressed, she felt better. She could almost pretend that the old remedy of a good night's sleep had actually put things right.

Downstairs, the house was empty and very tidy. Edward would be at work, of course. Martha Bateman had clearly been and gone, and on the kitchen table there was a note from Stephanie.

'Gone to lunch at the Wagstaffs. Back later.'

Well, that was normal enough. Steph had always spent half her time in the stables there, and Dora treated her like one of the family.

Martha had left the mail there too, in a neat pile. Incuriously, she flipped through it.

Mostly it was for Edward, boring letters with typed addresses or windows in the envelopes. There was one of those for her too, though she didn't bother to open it.

But there was one letter written in a strong, clear hand in black ink, addressed to her and marked 'Personal'.

She picked it up. She had had bitter experience of personal letters, and she had not read a letter which Edward had not vetted first since – well, for a very long time.

She hesitated. But that was behind her now. This was ordinary life again, humdrum and unexciting. She tore open the envelope.

It looked harmless enough. 'Dear Mrs Radley . . . .' No threatening block capitals, no wild accusations or insults.

She turned it over to study the signature, neat and unaffected. 'Frances Howarth', it read.

She felt the blood drain from her head, and she sat down heavily in a kitchen chair. Her hands were shaking; she had to lay the letter on the table to read it.

'Dear Mrs Radley, You may remember –'

Remember! She didn't want to remember. She had spent months perfecting the skill of not remembering. Yet now, like a sand wall naively built to repel the incoming tide, her defences were crumbling and the past swept back in all its hideous clarity. Recollection rose like bile in her throat, with a cold, metallic, poison taste.

PART TWO

2

Sky, Helena thought. Sky, and sky and sky. What in the world would anyone want with that much sky? It was positively bullying the meek, damp line of cringing Fenland earth into submission.

She had almost ducked as she got out of the car to stand beside Neville who, at a little over six foot, was the highest point in the landscape. The universe seemed to close over them with a clang, like the visor of a helmet slamming shut.

'It's a bit much, isn't it?' she called into the chilly wind, but Neville only shouted back, 'What?' Using the Method approach to the part of prospective country-dweller, he was thinking himself into it, working from the brogues upwards to the lovat thornproof jacket with the suede patches and the trilby with a fishing-fly tucked jauntily into the brim.

There was a hedge, then only turnip fields and more flatness, with a marshy pond in the distance. Somewhere a crow was cawing; another pecked in the field. The grass verges were wide, grey with dried traffic mud, and the ground scrubby with a few diseased-looking furze bushes.

It was a staggered crossroads, with no distinguishing features beyond two striped fingerposts, one at each road end, pointing in opposite directions off the main highway.

Yet Helena could see, with a sinking heart, why it had caught Neville's imagination. It was a very powerful statement, in its bleak isolation; so stark, so uncompromising, so ugly. And Neville, alongside his usual flirtations, was indulging in a full-blown love affair with ugliness. She could only hope that, like his other flirtations, it would burn itself out.

Now he came over to her, pointing to the signpost to the north-west, marked 'Radnesfield'. 'See that?' It was the smaller of the minor roads, flat and bare of habitation. He put his arm about her shoulders, pulling her to his side.

'That's it, Nella – that's my road. This is the one that says to me, "Neville, this is for you." '

She paused, uncertain how to reply. One of the crows, tiring of his quest, flapped up to land on the signpost with a harsh caw.

Neville's sudden laughter frightened the bird off, and it flew away with another raucous cry.

' "The raven himself is hoarse . . ." ' he began, and with instinctive, theatrical superstition, she shuddered.

'Don't quote *Macbeth*, Neville,' she said sharply. 'It's bad luck. And I'm simply freezing out here.'

She shrugged off his arm and returned to the car, irritated by her own reaction as well as by his behaviour. If he had decided to ham it up, she wasn't about to indulge him.

Neville did not turn to watch her go, but he was keenly aware of her withdrawal. Withdrawal was always the weapon she used, like a lance to jab his Achilles heel.

He needed to be the star: she knew that! He needed attention the way other people needed food, and warmth and shelter. And love.

Love – somehow, he'd never quite got it sussed. He'd read enough about it, god knew, talked about it, acted it – on and off the stage – and yet he still had never figured out how you knew it was there. Perhaps when your mother had dumped you in a children's home the first second she could, without doing you the courtesy of mentioning who your father was, you didn't really have a reference point.

So he had always been a pragmatist, and at least his unknown parents had given him one legacy – the sort of head-turning looks that gave him the edge on the other kids in that dreary, dismal hole. Being the centre of attention gave you the sort of warm, safe glow that seemed to be associated with love. But the indicators were more specific: you could tell when you were the star, when you weren't insignificant and powerless any more. That was when he had learned the great truth about acting, long before they taught him about Stanislavsky; act it, you became it, and you could convince yourself you really were Neville Fielding, not Norman Smith. Hell, he'd never had a proper name, anyway.

He was the star, all right, by the time he left for drama school, with old Ma Porter snivelling and making him promise to come back and see them. He hadn't, of course; bleakness and squalor were hardly what you'd call a draw, when you were headed for a life of luxury and fast cars and sexy women, or thought you were. She still sent him a Christmas card; probably Helena sent her one back, though he wasn't sure.

Helena. Oh, dear god, Helena. She was under his skin like some festering thorn. He had been mad for her from the first moment he spotted her, cool, aloof, beautiful, everybody's fantasy and no-body's prize. Getting her attention was his only early success.

Lust came into it, of course – he wasn't trying to deny that – but the obsession that gripped him was more than just the spoliation of the Snow Queen. She was assured, middle-class and seriously talented, with all the qualities everyone admired.

He wasn't, but he had got the ring on her finger, which should have settled it. She said she loved him – but how could he ever believe her? Some demon prompted him to push her to the point where his fears would be justified, and he had done some bloody silly things to see if he had the power to hurt her. He did, and she forgave him, so that was all right – for a time. But then the doubts would begin again, the need would come back, and the test, this time, would be stiffer than ever.

Surreptitiously, he glanced over his shoulder as he stamped his numbed feet. She was showing no sign of the impatience he was convinced she really felt. Sod it, why couldn't she open the window and yell, 'Come on, Neville, it's bloody freezing out there!'

But that wasn't her style, to meet him on his own ground. That might allow him access to her very private self. She always, ulti-mately, eluded him, even in their moments of closest intimacy, and sometimes his love-making had been brutal in his desperation to possess and dominate. But increasingly, whenever he turned up the emotional thermostat, she, so to speak, slipped out of the room.

But there had always been Stephanie to reassure him, looking up at her Dad with his own dark blue eyes, wide with wonder at his magnificence. In the days when having a real family seemed about as likely as winning the pools when you hadn't posted the coupon, that was what he reckoned it was all about – unstinted love and admiration, given as of right.

She didn't look at him like that any more. She would turn down an invitation from her father, who did just happen to be one of the best-known stars of television, only to go shopping with her scrubby friends.

So, if it weren't for Harry, he'd be feeling as unloved and as powerless as little Norman Smith. Harry had brought him the fix he needed, that warm glow which came now from the adulation of hundreds of thousands of fans. He didn't need Helena's approval or Stephanie's admiration now. Harry was freeing him to be himself.

For years he had blanked out his background, pretending all that ugliness and lovelessness didn't exist. But it was there, in his soul, burned deep, and it was Harry who validated his experience. And Radnesfield, he had felt with a profound sense of recognition, was Harry country.

And in Radnesfield he was planning to rub Helena's well-bred nose in it. He would be on home territory, and she, for the first time in their married life, would be at a disadvantage. Perhaps they could start again, on his terms this time.

Perhaps they couldn't. Harry, smart bastard, would have all the answers, if that was the way it went.

So that was where his crossroads came in. He could just get back in the car, say, 'Let's forget it. You wouldn't like it, and I've changed my mind.' He could do that.

He looked again at the signpost that said 'Radnesfield'. He believed, almost, that he took the decision at that moment, but the attitudes which made his choice inevitable were long-established.

The crow, seeing him move away, took possession of his perch once more, with three hoarse, minatory caws. For a bare second, Neville checked, frowning, then he shrugged and grinned. Blowing on his hands and stamping his feet to warm them, he went back to the car.

Radnesfield was even nastier than Helena feared. It was a mean little huddle of Fifties council houses, with a few older ones modernized in the fake-bow-window-with-bull's-eye-glass style, and a pub with a garish plastic sign proclaiming 'The Four Feathers' on a concrete front with aluminium frame doors and windows. There was a post office and a shop, with its owner's name on an orange and yellow advertisement sign.

There was a decent Norman church, and a square about a town cross with a couple of pretty houses, but Neville drove on, humming contentedly, and bore left up a slight incline.

Then, on the right, there was an old wall, broken down by tree-roots and badly maintained, and at last, at the top of the sort of rise that passed for a hill in this uncompromisingly flat countryside, was a house.

'There you are, Nella! Radnesfield House.' Neville spoke with pride of possession, as if it were his already.

In a different situation, she would have burst out laughing. It was late Victorian yellow brick and red tile, after the Legoland school of architecture. Nightmare patterns of hideous complication defaced the frontage, and a wooden trellis, apparently constructed by a giant with a fretsaw and a lurid imagination, was improbably grafted on to it, the wood rotted in places and the paint peeling. It was so revolting that it was comic, but she was, after all, going to have to live in this place.

'Neville,' she said faintly, 'it's unspeakable.'

He roared with satisfied laughter. 'Isn't it? Didn't I say so? It really is the pits, the purest sample of the worst sort of Victorian vulgarity. I love it! And that, on top of the village! None of your rubbishy, tourist-trap, picture-postcard places, just a real, un-spoiled, ancient English village. This guy has simply got to sell. It fits me like a glove.'

It wasn't Neville it fitted, of course. It fitted 'Badman' Harry Bradman, as if it were a new concept – the designer village.

It was three years since their marriage had become this weird *ménage à trois*, with the sinister shadow of Harry lurking like a paid heavy on the fringes of every conversation. Helena never knew when he would move stage centre, but she had no difficulty in recognizing him once he appeared, hard, bullying and blustering, as if Neville were using his *alter ego* as a suit of armour which became more impenetrable daily.

She recognized her own complicity. Harry had been spawned long ago in Neville's wretched childhood, but she had nurtured the monster by her own weakness in giving way to Neville's demands. It was a form of self-indulgence, because it had always been easier to sacrifice her own satisfaction than to combat Neville's selfishness.

The groundwork had been laid long before by Helena's father, Simon Groves, a joyless, self-styled Man of God, who filled the West Country vicarage with an atmosphere of sour, unloving disapproval of every blithe and youthful impulse his only child displayed. Her mother, gently-bred, weak and pretty, had died when the girl was twelve.

As Helena bloomed in adolescence to something of a beauty, she lived in terror of his icy rages. When she rebelled, taking a scholarship to the drama college which her father, his eyes bulging with rigidly-controlled fury, stigmatized a sink of iniquity, she turned her back on him for ever. She knew now that he was dead; she had not seen him since the day she left home.

At college she was studious, quiet, and possessed of the real dramatic talent which often lies in violently repressed natures. It appeared to her then incredible that Neville Fielding, with his glamorous looks and wild reputation should look twice at her.

Initially, though, it had worked surprisingly well. Perhaps he had wanted to prove he could melt the Snow Queen, but it was her helplessly maternal response to the wicked little boy in his character that made her indispensable to him. Neville, sunny side up, was funny and charming, with a demonstrative warmth which did, indeed, melt her heart, and when he behaved badly, absolution from her seemed almost a psychological necessity. She sometimes thought his was a schizophrenic nature, with a black side which intermittently forced its way to the top.

That, of course, was Harry, though it was only the television series that taught Helena his name.

It had not, she acknowledged, been easy for Neville. A profile born out of its time, he was Ivor Novello in an age which prefers its heroes short, bald or bespectacled. She had never lacked the early offers which might have led to real success, but faced with the physical brutality his envy engendered she denied her talent and got herself pregnant.

His career was a progression of small television parts, competently enough performed, but never yielding an income adequate for the standard of living he so desperately desired, as proof of success.

It was, paradoxically, his failures which brought success in the end. The harsh, disappointed lines about the chiselled mouth, the self-indulgence that pouched the deep-set blue eyes and blurred the classic line of the jaw were perfection for beautiful, wicked Harry Bradman.

' "Badman" Bradman, the villain you love to hate,' trumpeted the publicity machine. He appeared on Sunday evening television, scheduled against a favourite chat show, and Chris Dyer, producer and director, was a sharp operator. On to the framework of a soap opera, he had grafted an episodic series, relying shrewdly on the Baudelaire principle that evil and ugliness, glamorized, have a powerful attraction.

'He's Rhett Butler, without the fundamental decency. Or Dorian Gray. Find me Dorian Gray at the precise moment when the face starts to crumble,' Dyer told his casting manager, and in Neville Fielding, pushing forty, with his aura of fallen-angel seediness, they found him.

So Harry had rescued him from a thousand petty indignities – the betrayed husband in the last scene, the cigar-smoker in the commercial – and installed him at last on the throne of fame to which he had always pretended.

Helena was well aware that living the part is an occupational hazard for any actor in a long-term role, and as the series ran and the part became more tailored to Neville's personality, the division between other and self became, at times, not altogether clear in his mind.

Initially, he had talked of Harry as an amusing, attractive villain, a clever creation; of late, he had started finding excuses for Harry's fictional delinquencies, the sort of excuses he was inclined to produce for himself when he was in the wrong.

Her attitude to his success was ambivalent. Harry was, if not their bread and butter, certainly their jam, and even, as time went on, their caviare. Not only that, but, like most people, a happy, successful Neville was a great deal easier to live with than a morose, frustrated one.

But Neville's character had always had warmth; the nastiest thing about Harry was that he was cold, as her father had been cold, and she found herself increasingly anxious about the intrusion of Harry into their everyday life.

It was certainly Harry who had chosen Radnesfield. Helena recognized immediately his degenerate taste.

From the taciturn host of the Four Feathers Neville, on his previous visit, had prised a grudging history of the owners of Radnesfield House. The Radleys, who went back to sixteenth-century graves in the churchyard – and, by tradition, well beyond that – were on the way out. An accident with a shotgun to the elder son who had just inherited had incurred a double set of death duties; the younger son, a bachelor in his forties, living alone since the death of his mother two years before, was considered to be presiding over the family's dying throes.

Indeed, when Edward Radley greeted them, he seemed almost faded, as if ancient blood in him were starting to thin. There was a quality of stillness about him, and the long planes of his face were oddly unlined, as though untouched by the events of his forty years. Helena had seen that face before, on figures in East Anglian cathedrals, the knights in medieval brasses; the high, narrow brow with hair receding from the sides, the deepset eyes, the strongly-marked nose. Beside Neville's flamboyance, he seemed shadowy, though this was a phenomenon she had noted before, as if earning a living on stage gave actors a larger-than-life-size quality in everyday existence.

In any case, Neville was, in nursery parlance, getting above himself, greeting each fresh Victorian atrocity with exaggerated ecstasy.

'Helena, look at that absolutely glorious fireplace!' It was oxblood and black marble, mottled with varicosed grey veins set in a patchwork of rising suns.

Helena rebelled. 'Neville, you can't like it!' Then, recollecting the silent man at her side, she bit her lip. 'Oh, I'm sorry, Mr Radley.'

His amusement seemed genuine. 'I'm relieved you said it, Mrs Fielding. I've been feeling as if somehow I've been perpetrating a fraud. This place has always seemed to me uniquely hideous.

Neville gave his Bradman guffaw. 'Hideous? But of course it is! That's why it's magnificent. Can't stand all these sickly, chocolate-box places. Just look at the village – no tastefully-restored cottages, no Designers Guild fabrics at the windows and antique, frightfully-understated door furniture. No middle-class architectural watch-dog society. Practically no middle-class at all, come to that, thank god. There's nothing twee about Radnesfield. Give me reality every time.'

'Why,' asked Helena bleakly, 'is ugliness considered more "real" than beauty?'

It was a rhetorical question, but Radley looked at her with interest. 'People believe that, though, don't you find? Loving beauty is seen as retreating from life and refusing to face up to things.'

'Exactly.' Neville, only half-listening as he explored a cupboard, gleaned the impression that his wife's argument had been refuted. 'The man who built this house certainly wasn't interested in namby-pamby considerations like that.'

'I think the pathetic truth is that when my grandfather virtually bankrupted us to build this, he considered it the last word in elegance. Every tasteless embellishment was another step away from the harsh realities of his life.'

'But how sad!' Helena exclaimed. 'Don't you feel a responsibility to love it, in that case?'

Where another might have laughed at her, he smiled, and considered his reply, like a man unaccustomed to discussing his feelings.

'I was brought up to feel great responsibility towards the place itself, which goes back to the mists of time. There must have been a dozen houses on this site, and probably as many families – though we do have a conceit that Radley and Radnesfield both come from *Raed*, the Anglo-Saxon word for a council.'

'So you've been squires here for centuries?' Neville put the question eagerly, twirling imaginary moustachios. 'Droit de seigneur, and all that?'

While Helena groaned inwardly, the other man looked uncomfortable.

'It's not something I've ever considered, but they're not at all feudally-minded here. The Radleys have never been socially much above their fellows. We've got the Home Farm, of course, but it's been directly farmed, or managed as it is now, not put out to tenancy. And even before grandfather's attack of *folie de grandeur*, we were gentleman farmers, but only just, with the emphasis on the second part of the description.'

Neville, losing interest as the part of rural squire was denied him, wandered off rudely. Politeness dictated that Helena should linger; anyway, she was beginning to be intrigued by this quiet-spoken man. Where someone more sophisticated might have studied her covertly, he watched her when she spoke with meticulous attention, as if he might be planning to draw her face from memory after she left.

'Would it be very impertinent to ask if you mind selling?'

'Mind?' He looked quizzically round the room. 'This? I'd move to the Red House in the village, with enough money left after paying off the mortgages to mend the roof and fix the dry rot. It was my grandmother's house. She quarrelled with my grandfather – I suspect she was a woman of taste and discrimination – and moved out. It's perfect Queen Anne, and the relief to my aesthetic sense would be enormous.'

'It can't be as easy as that.'

He shot Helena a startled glance, like a horse shying, as if afraid of this approach to mental intimacy. His reply seemed at first inconsequential.

'My brother had thought about selling off land for building. Well, I suppose I could do that, and be financially a lot more comfortable. But I don't need that much money – there's no one to come after me. If I were to sell to a developer, the village would be swamped by strangers, when it's hardly changed since I was a child. By some sort of fluke, perhaps precisely because it's not remotely picturesque, it's escaped the influx of commuters bed-and-breakfasting during the week and getting up morris-dancing societies at the weekend. Your husband – forgive me – would be wealthy enough to pay for his privacy and satisfy my purist notions that it should stay as it is, unchanged.'

'You like the village as it is?' Her response held a note of impolite incredulity, and she coloured. 'Oh, I'm sorry. I didn't mean to sound rude. I'm sure it has charms which are hidden from me. But it did strike me as being a rather unappealing place, as we drove through it.'

'I suppose that's our fault. Grandfather let a nice little row of Georgian almshouses collapse, and then the council built that very unpleasing housing scheme. The village properties never had a controlling landlord, so they all did their own ghastly thing.

'And of course they were quite delighted when the brewery pulled down the old inn and built a nice new one in the Fifties, with aluminium windows and a sign saying "Gents' Toilet". We are not burdened with a middle-class interest in conservation around here.'

'I had noticed. It's what Neville loves about it, or at least, says he does. But you – you've been away from here, surely? Didn't you find it jarred when you came back?'

It seemed to be a question he had never asked himself. 'Well, I was away at school, and then the army, of course, until I – I had to come back. But Radnesfield's where I belong, they know me, I know them. Our families have lived together for a very long time, and we've always adapted to one another's foibles.'

'Like an old married couple.'

'Perhaps.' His glance lingered on her for a moment. 'Though of course, as a bachelor, I couldn't comment, could I?'

'So you really like it?' She was interested in his response; he was a thoughtful and civilized man, and if he could feel at home here, perhaps she too might find in village life the hidden charms she had flippantly mentioned.

For the first time, she sensed withdrawal. 'Like?' he said vaguely. 'Oh, I don't know about like. It's a funny old place. Seems a pity to mess it about. But I'm keeping you talking far too long. Let's go and see where your husband has got to.'

Neville, in the library which boasted French windows inlaid with stained glass, in trying hues of blue and orange, was talking about where his desk would go. Helena left them, and wandered drearily back to the big, old-fashioned kitchen.

It was at the moment a nightmare, with a floor of cracked flag-stones and a stone sink with a rotting wooden draining-board. But here, at least, the deadly hand of the architect had fallen lightly; it was simply a square, undecorated room, surprisingly light thanks to the great window at one end overlooking the big pond at the foot of the shallow rise on which the house was built.

It was the first pretty view she had seen. The trees, the water – it reminded her of something. Willows, reeds, and – ducklings, yes, there had been ducklings. From her bedroom window in the vicar-age all those years ago, she had watched ducks on a pond like this, delighting each year in their fluffy clockwork broods.

She had spent hours there, on the window-seat dreaming of all the glittering prizes – Juliet, Cleopatra, Hedda Gabler; the applause, the acclaim.

Well, it hadn't worked out, had it? She felt a sort of dim, detached pity for the little ghost with her long blonde pigtails. How lucky she had never been granted a prophetic glimpse of the future she imagined like a huge box, wrapped in shining silver paper and tied with a great gold bow. She never even suspected, poor innocent, that the box was empty.

'I must have a window-seat here too,' she thought, and only then recognized her own acceptance of Neville's decision.

A tiny quiver of fear touched her. What choice had she left, but to accept it?

Oh, for years she had given way to keep Neville happy, because she didn't really care, did she? Or not enough, anyway, to pay the painful cost of any fuss. It kept intact the fiction that, if she did seriously protest, Neville would fall into line. Perhaps, once upon a time, it had been true; she could not remember when she had last put it to the test.

She couldn't pretend that she didn't mind this time. But she knew she must do what he chose, or he would do it without her, and she wasn't ready to break up her marriage. The bridges were in flames behind her; she had made no provision for any alternative to life as Mrs Neville Fielding.

But still, the sensation of a snare-wire tightening about her neck was so oppressive that she was raising her hand to loosen the collar of her heavy silk blouse when Neville found her.

'Isn't it absolutely mind-blowing? Once in a lifetime stuff, I tell you. Now, I'm taking you down the pub for a jar, so you can get a real taste of English rural life without the frills.'

The pub smelled of stale beer, tobacco, and boiled cabbage, and the half-dozen men gathered round the bar viewed them with unconcealed hostility.

Neville was in his element. Flashing notes, he bought drinks all round, addressed the silent man behind the bar as 'landlord', and with much jocularity ordered pork scratchings for himself and Helena, who shrank into a corner as far as possible from the bar.

When at last, after an elaborate series of farewells, he tore himself away, she followed him to the car, wordless in her embarrassment and cold with shame.

'There you are – what did I tell you? The genuine article!' Neville, driving away, was still high after his performance as the Man with the Common Touch.

'Neville, they were laughing at you.'

'What?' A faint flush crept up his cheeks, and he shot her a resentful glance. 'Words of wisdom from Helena Fielding, well-known expert on rural psychology and social classes C and D! Since you didn't condescend to talk to them, you're hardly qualified to comment.'

He had not been unaware of the atmosphere, this time or on his previous visit; far from it. He wasn't looking for simple-hearted, apple-cheeked villagers in a charming country pub; that was a folk-fiction he despised. The petty nastiness so evident in Radnesfield was, in his personal experience, a true reflection of human nature, and he believed himself now to be, like Harry, something of a connoisseur of its less pleasant manifestations.

Here he had struck a rich and subtle lode, a situation ripe for mischief, ready for exploiting into real-life drama. Harry had always thrived on the open sores of imaginary existence; jaded now, Neville craved the stimulation of flesh-and-blood playthings. Here was rank soil in which the flowers of evil might flourish.

He had felt like this before when he abandoned himself to the first stages of an affair. Common sense dictated he should draw back, but he was wantonly deaf to these promptings. There was a glorious exhilaration in being swept along, like going faster and faster down a ski-slope. The suspicion that the only stopping-place was in a crumpled heap right at the bottom didn't help you resist the temptation to push off at the top. Well – Geronimo!

His good mood restored, he drove on, humming under his breath.

They collected Stephanie from a friend's house on the way home to their Docklands flat. For her sake, they talked normally, but the atmosphere was heavy with unasked questions.

They were clearing supper, with Stephanie tucked up in her pretty, chintzy bedroom, when Neville said, without preamble, 'It said something to me, you know, that road, the signpost.'

She shifted uncomfortably. She too had felt something of the stark attraction he talked about, but feeling it unhealthy, would not indulge the thought.

'Where does the opposite road go to?' she asked, as if idly.

In an instant, the clouds descended. He clenched his fists in a pantomime of furious frustration. 'God, Helena, do you always have to do that? I'm only talking about an important moment of decision – important for all of us – standing literally at a crossroads, and you come out with some crass vapidity about the other road.'

He glared at her, his face darkly suffused. Once she would have bowed under the onslaught, but experience had taught her that allowing him to lash himself into a rage led to the sort of violence she had no wish to endure again.

She withdrew her gaze from him, as if he had suddenly ceased to interest her, becoming apparently engrossed in tidying the kitchen.

It usually worked, this weapon of indifference, to the point where she sometimes felt guilty about making use of it. Neville's desperate need was for an audience to act as mirror for himself; without one, he vanished.

Tonight he came over to put his arm about her shoulders.

'Nella, darling Nella, I'm sorry. I didn't mean it. I'm a horrible person, and I don't know why I shout at you when you're the best wife I could have. Far too good for me.'

'Neville, you're so stagey,' she said in exasperation. 'It's all an act. You're even acting now! We might as well be playing *Hay Fever* – "say sorry to your wife in the manner of the word 'engagingly'." '

He grinned. 'But I am engaging, aren't I? Usually?'

She sighed helplessly. 'That's the trouble. Most of the time, yes. Except when you're Harry, and then you're not engaging at all. You're plain nasty.'

'Bad Harry. We'll put him in the dustbin for the evening, shall we? There. Squash the lid down. Now I'm nice Neville, and you're lovely Nella, and you're pleased with me because I'm good now.'

He drew her into his arms, and she didn't resist. But as he bent his head to nuzzle her neck, she said seriously, 'I'm worried about Radnesfield, Neville. I think it's going to be Harry who lives there.'

He raised his head, but did not turn to meet her eyes. 'I'm sorry, Nella. I can't explain, but somehow, I have to buy that house. It's – it's destiny, if you like. Kismet.'

'There you go, over-dramatizing again,' she protested, but something about the way he said it sent chills down her spine. Harry was back again, like someone standing just at the edge of her vision, and in an uncharacteristically fanciful moment, she felt that they were the actors on his stage, being manipulated into position for a drama of which only he knew the denouement.

3

He had done it again. She could kill him, preferably slowly. For the umpteenth time since they came to live in this godforsaken black hole, he had landed guests on her at an hour's notice. A drinks party – well, thank you. Thank you very much.

She could cope, of course. She had a freezer stacked by a local gourmet cook and a microwave; having sweated blood the first time he dumped her in it, that wasn't going to happen again. But this was the symptom, not the disease.

The little flame of anger flickered, then died. She had tried protesting, forcibly; his only reply had been some offensive flippancy about fish and chips. When she persisted, he had stared with cold, opaque eyes until she was frozen into foolish silence. Things were going wrong – badly wrong – and she didn't know why.

At first, the house had seethed with builders, joiners, plasterers, decorators, plumbers and electricians. She had studied shade cards and samples and swatches of fabric until she had spots before her eyes, and fell into bed at night to sleep the sleep of total exhaustion and dream of light fittings and bathroom taps.

Then, suddenly, it was finished. The last painter brushed the last inch of the last wallpaper border into place and left, and a mind-numbing silence fell.

Stephanie had started at boarding school. Neville, commuting to London for the series, was at home seldom, and seemed increasingly, and deliberately, remote. He stayed at his club or with Chris Dyer, and had insisted on selling the flat, a decision which, she suspected, had been designed to rob her of an excuse to join him.

Neville had never before distanced himself like this. In the good times, they had been lovers; in the bad times, he had tried her patience like a child, and, like a mother, she had always indulged him. Now he was more like a rebellious teenager, inconsiderate, withdrawn and unpredictable.

She had always believed that, as a consequence of his childhood, he had a need for mothering; now, for the first time, she questioned the wisdom of filling that role in the life of a man who must bear his own mother a festering psychological resentment. And once he had reached the independence of emotional adolescence, he might, not implausibly, seek revenge.

What if – the thought transfixed her – the hidden agenda which she sensed, but could not discover, were her own destruction?

She gave herself a mental shake. This was hardly the time for speculation more suited to melodrama than to real life. Real life was the tomato roses and lemon curls she was turning with practised hands and adding to the platters she had set out with her usual artistic flair.

The results were impressive, for under an hour. But looking at them, she found her eyes misting. It wasn't much to be proud of, not really. Not when there wasn't anything else.

In London she had never had to notice her own poverty of resources. There had been friends, and charity work, and the constant round of artistic and theatrical events, essential for keeping up illusions when absolutely none of it was happening to you.

He had taken that away too. And now, in case she had any ideas about making friends in Radnesfield, he had begun throwing his weight around in a stand-up row with George Wagstaff up at Home Farm this afternoon.

She had been giving tea to Edward Radley, on his first formal visit to see the house transformed when Neville came in, full of his latest bully's triumph.

'Had the bloody nerve to send for me – cheeky sod – then tells me I have an obligation to make him official tenant of my farm, instead of manager. How do you like that?'

Helena was bewildered. 'What does he mean?'

'Mean? I'll tell you what he means. That's my farm, right? Paid for with my money, and by god, I've earned it. He's my manager, and I pay him, and if I don't like the job he does, I can fire him. It might cost me, but I can fire him. I've a damn' good mind to do it. Told him this morning his stackyard was a tip, and it is, too.'

Edward's eyes were lowered unhappily, and Helena said feebly, 'Oh dear.' It didn't take an agricultural expert to work out that Neville was unlikely to have useful advice for a man who had been in farming all his life.

'So this afternoon, he tells me the situation is "unsatisfactory", if you please, and he's going to get a lawyer to draw up a tenancy agreement. Prepared to offer very good terms, he says, and is dumb enough to suppose I'll buy that.'

'Wouldn't it be easier, in some ways?' Helena suggested, not very hopefully.

'Easier for him, all right. That way, he gets rights over my property, so I couldn't do anything with it, or get rid of him, and not only that, but his son could take it on without me being able to say a dicky-bird. He reckoned he was going to pull a fast one, but I set him straight. Oh, I set him straight, all right.'

He was quieter now, and his dark blue eyes glittered as he moved to the hearthrug, the better to dominate his audience. Pure Harry, Helena registered with dismay.

'I told him he was manager, and he would stay manager just as long as I chose. Of course, if he wanted to quit, that was his choice.'

'But Neville, he's lived there all his life!' she cried, sensing an uneasy movement from Radley.

'So? He told me all that, then gave me a spiel about how it was only fair he should have what he called his rights. So I told him I'd heard more than enough, and I would phone this evening if I wanted him out by next month.'

He paused in satisfied contemplation, then stooped to pick up a scone.

'I won't, of course, but I've put the frighteners on him and there had better not be any more trouble. He's a good manager, though, didn't you find, Edward?'

It was the first sign he had given of noticing the presence of the other man. Edward coloured, murmuring pacifically that he had always found him so.

'Perhaps I should have given him the tenancy. But I was always anxious to keep the land management intact.'

45

'Of course you were. Thoroughly prudent move.' His rage, as usual, had blown over quickly. 'Nella, you look ridiculous, sitting there clutching a teapot. Do I get a cup or don't I?'

'Oh, of course.'

She was pouring his tea when Neville said, with elaborate nonchalance, 'By the way! I asked a few people in to drinks this evening – forgot to tell you.'

'You've – oh Neville, how many?'

'Just a few. You'll stay, naturally, Edward, and Jack Daley from the garage with his wife, dear old Mr Tiggywinkle, I mean Tilson, the padre and his perfectly gruesome lady, the Morleys – is that all? Oh yes, and old Chris. He's been so impressed with our rural existence that he's down negotiating a lease on one of the cottages. Have to have a party to amuse old Chris.'

'I suppose he'll be staying the night.' Her voice was flat.

'Oooh, yes, I suppose he will.' Neville was in high good humour now, stuffing a cake whole into his mouth, as if showing off to court disapproval. 'I said to them all about six, anyway.'

It was quarter to six now; she had met this challenge, but would challenges of the future merely become harder and harder, until he had the satisfaction of seeing her fail?

Jack Daley was whistling as he set the alarms and locked up the garage. Getting to be quite a snug little business, it was.

He was a contented man, comfortable with the way his life was shaping. It had been a gamble, no two ways about that, throwing up a steady job as a mechanic in Birmingham and going in hock up to his neck to buy the garage here. Well, he'd been right, hadn't he, and it had taken him less than two years to prove it.

Sandra wasn't so crazy about it. A real city girl, his Sandra, and Radnesfield wasn't exactly the Bull Ring. But now he was doing well enough to take a bit out of the business, there were the clothes and the holidays they'd never been able to afford before; she liked that, and she'd come round to it. And it would be a good place for kids, when they decided to start a family.

Tonight he had extra reason to be pleased with life. Sandra would be dead chuffed by the invitation – well, to be honest, he was chuffed himself. You didn't get to meet famous TV stars when you were a mechanic in Brum, still less get invited back for drinks. Sandra would be over the moon. He'd just pop into the Feathers for a packet of fags, then go home and tell her the good news.

But there was no such light-hearted atmosphere inside, where a huddle of men were united in concern around George Wagstaff, whose heightened colour suggested that the double whisky clamped in his fist was not his first.

'He's going to pay for this, that I promise you,' he was saying, with a belligerence only partially induced by alcohol. 'And who the hell does he think he is, not been here five minutes when –'

Bill Smith, the landlord, came to attend to his latest customer, and Jack raised an eyebrow.

'George is starting a bit early today, isn't he?'

Smith, never communicative, grunted, but his wife, a comfortable bosomy creature, came over from washing glasses to murmur an explanation.

But Wagstaff had spotted him. 'Jack! Jack! Come over here and help me drown my sorrows. What's yours? I'm in the chair tonight – I may be out of a job by tomorrow.'

'No thanks, George, I'm not stopping. Just in for a packet of coffin nails.'

But the farmer was not disposed to take no for an answer. 'Come on, what have you got to do that's so important you can't stop for a pint? Sandra's the last girl to grudge you ten minutes.'

This was hardly the moment to announce his plans for the evening, and Jack hesitated. He wouldn't be giving Sandra much time to get herself tarted up. But then Sandra always looked good; it was one of the things he liked about her, that he didn't come home to a wife wearing bedroom slippers and no make-up. It shouldn't take her a minute to run a comb through her hair, just for a spur-of-the-moment, casual drinks party.

'OK George,' he conceded. 'Just the one.'

Jennifer Morley appeared first, an old acquaintance from drama school days who had hailed their arrival only ten miles away with genuine delight. With undeflectable enthusiasm she appointed herself Helena's social sponsor, decreeing simultaneously that Stephanie would adore boarding at Darnley Hall with her own Emily.

In this, as in many things, she was absolutely right. One of Jennifer's more disconcerting attributes was her ability to hit the nail squarely on the head, usually in public and without, as Helena had once observed feelingly, the smallest consideration for the feelings of the squirming nail.

'Neville, what fun!' She kissed him on both cheeks, before sweeping him neatly out of the way to perform the same operation on his wife. 'Helena, you are looking quite unfairly *soignée*. I do think it's utterly disgusting – no one can say I don't try, and Charles has the overdraft to prove it. Then you come and make me look like two bob's worth of nothing at all. Doesn't she, Charles?'

Her husband, a stolid-looking man with a stoic smile, had entered almost unnoticed behind her. 'Helena is looking delightful, as always. How are you, my dear?'

Helena liked Charles, and smiled at him affectionately, asking about his beloved garden, while Jennifer pounced on Edward like a cat enjoying the serendipity of discovering a fieldmouse on the hearthrug.

'Edward, what a lovely surprise! You haven't invited me to the Red House yet, you wicked man. But we're free three days next week . . .'

Neville was greeting the Daleys with great enthusiasm, Helena noticed, with a certain weary suspicion, though perhaps she was being unfair. Jack and Sandra were, after all, their nearest neighbours.

He still had some of the big city 'wide boy' aura about him, which amused Helena by its incongruousness in this rural setting. Sandra, too, did not dress to suit her surroundings, appearing tonight in a short, straight red skirt with a tight-fitting matching blouse and city stilettos. She was pretty enough, but her blonde hair was brassy, and the bright lipstick on her small, discontented mouth did not perfectly match her clothes.

Neville was chatting her up now, and although Jack was smiling proprietorially, as if taking credit for his taste in wives, Helena moved swiftly.

'Sandra, Jack, how nice to see you. Now, Sandra, who don't you know?'

It would be cruel to deliver her into Jennifer's clutches, so, since she was still pinning Edward to the wall in one corner, that left Charles. At least she could rely on well-bred attentiveness from him.

Neville, with a cool, sidelong glance at her, was fetching drinks; she, busy with her introductions, did not notice the next guest letting himself in until arms as muscular as a stevedore's came round her waist from behind.

'Nella, darling, you're looking sexier than ever. Village life obviously suits you.'

Chris Dyer, onlie begetter of Harry Bradman. How was it he always contrived to take her at a disadvantage? She freed herself and turned with distaste to greet him.

He was a great bull of a man, thick-set and short-necked, swarthy-skinned and with a taurine poll of tight greying-black curls that grew low on his forehead and, at the back, almost down to the top of his spine.

'Don't call me Nella, Chris. And if that's meant to be flattery, forget it. I don't feel cut out for village life.'

Taking up a plate of *crudités* gave her an excuse to circulate, and once Mr Tilson, whom Neville would persist in calling Mr Tiggy-winkle, arrived, she could relax a little, since that entirely unself-conscious gentleman seized on Dyer as the only unfamiliar person, and therefore a source of fresh interest.

Edward Radley was looking in need of rescue. Ten minutes of Jennifer Morley undiluted tended to induce structural stress in even the most robust male, and Edward, Helena surmised, had fewer social defences than many.

'Don't you think Helena's been most awfully successful in toning down the worst excesses of this perfectly ghastly room? Neutral shades and those fabulous Persian rugs – isn't it funny how they pick out the colours of the fireplace, and yet they're so pretty?' Jennifer was saying as her hostess approached.

Edward was taking it remarkably well, agreeing with a slight smile, but he looked relieved when Helena intervened.

'Jennifer, you are appalling. It's dreadfully rude to say that to the former owner.'

'Darling, I know I'm appalling. I was born that way. But I'm paying Edward a compliment. His taste is far too good to have liked it the way it was.'

At this, he laughed outright, and Helena was forced to join in. Jennifer, satisfied with her tactics, cast about for her next victim.

'Helena, who is that sensuous-looking brute with the cruel mouth who came in and made a pass at you?'

Annoyingly, Helena could feel her face redden. 'Chris Dyer. He's the creator of "Bradman", and apparently he's trying to lease a cottage here. It would be very convenient for him to be near Neville when he's working on ideas for a new series.'

'Judging by the way he's still watching you, it's not Neville he wants to be near. He's – good gracious, who on earth is this?'

A slightly grubby child of about ten, probably, though not certainly, female, had materialized beside them and was staring up at the adults with round, black, boot-button eyes, and the expression of one waiting, not very hopefully, to be entertained.

'Oh, it's one of the vicar's children!' Helena exclaimed, hailing the distraction as if it were the bugles of rescuing cavalry. 'How nice to see you, dear.'

A faint look of surprise crossed the child's face. It was not often that the appearance of one of the vicarage children provoked any sign of enthusiasm.

'Tell me your name again – I'm afraid I've forgotten. It's very stupid of me.' She knew she was gushing, and deserved the reply she got.

'Yes, it is. I'm Tamara.' The child spoke without moving that fixed stare from their faces.

'Are your parents here? – Oh, there they are!'

The group standing awkwardly in the drawing-room doorway gave her an excuse to move away, leaving Jennifer skewered by the redoubtable Tamara's gaze, and, for once in her life, outfaced.

Peter Farrell, the vicar, was hovering, anxiously rubbing his hands when Helena reached him.

'Ah, Mrs Fielding! The door was open. We just . . . . So kind of your husband to invite us. I do hope you don't mind the children – baby-sitters, you know, such a problem . . . .'

The other two vicarage children, differing from Tamara only in height and, in the case of the younger, gender, stared up at her from identically grubby faces with identical round black eyes.

'Of course not,' Helena assured them with the closest she could come to sincerity. 'It's Nathan, isn't it – and – and Diana?'

'Dinah.' When Marcia Farrell smiled, her short upper lip disclosed a row of unfortunately crooked and prominent teeth, as well as more than the usual expanse of gum. 'I don't know why it is that

Peter always feels obliged to apologize for the children, do you, Helena? As I always say to him, our blessed Saviour didn't think anyone needed baby-sitters, did he?' She laughed her determined, religion-needn't-be-solemn-now-need-it laugh, and went on without waiting for a reply. 'I said to Peter, Helena's just such a sweet person, and a mother herself, and I expect having sent her own little girl away from home, she'll love to see some youngsters about the place.'

'Of course. Now do come and meet people. I think perhaps you know everyone, except Chris Dyer –'

She moved them smoothly on, setting the children on Neville for orange juice. Marcia Farrell was the kind of person she found it hardest to like, the kind who put so many people off religion; sugary-sweet at surface level, with always the sting of pure poison somewhere. Helena was meant to be feeling guilty now about having sent Stephanie off to school, but fortunately, though she missed her, she had no ambivalence about the decision. Removed from the tensions at home, Stephanie was thriving, and besotted about a school which let you keep your very own pony.

Helena derived vindictive pleasure from leading Marcia across to Chris Dyer. He, priding himself on being a connoisseur of feminine charm, would suffer merely from looking at the vicar's wife with her straggling black hair scraped into an elastic band at the back and her aggressively Oxfam couture. The vicar followed, his dark, sad, spaniel's eyes on his wife, contriving to look left out of the group even before he got there.

She found Neville at the drinks table, and hissed humorously, 'Did you have to ask the Farrells? You know they always bring those wretched children, and I dread to think what they may do if the mood takes them!'

He could have laughed with her. But his eyes were hard and bright as he said, 'Perhaps I should have spiked their squash – I hate it when parties get dull, don't you?'

He picked up the vodka and orange he had been mixing, and steered across the room to where Sandra stood, trying not to look as if she were eagerly awaiting his return.

Sandra took her drink with a lingering, suggestive glance, fluttering her heavily-mascaraed lashes, with her silly little mouth moist and parted. Neville looked down into the vapid brown eyes too long and too intimately, and when he brushed her bare arm,

Helena saw her jump as if his fingers were red-hot. At that moment she caught Helena's eyes upon her, and her cheeks flared guiltily.

Angry with herself, and with Neville, Helena spun away. How many foolish, dazzled little girls had she seen? Too many even to remember, she thought tiredly. These conquests meant nothing to Neville: they were as anonymous to him as the pawns in the decorative chess set in his study.

The game with Helena was darker altogether. He had always loved to see her jealous, and despite her carapace of indifference, he seemed still to see through to the delicious, shrinking vulnerability underneath.

To cover her confusion, she seized a tray of canapés, and, turning, noticed Mr Tilson installed in the wing-chair by the fireplace, and unattended.

He had been watching them all shrewdly from under shaggy grey brows, his bright and quizzical eyes, frizzy grey hair and age-rounded shoulders giving him the cosy look of the nursery figure Neville had mentioned.

But there was nothing cosy about the cool, active brain which still operated, almost casually, the business end of his electrical components factory at Limber, from theoretical retirement in Tyler's Barn, next to the Red House.

Half-hidden in the big chair he had chosen, he could indulge his favourite occupation of playing fly-on-the-wall. This, he had discovered, was one compensation for growing old; given the flimsiest of excuses, people pretended not to see you. They were afraid of boredom, afraid you might talk and they be forced to listen, trapped, like the wedding guest, by interminable reminiscence.

But you didn't learn talking, whereas under silent observation, human dramas would always unfold, more absorbing because of their authenticity than any that might pass across a screen.

He knew a lot about Radnesfield. He was not part of it, nor could he ever be – an incomer of only ten years' standing – but he knew all that anyone could know by watching, listening, and rarely, very rarely, asking the strategic question.

Tonight he was inundated with a delicious wealth of new material, in an atmosphere of oddly heightened tension. Emanating from host and hostess, he surmised, observing the interaction, or lack of it, between Neville and Helena. This intrigued him, and he observed with keen anticipation that Helena, lovely, poised, and with a hostess's proper concern for a neglected guest, was approaching him.

She was a bit too perfect, that girl. With her cast in the angelic role, lapped in universal love and admiration, there wasn't really another starring part for her husband, except Lucifer.

'Can I fetch you another drink?' she offered now with a smile, indicating the old man's empty glass.

'No thank you, my dear. I've had quite as much as is good for me already. That husband of yours is mixing some very powerful drinks this evening. I wonder why.'

It wasn't exactly a question, and he saw her, glancing round, realize that he was right. Voices were rising, Jennifer had two bright spots of colour in her cheeks, and even Marcia was laughing immoderately at something Chris had said.

'Oh dear,' she said helplessly. 'I wonder if I should –'

'Comfort yourself with the reflection that adults, in my experience, are usually well aware when they are being plied with strong drink, and only Charles Morley, who is a sensible man, has come by car, so you may as well relax.'

'I suppose you're right.' Helena, balancing the tray, sank on to a stool at Maxwell Tilson's side.

'That's when you learn all about people, when their guard is down.' Blinking aimiably about the room, he said, 'For instance, Jack Daley thinks he is impressing your friend Mr Dyer – but Mr Dyer isn't really listening.'

Helena followed his gaze. 'Oh, he's getting copy.' Her tone was unfriendly. 'I don't know if you watch "Bradman", Mr Tilson, but I would bet that the next series will feature an engaging young salesman, living on his wits, who will naturally be filleted by dear Harry going, oh-so-smoothly and elegantly one better.'

His interest made him incautious. 'How fascinating. Now, either you don't like Mr Dyer, you don't like the series, or you don't like your husband. Or perhaps all three.'

Her gasp of outrage alerted him. 'Oh dear, my wretched tongue! I forget, you know – as one grows older, people's reactions become so transparent that it's hard to remember that one's responses should be veiled.'

Helena's face still burned. 'You're a very dangerous man,' she said wryly.

'I watch, and people talk to me sometimes, because I'm interested, but I don't judge, and I don't gossip. But yes, I suppose it is dangerous in its way. Knowledge is power, and really the only sort of power that still interests me.'

A little silence fell, and his gaze went back to Neville, talking to Sandra Daley. 'But when you're still young – well, there are so many temptations.'

'Talking of temptations.' Helena was becoming desperate. 'Can't I persuade you to have a vol-au-vent? And shall I get Charles Morley across to talk to you? He's clearly a friend of yours.'

Jumping to her feet she made her escape. Why would people persist in trying to force her to look at things which it had taken a lifetime's practice to ignore? And this party seemed to be going on forever. Would they never leave?

Like an answer to prayer, Edward approached her, his face full of concern. 'I must be going – I've certainly outstayed my welcome, and it's time some of these others remembered they have homes to go to. You're looking tired.'

She looked up gratefully, only to find his eyes fixed on her in a way that depressed her further. She had seen that look before, and it always meant trouble. Now she would have to avoid even the most harmless intimacy, and that, in this barren social environment, would be a real deprivation.

'Not at all.' She assumed a light tone. 'It's always gratifying for a hostess to see that her guests are enjoying themselves.'

He smiled in polite disbelief, turning to Maxwell Tilson. 'I'm just on my way now, sir. Have you brought your car, or shall we walk down together?'

Helena could see that the old man was not entirely pleased; his reply had a sarcastic edge. 'Why, thank you, Edward. I feel sure that even my aged bones can make it down the hill unaided, but I have to admit that you did that very neatly.'

Ignoring the implication, Edward went on, 'In fact, I have an even better idea. The Morleys have to pass our respective doors; I'll see if I can hitch a lift for the two of us.'

Under such a quietly determined onslaught, the party inevitably began to break up, and Tilson got himself to his feet.

'He does get what he wants, that young man. I think you will have to be careful, my dear.'

But this time Helena was ready, 'He's been so helpful to us both. And whatever he says, it can't be easy to see your family home fall into other hands.'

'He must have felt very sure that your husband was the right custodian. Thank you for a most – enlivening – evening.'

His eyes twinkled on the adjective, and Helena could not help laughing, as he kissed her hand with old-fashioned gallantry.

Then they were, mercifully, leaving. The vicarage children had perpetrated nothing worse than black sticky marks on the new paintwork, and Marcia, flown with wine, was in full spate.

'What a marvellous, generous man your husband is! So good, so kind – we couldn't believe it, could we, Peter, when he said – oh, I mustn't let cats out of bags, must I? But I think, I really think, he has saved me from having a nervous breakdown –'

Wearily, Helena wondered what empty promise he had been making now. Once she would have assumed it was a naïve way of buying temporary popularity; tonight, she really wondered if he had given it for the pleasure of breaking it later. But meantime, to Marcia at least, Neville was all that was wonderful.

His popularity, however, was not universal. Amid a volley of giggling, tipsy protests from Sandra, Neville was kissing her fingers individually by way of saying good-night. At his shoulder, Jack's face was darkened by a cloud of suspicion; it was clear that Neville noticed, and was amused. The involvement of a jealous husband might add spice to a conquest that threatened to be all too easy.

With considerable relief, Helena escorted them all out. But when, ahead of her husband, she came back into the room, a figure still loomed by the window – Chris Dyer.

Her recoil must have been obvious, for he gave a short, harsh laugh. 'The welcome guest! Did Neville forget to tell you I was staying?'

'No, of course not. You just gave me a start as I came in.'

'That's a weight off my mind. I would simply hate to think you didn't want me.'

He was moving towards her as Neville came in. His eyes travelled from one to the other with speculative, malicious amusement.

'Don't let me interrupt anything,' he drawled, but Helena ignored him.

'If you'll both excuse me, I've got a bit of a headache, so I'm just going up to bed.'

It was Chris who expressed polite concern. Neville's face, she thought as she closed the door, displayed the thwarted annoyance of a spoiled child when the grown-ups have ruined his fun by taking away the sparrow before he could really settle to pulling off its wings.

Her steps dragged as she climbed the stairs. She was papering over the cracks. It was what she had done all her life; now the paper was peeling and the cracks gaping wider and wider, yet she still lacked the resolution to pull the whole rotten edifice down. She made a timid prayer that something would happen to sort it out, and despised herself.

The only thing worse, they say, than unanswered prayer, is being given what you thought you wanted.

4

The mirror in the old hallstand lent Martha Bateman's face a drowned, greenish tinge as she peered at it, but she had long ago ceased to notice that. It had been here in the hallway of this house when it belonged to Joe's parents, and Joe's father's parents before that.

In any case, it was a long time since looking in the glass had given her pleasure – not that she hadn't once been well enough. But now her interest was strictly practical, to ensure that the grey wool hat was set decently straight, covering the rigidity of the iron-grey perm.

This morning, she barely saw her image, though her fingers automatically twitched the collar of her Sunday coat into place. There was trouble on its way; she read the signs as surely as she would have deduced the otter's presence from the arrowhead of spreading ripples on Markham's Fen. It might be no more than the follies of strangers, as unthreatening as the posturings on the television screen. But some instinct was telling her it was not so, and there was wariness already in her hooded eyes.

With handbag and gloves in her hand, she opened the door of the front room. Joe Bateman was sitting in vest and trousers, with his tabloid Sunday newspaper in his calloused joiner's hands, in the nearest approach to squalor he could achieve in any house that Martha Bateman cleaned.

Her mouth, grim-set already, tightened further. He could be managed only so far – stubborn as Eardley's pigs, the Batemans were, in the village phrase.

'You see you remember to put on them potatoes, like I said.'

He took in her church-going outfit, and a slow, knowing smile crossed his face. 'Well, vicar'll think it's Christmas, with all the old hens coming in to cackle.'

'You're one to talk, Joe Bateman. When did you ever set foot over the threshold, except for your own wedding?'

His manner might be ponderous, but the reply was pointed enough. 'And the christening. Don't forget the christening. You set a lot of store by that, seems to me.'

Her eyes travelled involuntarily to the photograph on the mantelpiece in its brass frame: a boy, smiling, but with features which somehow testified to the fact that he was not quite as other boys are. Her mouth softened as she looked at it, but only for a moment.

'And for the funeral,' she said harshly. 'Well, three visits won't get you to heaven, not to my way of thinking.'

'I'll have good company where I'm going, then.' Unruffled, he chuckled coarsely as he waved the newspaper at her. 'Takes something out of the ordinary to get you there, anyways. Oh, there'll be a great old turn-out today, shouldn't wonder.'

Martha, ignoring him, went out into the street. She did not look round at the sound of hastening feet behind her.

'Martha, oh Martha!'

She neither turned her head nor adjusted her pace as the woman panted up behind her.

'Well, Martha, what do you reckon to it?'

Her lip curled a fraction. 'Reckon to what, Annie?'

'You mean you've not seen it? All over our paper, it were . . .'

'Oh, that.'

At the church a huddle of women, like Joe's barnyard fowls in their sober Sunday colours, were clucking at the lych gate, ignoring the vicar who waited to greet them at the church door, his hands rubbing unconsciously together.

The hush that fell when she arrived was a tribute to Martha, and she savoured it. She was very watchful these days; as housekeeper at Radnesfield House she had commanded an automatic respect which now she must exact by force of personality. Relishing the moment when she would toss them this juicy worm of scandal, she hesitated a second too long. She bridled at the sound of another woman's voice.

'It did seem to me we'd all be in our pews this morning. What do we think on it, then? Is he misbehaving, or are they a sweetly loving couple?'

'Oh, there you go, Jane Thomas.' Martha's tone was sharp with spite, resenting this theft of her small pleasure. 'You should know better than to pay any mind to what you read in them old newspapers, you should.'

'No smoke without fire, that's what I say.' One of the lowest in the pecking order had dared to speak, emboldened by the choice nature of the titbit of information she had to contribute.

'Them Daleys had a right set-to going home from the pub at lunchtime, and Jack Daley with some tidy names to call that Sandra. And there was my youngest, out playing in Wagstaff's field with Mary's Billy. And when she comes in, "Mam," she says to me, "what's a common tart?" '

Teeth were sucked in pleasurable shock, and scandalized breath indrawn. The subdued clucking rose again.

'Well, London ways.'

'Everso pretty, that actress is. Younger than Mrs, by what I saw on the telly last week.'

Sharon Thomas was hovering at the outside of the group. She was pretty, in the drawn, exhausted way of women who have married and had too many children too early, and drudged all their young lives. She lived in the shadow of Jane, her forceful mother-in-law, and certainly in awe of Martha Bateman and her vitriolic tongue. But now, exalted by her status at Radnesfield House, she could taste the delights of superior information.

'All I know is, that Mrs Fielding, she's a real lady. Ever so kind and thoughtful. But him – pinched my bottom, he did, when I were bending over cleaning the brass.'

'He never!' Incredulous eyes swivelled on to her.

'You've never said nothing about this before!' Martha led the accusation.

'Nobody's never asked me.' She tossed her head. 'Like I said, she's nice. And we'd best be getting into church, or vicar will wring those hands of his right off.'

Martha's face was blacker than ever as she brought up the rear with Jane Thomas.

'Changes, that's what this'll mean. You mark my words.'

'Talking's cheap,' Jane said comfortably. 'Takes a lot of believing, you said yourself.'

Martha was not appeased. 'We've had enough changes in Radnesfield. We don't want no more.'

In agreement for once, Jane nodded as they reached the vicar, who, with all the innocence of the reader of quality Sundays, was saying happily, 'How very nice to see you all, ladies! Such an encouraging congregation,' as he ushered them in.

Neville was brusquely uncommunicative as he and Chris Dyer set off for London early on Monday morning. Dyer was unsurprised. Fielding was a moody sod, and anyway, who made bright conversation at six a.m.? He pulled his French leather cap down over his eyes, leaned back and went to sleep.

Neville glanced at him in annoyance. Just because he had been a little crabby, it didn't mean he wanted to drive all the way up to London with only his thoughts for company.

He was obscurely disappointed in Radnesfield, which had promised, somehow, a lot more than it had got round to delivering. Helena, despite the dislocation, was still the same Helena. She had managed to convert his wonderful anarchic house into a sort of monument to good taste in dreadfully trying circumstances; when he had reckoned to reduce her to bread and cheese at the kitchen table or a chicken and chips carry-out from Limber, she had responded with entertainment as elaborate as anything she produced in London for expected guests.

He had tried to get her off balance; she had treated him like an experienced mother ignoring her child who is kicking and screaming on the floor. Now they didn't talk, they didn't fight, they didn't make love.

If Helena wanted to play the 'don't care' game, then he was happy to raise the stakes. Don't care, as they had been accustomed to say in the Home, was made to care, and god! he was going to enjoy watching her break. He'd like to see her attempt the sort of toffee-nosed lack of interest she'd shown about Sandra Daley.

She was right there, of course; Sandra didn't matter. Sandra was a zero, like a dozen other zeros, and her eagerness had about as much appeal as an over-ripe plum that squelches into the hand that plucks it. He would have dropped her long ago if it weren't for the husband, who provided fresh entertainment each time Neville saw him with some new evidence of tortured suspicion.

Daley, mad with jealousy. Cool, self-possessed Helena, helpless and pleading. That would provide two delicious illustrations of his power, and a tiny taste of the fictitious satisfactions Harry Bradman so regularly enjoyed.

Helena heard the front door slam as Neville and Chris left, and tried to get back to sleep, but as tormenting thoughts cartwheeled behind her closed lids, she accepted the inevitable, and got up. Bundling on her jade dressing-gown against the morning chill, she pattered through the silent house to the refuge of the kitchen.

The red Aga glowed warm and welcoming, and she pressed herself against it like a cat as she made her coffee.

Sipping it gingerly, she went to perch on the cushioned seat in the window that took up almost the whole end wall of the kitchen.

The sun was dragging itself lazily above the horizon, and a wraith-like mist was rising from the pond in the hollow beneath the house. The tops of the beech trees in the coppice that straggled down towards the village, showing a lively green just now, were barely swaying in a light dawn breeze, and somewhere a blackbird was calling. Over it all, the great span of sky was clear, brilliant silver. It was going to be a lovely day.

Helena gazed hungrily at the beauty before her. Somehow beauty seemed to be a very scarce commodity these days.

She had wakened with a headache, the sort that tension clamps like an iron circlet about the forehead. It came on, sometimes, before a thunderstorm, and this weekend the house seemed filled with the same sort of brooding, electric anticipation.

She had scolded herself for being melodramatic, but this was not imagination. The balance of her relationship with Neville, so precariously maintained over the years, was shifting. It was as unmistakable as the wind veering round, though she was still unable to identify the quarter from which it came.

She had once fasted for three days, in a fashionable attempt to rid her body of toxins. At the end, she felt weak and disorientated, but strangely perceptive. Solitude, it seemed, was having the same purgative effect on her. She was becoming painfully sensitive to atmosphere, as if every mood vibration acted on her like ice on a tooth with an exposed nerve.

On past experience, there should have been weeks of tranquillity and sunshine, while Neville, having got his own way, sweet-talked himself back into favour. This time, he seemed to have kicked the craving for approval.

Yet again, Harry's shadow fell. She had heard them talking on the terrace, Neville and Chris.

'It's got to convince,' Dyer had said. 'I'm going to be asking more from you, Neville – more sense of danger, more anarchy. The punters have got to see you uncontrollable, in free fall. They have to believe you're capable of absolutely anything.'

And Neville, in the slow, deeper voice he used for Harry, had drawled, 'Oh I am, believe me, I am.'

Helena, clearing cups from the study, had shuddered as if a goose walked over her grave, and couldn't shake off the thought.

It was uncharacteristic, too, that Neville should be indifferent to Chris's blatant attentions to her – Neville, always one of the great modern proponents of Victorian double standards.

He knew of Helena's fastidiousness, so was this another Bradman development, a psychological game to attack what she was and break down her personality, or was he trying, at last, to provoke a crisis in their marriage? Until now, she had been essential to his comfort, his safeguard against the Sandra Daleys who persisted after he had tired of them.

Or was there, perhaps, someone else, someone with whom he might genuinely have fallen in love? Given the rest of his behaviour, it seemed unlikely, but she had her headache to convince her that somewhere, storm clouds were indeed massing.

The click of the letter-box, telling her the newspaper had been delivered, roused her from her depressing reverie. Beside the paper on the mat lay a large brown envelope, addressed to herself in anonymous black capitals.

When she slit open the envelope and drew out newspaper clippings, she checked, with a churning of the stomach.

They came from the bottom end of the Sunday newspaper market, and, in essence, all carried the same story. There were photographs of Neville, escorting a young and very glossy blonde, which showed them tête-à-tête in a restaurant, entering a theatre, or leaving a nightclub with her on his arm. Several shots revealed them gazing into one another's eyes.

' "Badman's" latest victim?' the largest of the headlines ran, 'Or is it true love for TV's anti-hero?'

Sickened, she read every loathsome word. She knew who the woman was; Lilian Sheldon, a minor television star playing Bradman's latest mistress in the series, and Helena could see the publicity machine grinding away behind it all. The public were to be led to believe that this might be, at last, the love of Harry's life, and to help the thing along, rumours of True Romance would undoubtedly be generated. It had happened before.

But always, she had been warned; always, Neville brought her into the act, feeding her the right lines to say to the press. She had even been known to enjoy these little bits of live theatre. Keeping her hand in, she called it.

This time, he had said nothing. Perhaps, she tried to tell herself, he had hoped she wouldn't find out, knowing her policy of avoiding sensational newspapers.

It was only at that moment that the obvious question occurred to her. Where had the cuttings come from?

She turned over the envelope. The printing was fairly neat, done with a broad felt-tipped pen, and the envelope was like a million others. But it had been delivered by hand, not by post.

Either someone in the village had taken it upon themselves to spread a little misery – which would be in character – or Neville had left it himself, this morning.

She was afraid she knew the answer; that Neville had chosen to tell her their marriage was over in the most humiliating and hurtful manner possible. She was, for once, underestimating her husband.

At quarter past nine she managed to speak to him at the studios.

'Ah, Helena! Now, what little bird told me you would call?'

She had phoned Neville, but it was unmistakably Harry who answered, silky and cruel, with a hateful smile in his voice. She had managed, she believed, to sound neither tearful nor accusatory with her opening, 'Neville?' but despite hours of agonizing she was still unsure what she would say next.

She could have spared herself. Without waiting for her reply, the voice went on, 'Terribly sorry, I just can't talk just now – dozens of bods all breathing down my neck as I speak, darling – but I'll see you next weekend. Chris is coming down with me, and perhaps someone else. OK?'

She replaced the buzzing receiver slowly, and automatically switched the answering machine back on. The tape was already loaded with optimistic requests that she should contact this newspaper or that, with financial inducements attached. She could be a rich, if undignified woman by this time tomorrow.

It was strange, she observed dispassionately, how much it did hurt. She had thought of divorce lately in much the same way as a sailor views the harbour lights at the end of a long and particularly stormy voyage. Yet here she was quivering in shock that the man she had lived with, and, in their fashion, loved for so long, could dismiss her as casually as an importunate telephone caller selling kitchens.

'Someone else' – was it at all possible he meant Lilian Sheldon? Even with Neville locked into Harry mode, she found it hard to believe he would bring his mistress to meet his wife, but she no longer felt confident to predict his behaviour. They were entering new territory now, and the old maps were useless.

Huddling her misery about her like a black cloak, Sandra Daley stared into the window of the Limber department store, at the anorexic dummies with their sinister white embryonic faces and their glitzy frocks, seeing nothing.

But at least pushing past and round her were strangers whose eyes didn't stick to her like vacuum cleaners trying to suck out her secrets. Radnesfield was laughing at her now, hidden cruel laughter behind faces as closed as the dummies' were.

She had fled here today because you needn't think when you were shopping. You could look at the pretty things, and simple childish greed would blot out everything else. But today the brain-numbing magic wasn't working, and she was still hurting as she had never hurt before.

But then, she'd never been so high before, floating on a pink cloud. She had lived a paperback romance – the veiled looks, secret phone-calls, stolen afternoons at a little country hotel where there was champagne waiting for them. Best of all, he could have had anyone, and he had chosen her.

Oh, she wasn't dumb. She knew she was being given The Treatment, and he sure as hell hadn't invented it just for her. She'd told herself all along it couldn't go on for ever – but only three weeks! And no warning about the photographs with glamorous, sophisticated Lilian Sheldon.

Worst of all, was the dark, poisonous suspicion that the great romance of her life had been just a squalid little affair where she had been used, unvalued, and then discarded like some cheap hooker. Well, you couldn't say he was wrong, after what she had done to Jack, who was faithful and decent.

And Jack knew. She had denied everything, of course, but once or twice Neville had been careless, and Jack knew as surely as if he had been a witness to their love-making. With her head full of impossible dreams, she hadn't really cared.

But reality was Sunday morning, with Jack rubbing her nose in the pictures in the paper. She had tipped her chin and said, 'Must be a barrel of laughs for his wife, mustn't it?' but she knew she had gone white.

Jack's eyes had scorched her like a blow-torch. 'That'll put your little nose right out of joint as well, won't it?'

She had been bred tough. 'That just shows what a small-town mind you've got. I'm sorry for you, really. I told you before – big stars go on the way he does all the time, and it doesn't mean a thing. Maybe now you'll believe me.'

But now she was left with the pain, the agony of loss and humiliation and shame. The sequins on the dummies' dresses shimmered into a blur as hot tears came to her eyes.

'Goodness, Sandra, surely you don't need another new dress!'

The tone was arch, the voice that of the vicar's wife. Startled, Sandra swung round, blinking rapidly.

'Oh, just window-shopping,' she said, attempting a side-stepping withdrawal.

With the expertise of long practice, Marcia Farrell had positioned herself so that without physical contact it was almost impossible for her victim to escape.

'That is smart, that black dress, isn't it? I'd love to be tempted, but of course . . . .' she sighed, but then continued brightly, 'Still, I really mustn't complain – it's not one of the important crosses one has to bear, is it? When you see the trouble other people have –'

Was there a knowing look in the sharp black eyes? Mrs Farrell was such a busybody that no one in Radnesfield told her anything, so perhaps she hadn't heard the latest nasty whispers.

'The poor Fieldings!' she went on. 'Isn't it appalling what they print in papers these days, probably without a scrap of real evidence?'

The question mark hung in the air, and Sandra stonewalled. 'I couldn't say, I'm sure.'

'Of course, he's such a charming man, women must absolutely throw themselves at him. And Helena, well, she's absolutely sweet of course, but between ourselves it has just once or twice occurred to me that she's a teeny bit shallow, perhaps? Just a fraction lacking in the sort of spirituality that such a sensitive man might need.'

Sandra had no option but to listen, as the gushing torrent flowed on.

'He saw at once, you know, at once, how burdened I was with practical problems, said he must liberate me to use my real, God-given talents. He's made the most wonderful offer – but I mustn't say too much! Except that not many people with his wealth would be so ready to see it as a privilege to use for others. "Peter," I said to the vicar, "he has a great soul." '

Then what could only be described as a simper crossed her face. 'Not that one could be blind to his other attractions! "It's lucky I'm not a jealous man," the vicar said to me.'

She gave a girlish giggle, and Sandra stared in sudden, contemptuous comprehension. The silly cow was in love with him herself, and was dumb enough to imagine that he fancied her too. And for all her yammering about spirituality, it wasn't Christian love she was on about.

Suddenly, the image of Neville shortening his own upper lip in an imitation of Bugs Bunny, as he called her, struck Sandra with such painful force that she thought she might either laugh or cry hysterically. The fear gave her strength to extricate herself, almost pushing the other woman aside.

'I'm sorry, I've got to go, Mrs Farrell.'

Sandra heard the cry behind her, 'Oh, just Marcia, please! Mrs Farrell always makes me feel like the vicar's wife!' as she scurried thankfully away.

5

By Friday afternoon, Radnesfield House was well prepared. For the unidentified visitor, Helena had chosen the yellow bedroom, opposite their own. Chris she would put in his usual room which, by no coincidence, was as far away as possible at the other end of the house. At least he had now found a cottage; perhaps next time he would be staying there.

When she went upstairs to change, Helena was almost certain Neville and Chris would be alone. She was resigned to Neville's eyes sweeping round in triumph as he noted the signs of preparation that would show his bluff had been successful.

But she had, once again, misread her husband. It was, she reflected bleakly, becoming a habit. As she smoothed her hair in front of the glass on her dressing-table, she heard the wheels of Neville's Jaguar crunching on the gravel below and, feeling foolish, stepped behind a curtain to peep out.

Neville's eyes flickered immediately to the window as he stepped from the car, but he did not see her. While Chris, stretching, climbed from the back, he went round to help his other passenger gallantly from her seat.

Lilian Sheldon was wrapped in a luxuriant pale fur, its deep collar making a frame for her golden cap of hair. She laughed up at Neville as he opened the car door.

As Helena crossed the upper landing, she recalled her old drama school coach's advice. 'Deep breaths, petal – take it in, let it out slowly. Three of those and you're ready for anything.' She was, she felt, about to make the most difficult entrance of her career.

Lilian was experiencing a certain reluctance to get out of the car. She was like a cat in her appreciation of comfort, and in here the seat was soft, she was warm, and the atmosphere was peaceful.

One of her few consistent principles was never to go looking for hassles, and meeting Neville's wife struck her as the perfect scenario for heavy hysterical scenes. She'd given those up for Lent ten years ago and managed to stick with it.

It was, she had suspected, one of Neville's little Harry-games. She didn't usually mind Harry-games, which had a faintly sadistic edge that she found exciting; she'd never been what you might call a nice girl, and nice men made her eyes glaze over.

She didn't really understand Neville. He and his wife seemed to have sort of a weird relationship; the way he talked about her was like the way some guys talked about their mothers, and she'd really rather they cleaned this up with her included out.

Neville, however, had been hell-bent on her coming, and for the moment at least, what little Neville wanted, little Neville would get. Neville was her current meal ticket, and Lilian had her stomach set on some pretty fancy gourmet banquets in the future.

She wasn't at all sure where the relationship was headed, on screen or off, but for the moment the press attention was doing her nothing but good. She'd string along, and if he did divorce his wife – well, marrying him would surely be good for an extended run in 'Bradman', and he was as attractive a man to play serial monogamy with as any other. Better than most, in fact: in lots of ways, they were two of a kind, with strong appetites and few illusions, products of the same tough upward struggle. They played by the same selfish rules though Neville seemed to prefer a nice layer of cosy self-deception between him and the naked truth which was always her own bottom line.

She sighed, and prepared to swing her long, expensively-stockinged legs out of the car. He hadn't said anything, and she had picked up only the sketchiest indication about the way Neville wanted her to play this scene; she would have to busk it. His wife's reaction was Someone Else's Problem.

The hall was dark, despite the tall lamp on the chest at one side, which Helena always left burning in this shadowy part of the house. Neville and Lilian were laughing and talking as they came in, with Chris behind them. She moved to the chest to set down her handbag, and consequently appeared, as it were, spot lit.

Helena had believed herself prepared, and the newspaper photographs had not lied about the good looks or the glamour. What they had entirely failed to transmit was the resemblance.

Like a clever caricature of me, Helena thought wildly, with just that mild exaggeration of everything: the hair a more metallic shade of blonde; the features coarser; the complexion more highly-coloured; the eyes a more strident shade of blue. She was taller, of course, but the likeness was there, in the curve of the cheek, perhaps, or the line of the eyes. She felt the superstitious dread of the *doppelgänger*, as she descended the last few steps.

Then Neville, too, stepped into the pool of light, ready to take Lilian's coat, and Helena had to suppress a gasp. His hair, thick and straight, had always been worn combed back from the temples, but for Harry it was, as now, brushed forward to fall across his brow. His tweed jacket was of a pattern Neville would once have dismissed as crude.

A blessed sense of unreality descended. From somewhere a long way off, she saw herself walk across the hall to greet them, all serene confidence.

There was admiration in Chris's eyes, and for once she allowed him to kiss her without forcing him to arm's length.

She did not go to kiss Neville, and he made no move towards her. He did not take his eyes off his companion as he said, 'Lilian, sweetie, you've heard all about Helena.'

Helena smiled, saying nothing, experiencing only a mild curiosity as to how the other protagonist would react.

Reaction was too strong a word for Lilian's behaviour, suggesting that another person's attitude had impinged on her consciousness. Lilian operated like an emotional tramcar along the grooves of her own needs and desires.

She surged forward gracefully, a tidal wave of fur and expensive scent, putting out both hands to Helena and kissing the air four inches above her right ear.

'Darling, what fun to meet you at last! And what a wickedly amusing house! Neville's told me all about it, and you simply must show me every last horror.'

Astonishment almost overcame Helena's sense of detachment, but catching Neville's eyes upon her, dead as glass, she found a professional social smile.

'Have you had a reasonable journey? Do come in to the fire. Or would you prefer to go upstairs first?'

'Oh, a fire, and tea – is tea by any remote chance on the schedule? Oh, angel! I've been dreaming of a cup of tea all the way down, haven't I, Neville darling?'

She drifted past Helena into the drawing-room, slim as a wand in her cream suede suit, her head set like some exotic flower on her long neck, then collapsed gracefully into a chair, stretching uninhibitedly, cat-like, in the warmth. Helena could almost fancy she heard the rumble of a purr in her lazy, low-voiced laughter.

The extraordinary thing was, Helena found that she could not entirely dislike the woman. There was something almost refreshing in her frank enjoyment of her creature comforts and the naked egotism of her conversation.

She called Neville 'darling', ordered him to light her cigarettes, and blew him kisses when she went to change for dinner. On the other hand, there was none of the emotional or sexual tension between them which would have made the evening hideous with embarrassment. It even crossed Helena's mind that this was meant to demonstrate that there was nothing between them after all.

Almost she might have believed it. But Neville's eyes never met her own, and his behaviour seemed cold, yet excitable, as if he were waiting, with ill-restrained impatience, for the next act of the social drama to begin.

Chris, too, was ill at ease. He seemed to be out of patience with Neville's more boisterous exchanges.

Helena could, very nearly, derive sardonic amusement from it, shielded by the detachment that had fallen about her like a protective cloak. In this surrealistic situation, she had discovered that playing the role of a mother meeting her son's girlfriend for the first time meshed perfectly with Lilian's performance.

But Neville's eyes, still and watchful as a snake's, chilled any laughter, and despite Lilian's artlessly selfish prattle, the evening limped slowly and awkwardly away.

At last the clock chimed eleven, and Lilian rose, stretching luxuriously in her tactile pink cashmere, and patting a yawn that showed neat white teeth.

'Definitely my bedtime, darlings,' she proclaimed. 'I simply love my bed, Helena, and I can't wait to get below that puffy comforter – such heaven! Wherever did you find it?'

Helena knew better than to reply, Lilian by now being engaged in blowing streams of tiny kisses to the men. 'I'll show you up,' she offered, seizing the opportunity to get herself out of the room. 'Lock up, will you, Neville, when you're ready to go to bed.'

He had hardly directed a look or a word to her all evening; now he stared at her silently. He had been drinking steadily; his face was flushed and his eyes glittering.

It was Chris who got to his feet. 'I will,' he said. 'Does that earn me a good-night kiss?'

'Oh for goodness' sake, Chris,' she said, closing the door before he could move.

Lilian yawned again, much less delicately, as they crossed the hall. 'Don't you think Chris is gorgeous? He always looks as if he might beat you up, if you didn't do exactly what he wanted. It gives me the most delicious shivers up my spine when he calls me a stupid cow on the set.'

'I'm afraid I don't find that sort of thing appealing,' Helena said flatly. She felt exhausted by her efforts to sustain this ludicrous, artificial atmosphere, and, like the anaesthetic wearing off after a tooth extraction, the comfortable feeling that all this was happening to someone else was beginning to disappear.

Lilian did not pursue the conversation; she withdrew to the yellow bedroom, leaving Helena, her body suddenly leaden, to drag herself through her bedtime routine.

This couldn't go on; she must talk to Neville. But she felt sickening uncertainty as to his reaction, and as a roar of inebriated laughter rose from below she shivered. She had learned the painful folly of arguing with Neville when he was even slightly drunk.

Her courage failed her. He would be no more convinced by a pretence of sleep tonight than he had been other nights, but if she were in bed with her eyes shut and the bedside lamp at her side switched off, it should not provoke an outburst. Unless, of course, that were part of a plan over which she had no control.

It was after midnight when she heard the loud good-nights on the landing, and Neville came in. He sat heavily on the bed to take off his shoes, and opened drawers and cupboards noisily as he undressed for his shower, but he did not speak. When the rushing of water told her he was safely in their bathroom, she risked sitting up to stretch her cramped limbs, before lying back in the same position on down pillows that felt like concrete. In the silence that fell when the shower was turned off, she found her hands clenching in tension.

After the bathroom door opened again, she could hear no sound, though she strained her ears for any stir of movement. Perhaps he was standing, staring at her: by a huge effort of will, she stopped her eyelids flying open to look. But she lay still, and heard at last the bare footsteps rustle on the soft pile of the carpet, moving as slowly as a big cat stalking its prey, round to her side of the bed.

Still she did not move, and barely breathed, until without warning his hand, hard as bare bone, gripped her chin.

In one movement, she jerked upright, her eyes blazing. 'Don't touch me,' she said, her voice automatically lowered, but savage in its intensity.

He loomed above her, his eyes almost as dark as the navy of his bathrobe. 'So you are just indifferent, not actually clinically dead. I did wonder.'

'What do you want, Neville?' She shrank back, at bay against the headboard.

'Oh, I don't know. Just a little reaction, to show you care, perhaps? Just some sign that somewhere, under all that perfect self-control, there actually is a flesh-and-blood human being. Why didn't you fight for me, Helena? Why didn't you scratch the bitch's eyes out?'

He was almost shouting as he bent closer, and outrage gave her courage. 'Neville, you're drunk. I'm not going to talk to you now.

We can discuss it in the morning – if you can tolerate the sound of anything other than an Alka-Seltzer fizzing in the glass.'

The emotion went out of his face, leaving it expressionless, and his voice was flat as he said, 'No, Helena. No, I don't think we will.'

Suddenly, as if a switch had been thrown, his mouth curved in Harry's malevolent, mocking smile. 'Come on, darling, give us a good-night kiss. It's every wife's duty to kiss her husband good- night.'

He bent over, the smell of whisky raw on his breath, and tipped her face ungently to his, bruising her lips with a hard, unloving kiss. ' "Good-night, good-night! Parting is such sweet sorrow," ' he said. 'Sleep well, won't you, my pet?' and he was laughing as he walked to the door of the bedroom and went out, leaving it open behind him. She heard his footsteps cross the landing, his tap on the door – 'Lilian?' – and a gurgle of laughter from the other side.

She threw herself out of bed to slam the door against their mingled voices and stood, leaning against it, shuddering and scrubbing her mouth with her hand, like a child. She need no longer imagine there was any humiliation too gross for him to commit upon her. The metamorphosis was complete: Neville was gone, swallowed up by the monster he had created.

Indeed, in her first wild unreason, it seemed that Lilian, too, was a mutation; that Helena and the Neville she had once loved had no more substance than wraiths, adrift forever in the limbo of things past.

She did not know how long she had huddled, cramped against the door into a tight, agonized ball of suffering, but the sound of footsteps brought her to instant awareness.

The tap on the door, when it came, was gentle, even tentative, but still she fumbled for the awkward old key, persuading it to turn in the lock.

She succeeded, but the handle was not tried. Instead, Chris's voice spoke softly but urgently through the thick panels. 'Helena – Helena –'

'Go away,' she whispered fiercely. 'If this is all part of the plot, I can only say that you disgust me. For god's sake, leave me alone.'

She heard what sounded like a sigh, but he said nothing and the footsteps retreated. In a sudden frenzy, she rushed to the wall of cupboards, flinging open doors, dragging out suitcases and filling them, almost at random, with all that they would hold.

It was seven o'clock when at last she crept out to ferry her cases down to the garage. She was on her way by ten past seven, leaving no note, and driving through the sleeping village as if all the devils in hell were at her heels.

Sandra Daley, sitting listlessly at the uncleared breakfast table on Tuesday morning, did not jump to answer the phone when it rang. It was more than a week since she had last scurried eagerly to pick up the phone.

Now her voice was flat as she said, 'Hello?' indifferently.

'And what sort of greeting is that?'

A shockwave seemed to course down her spine as she recognized the teasing, familiar, dark-brown voice.

'Enough to make a fellow think you didn't want to speak to him!'

'N–Neville!' she stammered. She struggled to sound cool, sophisticated, in control. 'I – I wasn't expecting to hear from you.'

'Now, how can you say that?' His voice was caressing. 'Not expecting to hear from me, when we haven't had a chance to talk for ten days? I've been thinking of nothing but how to make time to call you, but I haven't had a moment alone when I didn't know Jack would be at your end with his hand out, ready to pick up the phone.'

'Oh, Neville!' Her eyes filled, and she didn't care any longer that he would hear the tears in her voice. 'What was I to think? Never a word from you, and all those pictures in the papers –'

'Oh, my sweet, I forget what a precious innocent you are! Look, the world I live in – it's different. Lilian's part of my job, and my public life – well, that belongs to my public, and to a large extent, I'm their slave. They have to get what they want, or that's the end of the track for me.

'But my private life – our private life – that's another thing. That's special; you don't need me to tell you that. That's the well of freshness that gives me my inspiration.'

Lips parted, she listened, letting him seduce her as much by the sound of his voice as by the words he used, and the remembered excitement flooded through her.

'Neville, I don't know what to say . . .'

'Just say you'll meet me – our own special place, three o'clock, Friday?'

'Three o'clock, Friday,' she repeated obediently. Did she hear him laughing at her confusion as she put the phone down?

Three o'clock, Friday. It wasn't over, after all. He hadn't ditched her. She was his secret inspiration, he had said so, and of course she understood about his public image. It was like royalty, really; he wasn't free to do what he truly wanted to do, in his heart, but that was all right with her, whatever happened. He had given her back her dream of herself as special, desirable. The wicked, delicious exhilaration fizzed up in her, like champagne.

London received Helena back with its characteristic indifference, which was balm to her violated sense of privacy.

Old friends had been both kind and tactful, and contacts yielded a publicity job in one of the larger theatres. It was menial work, but she was self-supporting and still in contact with her old acting world, and its undemanding nature was, for the moment, ideal. She needed time to get to know Helena Fielding, *feme sole*.

On Charles Morley's recommendation, she had refused to speak to Neville except through Henry Stanton, the solicitor he had found for her for whom she felt no personal warmth, but who, having a criminal as well as a divorce practice, was more than a match for Neville, despite his determination to behave as badly as possible. As a result, Helena was able to move into a pleasant garden flat in Highgate just in time for Stephanie's summer holiday from school.

Stephanie, despite an attempt at sophisticated acceptance of the realities of modern family life, took it badly. She had hoped to spend the first fortnight at Radnesfield House, with Angel boarded with the Wagstaffs at the Home Farm, but Neville was unhelpful. He and Lilian opened the house up only at weekends, and agreed to her coming without much enthusiasm.

When she arrived, afterwards, in London it was clear that her poise had been considerably shaken. Stephanie's veneer of indifference was not proof against seeing another woman in her mother's place, and neither Neville nor Lilian had done anything to make the child's awkward position more bearable.

Neville, after an initial, extravagant fuss over her arrival, had hardly been there, sometimes out in the village ('Playing squire,' observed Stephanie acidly), sometimes further afield. Lilian slept late, exercised in the mini-gym, then prepared herself to be taken out in the evening. Stephanie had spent most of the weekend in the stable, the rest in her bedroom.

Helena did her best to organize a pleasant holiday, with tickets for shows and excursions every day, but the girl was lonely while she was at work, and though Emily Morley came to stay for a week, she clearly had far too much time for brooding. By the end, she was thin and tense, longing to get back to school and desperate to be reunited with Angel, since, apart from a few days when she was visiting the Morleys, she had not seen her pony at all. She had refused to return to Radnesfield House; Helena did not force the issue, and Neville offered no specific invitation. 'Daddy's different,' was all Stephanie would say.

It was a relief to them both when she returned to Darnley Hall, and an anxious visit midway through September reassured her; Stephanie had regained weight, and seemed happily absorbed in the familiar world of school. In times of stress, children liked what they knew, and temporarily at least her friends had more influence than her family.

Helena returned to London feeling lighter of heart than she had felt for a very long time. She was very grateful for the bossy determination with which Jennifer Morley had insisted that Stephanie be sent to Darnley Hall.

She was, however, considerably less delighted at that lady's next attempt at running her life.

6

It was one of the warm, still nights of an Indian summer, and since the flat boasted a little walled courtyard, Helena went out to sit in the dwindling rays of the sun, sipping a glass of white wine and admiring the plane tree in a neighbouring garden whose leaves were beginning to show the first streaks of gold.

The buzz of the doorbell was an intrusion, but she went light-heartedly enough to open the door, blinking in the darkness inside.

She had to shield her eyes before she could make out the details of the figure on the doorstep, and when she did, made no effort to disguise her distaste.

'You!' she said. 'How did you find my address?'

Chris Dyer, resplendent in a vivid pink shirt open almost to the waist, a gold medallion lurking in the mat of hair on his chest, regarded her with mocking assurance. 'And to think I thought you might be pleased to see me! Jennifer Morley was sure you would be delighted to catch up with an old friend.'

Damn Jennifer, she thought, but said only, 'Old friend?' as she stood squarely in the doorway, determined to make no gesture, physical or verbal, which could be construed as an invitation to enter.

'Still the same lovely Nella, prickly as a handful of barbed wire. It does lend a certain spice to the chase, and you always secretly liked it, didn't you, my darling? Go on, admit to yourself that you enjoyed our little spats.' He leaned against the doorpost, oppressing her as much by his aggressive masculinity as his bulk.

She drew a deep breath. 'Chris, may I be perfectly frank with you?' This was one occasion when she felt, like Gwendolen Fairfax, that speaking one's mind ceased to be a moral duty and became a pleasure.

'While I was Neville's wife I had no option but to tolerate you, for business reasons. I disliked having to do that, very much. I hated the coarseness of your attitude to me, and I hated what you did to Neville through your unspeakable Harry. You encouraged Neville to glory in decadence and sadism and depravity and – and sheer nastiness, and though I can't blame you for the break-up of our rather shaky marriage, I do blame you for the manner of it.

'But now, thank god, I'm a free agent, and one of the joys of my freedom is that I only have to suit myself. So no, I'm not pleased to see you. I never have been, and I would like you to go away and leave me alone.'

Surely a few sips of Chablis couldn't have quite such an uninhibiting effect! The old Helena Fielding had never in her life been so blatantly rude to anyone; to discover that she could do it was an experience as invigorating as a cold shower.

She had given no thought to his reaction, but she no longer cared. Bluster, anger, even violence: she felt ready for anything he might chose to do.

He surprised her. The bull-like head dropped, like that animal overpowered, and when he raised his eyes to meet hers, they were free from any glint of sexual challenge.

'You don't pull your punches,' he said ruefully. 'OK, I had you figured wrong, and I'm sorry. You're difficult to read, you know that? I thought it was a touch of the old *odi et amo*, to tell you the truth.'

'Well – no.' His response deflated her; feeling, now, that she had been needlessly cruel, she added more temperately, 'I'm sorry too. I shouldn't have been so rude. Let's just say that we simply have nothing in common.'

'Neville.' He said it flatly, and though she shook her head in vehement denial, she fell back a pace, weakening her intransigent posture.

'Look, can I come in? You've got a bottle of wine on the table out there that looks inviting, and you'll have a headache if you drink it all by yourself.'

His rallying tone had returned, and she was quick to reply tartly, 'I was planning to cork the bottle and keep the rest for another day,' but she was standing aside as she spoke.

His male presence was almost overpowering in the little court-yard as he took the second chair, looking awkwardly large for its delicate wrought-iron frame. She poured him a glass of the cool wine, and he emptied half of it in a long swallow before he spoke.

'Cards on the table, Nella – Helena, sorry.' He changed it hastily, seeing her expression. 'I had two reasons for coming tonight. First of all, I thought the dust might have settled, and I wanted to get to you before someone else did. That stand-off-don't-touch-me act drives strong men mad, you know.'

Helena, suddenly very aware of his proximity, felt the warmth creeping up her cheeks and lowered her eyes, hastily taking a sip of wine.

He smiled sardonically, but to her relief added, 'Still, we'll let that pass. Neville is the other reason.'

Here she was on firmer ground. 'Neville Fielding, I am thankful to say, has nothing whatsoever to do with me – '

'Don't be facile. You were married to him for – what? Sixteen, seventeen years? Just because you're getting a nice, quick, uncontested divorce doesn't mean you can shrug it off. Helena, I mean this. I am really, seriously worried about him.'

After her outburst she was silent, only pursing her lips, and he went on, 'OK, I'll accept that I was a bad influence, or at least Harry was. I agree with it all, decadence, sadism – what was the other word you used? Oh yes, depravity. That too. But I swear by every successful series I ever hope to have, Helena, that what I created was a character, not a person. When I found Neville, he seemed great for the part. How was I to know he would try to be Harry?'

'Oh, Dr Frankenstein, how awful for you.' She was still unsympathetic.

'So if the guy acting Faustus sells his soul to the devil it's Marlowe's fault, is that it?' He controlled his rising temper with difficulty. 'Helena, I'm in deadly earnest. What I'm trying to say is that something is going to blow up with Neville. It's as if each new thing he does has to be more outrageous than the last – as if he's trying to see how far he can go before the sulphurous flames actually spring up and engulf him. And there's nothing to stop him now.'

'Lilian –'

'Lilian!' he jeered. 'As long as Lilian has the limelight and every glamorous luxury she can think of, she won't rock any boats. They're quite a good match, actually; both totally insensitive, totally self-absorbed, and quite indifferent to anyone's interests but their own.'

His concern for Neville seemed genuine, and against her will she found herself relenting. 'Chris, I'm not saying I don't believe you. But I wasn't having any effect on Neville anyway. Oh, I used to, but that was before Radnesfield and all it stood for came into our lives. After that, I was only another victim, and playing fly to his wanton boy wasn't one of the roles I fancied. So –'

He looked awkward. 'I know, I know. After that night –'

'No.' She rose, decisively. 'I'm not going to discuss that. Finished, OK? I think you'd better go, Chris. I'm sorry if things are going badly.'

'Badly? Christ!' Chris struck his forehead with a clenched fist. 'He's baiting George Wagstaff about the Home Farm. He's carrying on an affair with Sandra Daley under Lilian's nose, and driving

Daley off his head with jealousy. He's leering at every passing village maiden – and that's only the things I know about.'

She sighed helplessly. 'All right, it's disastrous, but he's got his head now, and I shouldn't think anyone can stop him. If there are consequences, so be it. Maybe he'll learn something. I'm sorry if that sounds callous, but I don't know why you think it's the end of the world if Neville has to face the music.'

He had followed her, without demur, to the door. 'I think he'll kill someone, eventually, because that's all that's left that he hasn't done,' he said sombrely. 'Or someone will kill him.

'Still, I daresay you're right. There's assuredly nothing I can do to stop him. Good-night, Helena. A kiss for old times' sake?'

For once, she did not mind turning her face up to him, and he did not take advantage. Kissing her lightly on both cheeks, he said, 'Another time, perhaps?' But Helena said only 'Perhaps,' and shut the door.

'I'm beginning to feel exactly like the Salvation Army,' Jennifer began her phone call.

'What, all of it, Jennifer?' Helena, recognizing the voice at the other end, found herself amused despite her current exasperation with her caller.

'Well, the Missing Persons Bureau, anyway. Did the rather luscious Chris Dyer catch up with you?'

'I would quibble with the description, but yes, he did. And I would appreciate it if you could be a little more circumspect with your information service.'

'Oh, don't be stuffy, darling. I thought he would be good for you. You're far too young to be living like a nun anyway.'

'Who else, Jennifer?'

'Who else? Oh, I see what you mean. Well, only Edward, actually. He's popping up to London for a few days and said he'd like to pay a neighbourly call. So I thought I'd better warn you – I don't suppose he's everybody's cup of Earl Grey, and you might want to be out, or something.'

She found herself surprisingly cross at Jennifer's patronizing tone. 'He was extraordinarily kind when we first went to Radnesfield, and I'll be delighted to see him. He's a very interesting man.

If you'd run a check before you left me a prey to Chris Dyer, it might have been more to the point.'

'Nonsense, Helena. You really are developing a distressing tendency to be prissy and middle-aged. You can't spend your whole life copping out. Edward's very sweet, of course, but he's one of the bloodless kind, whereas that caveman type is every woman's secret fantasy.'

'I'll give Charles a hint next time I see him,' Helena retorted snappishly, stung by her remarks. She felt quite out of charity with Jennifer as she put the phone down.

She had been expecting Edward's telephone call. It would have been unlike him to take her by surprise.

'I'd hate to impose on you, if you'd rather be left alone, but I wondered if there might be a chance of meeting up while I'm in London? Of course, I know you must be busy – lots of other friends . . .'

Perversely, Helena felt irritated by this excess of diffidence. 'It would be lovely to see you, Edward,' she said robustly. 'When can we meet?'

His voice changed. 'Oh, that's – that's marvellous. What do you like to do – opera, theatre –?'

Not knowing his tastes, she suggested a play she knew to be light-hearted and competently performed; they could eat, after the show, in an unassuming bistro unlikely to be patronized by Neville or his friends.

The evening proved surprisingly successful, and in the three days that followed, she rediscovered a sort of undemanding pleasure that she had almost forgotten. She had not felt so much at ease in male company for a very long time; with Neville there had always been an uncomfortable tinge of danger, of unpredictability.

She had seen herself supplanted by a younger woman, and felt the cold winds of indifference that blight any middle-aged woman's aspirations to a new career. Basking now in Edward's uncritical admiration, she felt like a cat, bedraggled from living rough, who had been taken in, put on a silk cushion in front of a roaring fire, and given a saucer of cream.

The last evening, after another glorious September day, they ate in the courtyard, Edward looking at ease in the chair Chris had so awkwardly overflowed. Helena had produced a simple cold meal, with strawberries and cream, and they lingered over the coffee and the last of the wine, reluctant to leave the fading sunshine and go inside. At last, a chill wind began to ripple a few leaves off the plane tree, and Helena shivered.

As they cleared the plates away in the narrow galley kitchen, he said, 'Well, back to Radnesfield tomorrow.'

Perhaps it was simply the cold; Helena shivered again. By now, Radnesfield had begun to seem a strange aberration, her memories of it faint and fading like yellowing snapshots curling in a drawer.

'Do you want to go back?' she said.

He turned to face her, hesitated for a moment, then, seeming to make up his mind, took her unresisting hands.

'You've got an unfortunate impression of it, you know. It's just an old-fashioned village, set in its ways by isolation, perhaps.

'But no, I don't want to go back, because I'm leaving you here.'

She made an involuntary movement of withdrawal, but he imprisoned her hands.

'Of course, of course. I know it's far too early for me to say this, Helena. But I daren't let the moment pass; I've been patient for such a long time. I've wanted you, you know, since the minute you stepped into my house, bringing colour and warmth and beauty, making me realize how narrow and cold my own life had been. I recognized you at once, knew you were for me – that sounds ridiculous, doesn't it, in the circumstances? – but I knew. If you want something enough, you can always make it happen.'

'Edward, please don't . . .'

He put a finger gently across her lips to silence her. 'I'm not trying to hurry you – time isn't important, you can take all the time in the world – but in the end, I'll persuade you to agree. Oh, you're far, far too good for me, I know that, and don't think I'm expecting you to fall madly in love with me. I don't suppose I'm what anyone would call a romantic figure.

'But I can look after you, offer you – and Stephanie, of course – a secure home with a husband who adores you. I can see it all so clearly, Helena. When I'm in the Red House, I see you there, in the chair by the fireside with your hair shining gold against the panelling. It's a timeless picture, so I don't know when you'll feel ready, but it's not a dream. It's a promise, and it's going to happen.'

She could not move or speak, only gazing at him, wide-eyed, and he laughed tenderly. 'I didn't mean to make a speech. I'm sorry. But at least I've declared myself, and you can start getting used to the idea.

'No, don't say anything. I'll see myself out, and I'll be back in London soon.'

He kissed her fingers, then touched a light kiss to her lips, and left her in the kitchen.

She stood, almost transfixed, for a long moment, then moved slowly outside to the darkening courtyard and sat down again, oblivious to the cold.

Reason told her she was in no state, as yet, even to consider the future. She needed time to adjust to the death of her marriage; she had only just regained that freedom which was a modern woman's most treasured right. And yet, and yet . . .

It was a wonderful feeling, being cherished, and there was such a promise of security in Edward's undemanding adoration. They didn't seem to be handing out prizes for uncomfortable self-sufficiency this year. And he seemed so sure.

Oh, she wasn't deluding herself that she was 'in love'. The remembered headiness of high romance, the stomach-lurching ecstasy that was pain as well as pleasure, formed no part of her feelings for Edward.

But somehow, the ancient words kept floating back into her mind: 'Stay me with flagons, comfort me with apples.' Love, for her, was a sickness she had outgrown.

They were married in December, with Stephanie's blessing, just before the much-publicized media marriage of Neville and Lilian. Bradman's marriage took place on screen, before record audiences, a week later.

Just before Christmas, Helena, trying to dismiss her misgivings, returned to Radnesfield once more.

Martha Bateman did not look full of the Christmas spirit when Jane Thomas caught up with her on the way to their places of work on the morning of Christmas Eve.

'Well, Martha,' she said cheerfully, malice spicing her speech like the cinnamon in the biscuits she was taking in to Mr Tilson, 'you'll be enjoying having a family in the house for Christmas, I dare say.'

Martha's sniff was eloquent. 'I never did think to see Mr Edward fix to marry. His mother, God rest her soul, wouldn't be resting easy, like she's every right to, if she knew.'

The look Jane gave her held understanding, but she said only, 'Not much harm in it, surely? He's not a lad, and she's not a young woman. Stands to reason he'd be lonely, with his mother gone and all. And not having other friends, neither.'

'Weren't no call for other friends, you know that, Jane Thomas.' Her voice was sharp. 'Kept themselves to themselves, they did, as were right and fitting. She never reckoned to go so soon, poor lady – shouldn't have, not by rights. And nothing been right here since.'

They were nearing their destinations now, the two houses next door to one another. At the gate of Tyler's Barn they both stopped, and Jane said slowly, 'Other days, other ways, Martha. I reckon old things got to turn over to new sometime.'

The other woman's eyes were hard as pebbles. 'Never knew a plough turn over a furrow without all the nasty crawling things come up to the surface. You mark my words, Jane, best leave things just the way they are.'

'I never held anything different, Martha.' Jane sighed, closing the gate behind her. 'Not a great old lot we can do about it, though.'

With a tightening of her lips, 'Them as lives longest sees most,' Martha said, in a favourite phrase, and stalked on to let herself in to the Red House.

'Martha hates me,' Helena said. 'She really hates me.'

'Give her time.' Edward bent to kiss her cheek reasuringly.

'Perhaps she'll come round once she sees I'm making you happy,' she said hopefully. She was feeling optimistic; they had spent a domestic fortnight in a quiet Devon hotel and were already, almost against her expectation, contented, like a long-married couple. There had been no surprises; Edward, if not exciting as a lover, was tender and thoughtful, and if Helena ever thought of the almost sick excitement of her relationship with Neville, she did not admit it, even to herself.

Edward laughed, patting her hand. 'She sometimes gets a bit carried away with the old retainer part. But you'll be accepted eventually. They'll even accept Neville, you know, given time, once they understand he isn't going to turn everything upside down. Though quite honestly, I think he's almost an irrelevance. He's only there at weekends, after all.'

Helena looked at him sharply, but he seemed genuinely unconcerned. Well, she wouldn't trouble him by putting the idea into his head, but she could not see Neville, who was becoming less and less amused by his plaything, considering Radnesfield House as a home for generations of Fieldings as yet unborn. When he eventually grew terminally bored with the entertainment it had to offer, he would sell up.

Even so, she could claim no premonition as to the scope of Neville's next disastrous enterprise.

The vicar's hands were black as he turned round from groping in the open flue above the stove, and across his face a sooty streak had given him a Hitler moustache.

The three children, jostling to get the best view of what was going on, shrieked raucously, and their mother laughed too, but to Peter Farrell's anxious ear the tone of her laughter was almost hysterical.

'But can't you see what's wrong with it, Peter?' Perhaps the tears in her eyes were still tears of laughter, but he wasn't sure.

'I can't see anything,' he said wearily, wiping his hands ineffectually on a rag. 'We'll have to get a man to come and take a look at it.'

'And what are we going to do for baths and heating meantime? Nat! Nat, will you get out of there, you naughty boy! Now look how filthy you are, and how I'm going to get the soot off your school shirt with cold water, I don't know. Oh, just go to your rooms, all of you, and see if you can manage to keep out of trouble for ten minutes.'

There was an astonished silence. Clean clothes had never been an obsession of Marcia's, and curiosity was considered sacred evidence of an enquiring mind. While the vicar was not sure that intellectual stimulation was invariably the primary motive for messing about with things, he was as unsettled as the children by their mother's uncharacteristic reaction.

84

'You heard what your mother said,' he pitched in, with an assumption of authority, 'off you go,' and to his surprise, they obeyed, with only Tamara whining, 'I don't see why we should go to our rooms, just because Mum's in a filthy mood,' as she shut the door.

Marcia turned, looking stricken. 'Oh, she's quite right, Peter. That was entirely unfair. I was punishing them for my own unhappiness. I'd better –'

He grabbed her hand, incidentally covering it with soot, though neither of them noticed. 'Look, sit down. Never mind them; it might do them good to think of other people's feelings, just for once. I'll make you a cup of tea.'

Blinking back the tears of sheer misery, Marcia for once did as she was told. 'I can't bear it, Peter; no heating, no hot water, and it's going to be one of the coldest nights of the year, they're saying. I'm sorry to be so feeble, but it was just that I had really counted on not having to cope with another winter of this. Double-glazing and proper central heating, by now, I thought . . .'

Farrell, warming the pot, chose his words carefully. His wife had been defensive on this subject before.

'Did – did Fielding give you any clear indication of when he would actually be lending us this money?'

Marcia's face flamed into two unbecoming Dutch doll patches of colour.

'How could I speak to him again, Peter, when I told you he said that Helena and that fancy solicitor of hers were simply bent on bleeding him dry! His accountant's hardly going to encourage him to go making deferred-payment, interest-free loans in a situation like that. But he did say he wouldn't forget. 'Now I've put my hand to the plough,' he said, remember? And I said I didn't know why everyone always thought they had to quote scripture to the vicar's wife, and he laughed.' She smiled herself, reminiscently.

'But now Helena's managed to get Edward into her clutches, perhaps we can hope she'll take her claws out of poor Neville. I trust him absolutely, you know, to do whatever he can.'

She sipped tea from the mug, rimmed with greasy black fingerprints. It seemed to do her some good; after a moment or two, she blew her nose fiercely.

'Well, I'll just have to soldier on, won't I, and trust in the Lord to see us through.'

She managed an unconvincing smile, but as her husband turned to fetch his own tea, added, 'But oh, Peter, I really don't think I could bear it, if there was no end to this in sight.'

Seeing himself as at the same time helpless and responsible, he found he could say nothing. He felt awful about it, simply awful, as he so frequently did about almost everything.

'Do you know what your ex-bloody-husband has done now?' Chris Dyer shouted. 'Do you know?'

It was a Thursday afternoon in April; opening her front door, Helena took an involuntary step back at this verbal assault. It was despite an inner cringing that she managed to sound unruffled.

'No, I don't know, Chris, but I can't imagine that shouting at me will help.'

'Sorry.' It was a perfunctory apology.

'I think you should come in.' Helena led the way into the sitting-room. 'I think we'd both be better to sit down.'

She sat as she spoke, but Chris was too overwrought to follow her example. He strode about, conducting a taurine progress past the delicate porcelain collection which had belonged to Edward's mother.

'He's hi-jacked Harry, that's what. And does he have the decency to tell me face to face?' He glared at Helena, then answered himself. 'Well, of course not. He knows he'd have got this,' he doubled up a massive fist, 'straight in the middle of the face he considers his fortune. I hear of it from my assistant producer – and he's fit to be tied, as you may imagine. But Neville's gone mad – stark, raving mad. I think he's got a death-wish, and he won't be satisfied till he's reduced everything to rubble. But I'll be damned if he'll destroy my life without paying for it.'

Helena was listening with growing bewilderment. It was plain enough that there was some major upheaval going on in their television world, but she did not see how it affected her. Surely he could not want her to intercede with Neville; Chris would hardly be naïve enough to expect results from that.

'I don't understand what you're saying, Chris, and I certainly don't see what I can do about it.'

He stopped short, whirling to face her. 'Ha! that's rich! It's not what you can do about it, my lovely. It's what it's going to do to you.'

For the first time, she felt real disquiet. 'For heaven's sake, Chris, stop striking poses, sit down, and tell me simply and clearly what this is all about.'

At last he told her.

When Edward came in, his eyebrows rose as he paused on the threshold. In another man, this would have been a violent exclamation of astonishment at seeing his wife, not only entertaining, with apparent equanimity, a man she cordially disliked, but holding a large Scotch in her hand at five o'clock in the afternoon.

It was clear, however, that here was trouble of some kind, and he crossed to kiss her first, then, perching protectively on the arm of her chair, nodded coolly. 'Afternoon, Dyer. This is an unexpected pleasure.'

Helena's face was white and shaken. 'You'd better tell him, Chris.'

It was simple enough. Neville, Chris said, had become increasingly restive about the storylines on 'Bradman'. Harry, he claimed, was being shown in an unsympathetic light and he started to blame Chris whenever he felt Harry was getting what he termed a bad press.

Chris had, in fact, paid little attention. The network was satisfied, the ratings were terrific, and Neville had his own success so bound up in Harry that he could not afford to walk off the set.

He had therefore been completely unprepared when his assistant producer, gibbering with rage, phoned from London to tell Chris he had just been carpeted by the Head of Light Entertainment, waving an embargoed press release to say that Neville was pulling out of the television production of 'Bradman' and – wait for it – making a Harry movie instead.

Edward, listening intently, interrupted at this. 'But surely he can't do that? Surely you have him under contract?'

Chris groaned. 'Only for one series at a time. When you're as hot a property as Neville, you can dictate your terms. And his agent was smart enough to keep the character of Harry as Neville's property – they insisted on that, right from the start – and frankly, Neville *was* Harry. The public would never have accepted a substitute if Neville had quit.'

'Go on, Chris.' Helena had drunk more than half the whisky in the big crystal glass.

It got worse. Neville wanted more scope, but they weren't queuing up to offer finance even for a low-budget film. So – 'And this,' said Chris maliciously, 'is where it suddenly becomes your business' – he had decided to liquidate everything and put up the money himself.

'Straight from the horse's mouth, I got this. Naturally, I got on the blower, and there he was, incredibly pleased with himself in that bloody insufferable way he has. He's going to sell everything, right down to the shoes on his feet, and put everything into a Bradman Trust. That way, he has no money, and no one can make any claims on him. According to him, anyway.'

'That's Stephanie,' Helena interpolated, her knuckles white round the glass. 'Chris asked him about Steph, and all he said was, "It won't do her any harm to forget about that fancy school. I didn't have ponies and gracious living at the local comprehensive." '

Edward's arm went round her shoulders. 'Perhaps we can manage something –' but Helena cried in fury, 'Why should you? Why shouldn't Neville support his own child? It's only to feed his appalling, overweening vanity, and I don't see why you should be sacrificed.'

'So he'll be selling Radnesfield House.' Edward was troubled. 'Well, I only hope he can be persuaded to take care who he sells it to. The village needs someone who will have the right ideas.'

Dyer sneered. 'Oh, he's been careful, all right. That, Radley, is the cream of the jest. He's got an offer with god knows how many nothings on the end from a developer who has the planning department in his pocket. They've been looking for a new development area. Three hundred executive homes, they reckon, including the acreage of the Home Farm. So George Wagstaff will be ready to plant a ploughshare in his skull. And won't Radnesfield be pleased? The Old 'Uns, as they always put it, will be whizzing round in the graveyards like spinning tops.'

On Friday afternoon, Sandra was in the stuffy little office behind the petrol pumps, going through the garage accounts. She had always had a good head for figures and it saved Jack the expense of a book-keeper. But today she was finding it hard to concentrate.

It was still brilliant with Neville, of course it was. There were a million women who would give anything to be in her size fours. And when she was with him, it was still as romantic and fantastic and exciting as ever.

But somehow, she was uneasy. Neville made all the right noises, but sometimes he left her without a word for days, and then reckoned she would come running. And the trouble was, she did, didn't she?

And then there was Jack. Jack had stopped giving her the third degree, but he'd stopped making love to her, too. He was a different person these days, surly and bitter instead of sharp and quick and funny the way he used to be. She felt really bad about that.

The other thing that was getting to her was the thought of the future. At the start, she'd been happy to live for the moment, but now she was wondering unhappily where this affair was leading. Could she bear it if he dumped her, and she was left with nothing but a ruined marriage? Or even no marriage at all. Jack sure as hell wouldn't put up with this for ever.

Impatiently she shook her head, and was tapping figures into a calculator when Jack came into the office. He came round to stand silently in front of her, leaning on the desk.

She would not look up until she had finished the column of figures. When she did, he was regarding her with an unpleasant smile, his face too close to her own.

She drew back. 'Whatever's got into you, Jack?'

'So you haven't heard.' He laughed harshly, and stood up. 'You wouldn't be looking like that if you had, would you?'

'Heard what?' She composed her face into a hard, defensive mask.

'Your precious Neville. Selling up and going away, isn't he? Oh, didn't he tell you? Well, that's tough. Perhaps he doesn't think you mattered that much.'

She bit her lips together. She wouldn't reply, she wouldn't react, she wouldn't!

'Sold to a developer, he has. Five hundred houses, they say, going to fill the village with strangers.'

'Good thing too, as far as I'm concerned.' She picked up a sheaf of invoices, pretending to study them.

'He's got a lot of people not very pleased with him, come to that.'

Her 'Oh?' was as indifferent as she could make it.

'Jenny Bateman's dad's not very pleased with him. Been carrying on with her, it turns out – ooh, six months or more. The silly little bitch burst into tears when she found out he was going, and told her mum. Her dad's taken a strap to her, and they're saying Vic Ede's doing the same to his wife, for much the same reason.'

It wasn't true, it wasn't true! She wanted to put her hands over her ears, blot out the hateful stories Jack was making up.

'Talking about seeing if he's got a taste for a bit of rough music, they are. Not that I'd have anything to do with that kind of thing. I wouldn't have any call to, by what you've said. Though they do say actions speak louder than words, don't they?'

Then he bent down, till he was only six inches away from her averted face; she could smell the beer on his breath. 'You poor, silly, dirty little cow,' he said with venom, and left, slamming the door so that the plate glass rattled.

She did not move after he had left, for a long time. She sat, with head bent, staring unseeing at the accounts for spark plugs and shock absorbers and replacement fan belts, and slowly her smooth, white, manicured hands curled into little scarlet-tipped claws.

7

There was an almost tangible atmosphere in the car coming from London to Radnesfield on Friday afternoon. Lilian, in lilac mohair, was hunched in her seat, her mouth curved down in pettish lines. Every so often she threw a smouldering glance at Neville, which seemed only to have the effect of deepening his contented smile.

At last, finding silence unrewarding, Lilian spoke. 'You won't have a friend left in the world once you've done this, you know. And you won't have a wife, either, because if you go on with this – this lunacy, I shall walk out.'

Neville threw back his head to laugh with genuine amusement. 'Now, my sweet, aren't you being just the tiniest bit impulsive? It might be wiser to wait and see how successful I am first. Think how utterly infuriating it would be if you left me just before I made a real killing.'

She checked noticeably at the suggestion, but only for a moment. 'Everyone knows you're going to fail,' she said scornfully. 'You're nothing on your own, nothing – without Chris, without me.'

It nettled him to spite. 'Now that, blossom, is true self-delusion. Didn't I mention it? Even for the TV series, even for "Bradman" as it stands, we had all agreed you'd served your turn. Death or divorce – we hadn't decided which, but you were definitely being written out of the next series.'

'That's a lie!'

Neville shook his head. 'True, alas. Ask Chris if you don't believe me. You were starting to cramp Harry's style, and his public wouldn't stand for it.'

He shot a sideways glance to assess the effect of this barb. The look of purest hatred she directed at him was clearly satisfactory, since he shouted with laughter once more.

'It had occurred to me to wonder whether any emotion you felt was genuine, and now I know, don't I? Damage your interests, and you'll fight like a wildcat. Is that right?'

She only glared at him, relapsing into a seething silence. All right, so it might suit her to play the dumb blonde, but he didn't have to treat her as if he believed it, did he? She was his wife, after all, entitled to be consulted about their joint future. That patronizing bastard had made it clear he didn't rate her enough even to sweet-talk her once he had made up what he was pleased to call his mind. He had got a lot to learn, and he was about to learn it painfully, if she had anything to do with it.

As tough, grubby little Lily O'Connor with her scouse accent and her buck teeth, she had needed resourcefulness and determination to get where she wanted to go, not to mention the courage to get in the way of her father's drunken fists so she could get her teeth fixed on the National Health. He'd landed in gaol over it, too, which just went to show that you shouldn't underestimate children and dumb blondes.

Milking situations was her big talent. It had needed to be. And if you wrapped self-interest round you like a comfort blanket, life became a whole lot simpler. In the end, everyone stopped expecting all the fiddly boring gestures to other people's concerns and it saved a lot of hassle. It left you free to concentrate on getting what you wanted.

So now the question was, what could she get out of the present mess? She didn't care a stuff about Neville; didn't begin to understand him, in fact. 'My wife doesn't understand me.' He'd used that corny line often enough, but then she hadn't tried, had she? Other people's hang-ups were deathly boring – until, as now, they posed a threat.

She had suffered, all her life, from what she simply called The Dream. It happened when she felt stressed or vulnerable, this dream where she stood outside, naked, in a biting wind with frost on the ground and a cold merciless moon shining in the night sky. She couldn't move, even to rub her arms or huddle for warmth, with the breath which was freezing on the air in front of her face beginning to freeze in her lungs until at last she would wake, gasping and shivering in terror. She kept brandy at her bedside, and a thick folded mohair rug; she would sit, swaddled, until the warm searing of the drink reassured her and the tears of fright dried.

For a moment, now, she caught a glimpse of a bleak future, and felt that familiar cold paralysis of fear. But she hardened her mind against the image. He would find he had a fight on his hands, even if she wasn't yet sure of the best way to go about it.

She could try taking him to court, but the man Neville had re-tained was the sharpest operator in the business, and she didn't fancy her chances. Lawsuits were the surest way to ruin, and any-way, once the word was out that you were likely to sue, any future prospect would have a lawyer along on every date and a palimony agreement ready to sign before you exchanged the first kiss.

She had never, god knew, been romantic about marriage. Life hadn't encouraged her to be romantic, and anyway, what did mar-riage to Neville really consist of? In private, they shared some fairly expert love-making and a lot of discussion of 'Bradman'; apart from that, it was a relationship conducted almost entirely in public.

The best thing about it was that it had given her, on a silver plate, all she needed at present. He was her passport to success and financial security – and he had, she knew, his reasons too, selfish and probably perverse, though she had never really bothered to wonder what they might be. It had been a bargain, no less binding because it had been dressed up in the language of soap opera.

She had been content to be used, provided that payment was made in full, but anyone attempting to bilk languid Lilian Sheldon was going to find her true to her ancestry of street-fighters who had come over on the Irish boat and never learned the meaning of a clean fight.

The asthmatic tick of the long-case clock in the Red House sitting-room had always seemed to Helena an almost uncannily soothing sound, easing away the cares of the day with every swing of the pendulum.

Tonight, however, the charm had lost its potency. She was restless, deeply troubled about Stephanie's future, and Edward, unnaturally silent, was clearly both worried and depressed.

It was shortly after nine o'clock when she first became aware of the noise. Uncertain at first, she glanced at Edward, and realized that he too had heard it, and stiffened.

'What on earth is that?' she said, getting to her feet as the sound became more distinct; the noise of a crowd in movement, with shouts and a strange, metallic banging.

It was dark now, though they had not yet closed the curtains, and she could just make out a mass of people moving in the little square outside.

'Switch off the lamp, Edward – I can't see properly,' she said over her shoulder, and as he complied the scene sprang into sharp focus.

Under the yellow street-lamp by the old horse-trough, about twenty-five dark-clad people had gathered; men, she imagined, though, since their faces were covered by hoods or black balaclava-style masks, it was impossible to be sure. Four or five held up pitch torches, flaming smokily; the rest carried pots, pans, or metal bin lids which they were striking with thick wooden sticks in a rhythm almost tribal in its intensity.

As she gazed in horrified incomprehension, a ragged cheer went up as another group marched into the square together, carrying on their shoulders a chair on poles in which lolled an effigy, stuffed and dressed as if in early preparation for Bonfire Night.

The crowd parted before it, and it was carried in triumph to the centre under the street-lamp, where a phalanx formed about it. It was only at that moment, as the light fell on the guy's tweed jacket and jaunty trilby hat, that Helena understood.

'Oh, dear god,' she whispered. 'It's Neville – it's meant to be Neville!'

She sensed Edward shifting uneasily in the dimness behind her. 'Yes, I suppose it is.'

'But Edward, whatever is going on? We must do something, stop them – oh no, look, they're moving off!'

At a brisk, determined pace, they were marching off in the direction of Radnesfield House, the shouts more threatening in tone now, the banging louder and more insistent than ever.

Instead of answering, Edward pulled across the curtains, then switched the light back on, leaving them blinking like owls. 'I don't think we saw that, my dear.'

Helena gaped at him. 'But – but do you know what's happening? What are they going to do?'

'Now, don't get upset. No one's going to come to any harm. It's a very old custom, one that ancient communities used for hundreds of years to demonstrate their anger when one of their number behaved in an intolerable way.'

She was still bemused. 'But what are they going to do?'

'All they'll do is to serenade him with the pots and pans – rough music, they call it – then they'll set fire to the effigy, and that will be that. It's an uncomfortable experience for the person at the receiving end, I grant you, but then Neville hasn't exactly been considerate of other people's feelings. It may be quite salutary.'

'Edward, it's barbaric! What if it gets out of hand – what if they attack Neville and Lilian? We've got to warn them, at least, or phone the police.'

'I think that would be asking for trouble. If you let things take their course, nothing will get out of hand. But if you warned Neville, he would probably go and fetch a shotgun. If he wants the police, he can phone them himself.'

She felt a frightening gulf opening between them, a sense that they were talking across the divide of centuries. 'You're on their side, really, aren't you?'

Distressed, Edward tried to bridge it by physical means, drawing her to him. 'I sympathize, yes. But I can see why you would find it threatening. In today's world we are used to demanding that outside agencies do all our social discipline for us, whereas Radnesfield has its own rules, and unlike modern fragmented communities, has unified support for those rules, and consensus on when enough really is enough. They don't often do this, you know; I've only heard of it once before.'

She hesitated, put under pressure by his need that she should see his point of view. And yes, in a way, she could almost understand it, if not quite sympathize.

'You mean, this is a sort of safety-valve? It just seems so – so primitive!'

'Ah well, there's no denying that.' Sensing her softening, he laughed gently. 'We don't like to acknowledge it, but an awful lot of our behaviour is primitive, even in civilized society, so-called. Just look on it as a rather dramatically-presented opinion poll. Neville and Lilian will be perfectly safe, I promise you.'

She moved out of the circle of his arm to face him. 'But Edward, think of it from the other point of view. Neville and Lilian won't understand that it's only a gesture. They won't understand that the violence will be confined to banging pots and pans.'

The sound was more muffled now. Edward, busying himself with folding a newspaper, did not meet her eyes.

'In that case, perhaps he'll give a little thought to the violence he's inflicting on the community, and realize that he can't hope to live in a selfish vacuum.'

She drew breath to reply, but before she could speak he went on, trying hard to lighten the atmosphere, 'Just "watch the wall, my darling!" It's one of the oldest and wisest of village commandments.

'Now, I know it's early, but we might as well start getting ready for bed, don't you think? We've had a stressful day.'

Weakly, she allowed him to change the subject, though she could still hear the thump-thump-thump of the improvised drums. 'That's putting it mildly. And tomorrow is going to be worse.' She signed heavily.' I'm going to have to go and see Neville. I just can't bear the thought of uprooting poor Steph, when she's had such a difficult time already. I think I'll phone and ask if we can have her home tomorrow. Neville has always professed to adore her, so she might manage to coax something out of him.'

'I could collect her before lunch. I said I'd go and see the vicar in the afternoon. He muttered something about the roof of the church porch, but I'm sure it's more than that. He's in a state about something – wringing his hands even more than usual. He said Marcia had been very much upset by Neville's decision.'

'Hasn't everyone?' Suddenly, Helena found herself yawning hugely. 'You should never have mentioned bed so early. All at once I feel absolutely shattered.'

She glanced at her watch, then shook it in annoyance. 'Oh, drat the thing – it's stopped again.'

'Give it to me. I'll take it in to Willie Comberton on the way to the church tomorrow. He still takes such a pride in his clock-making skills, poor old boy.'

She took it off obediently, struggling with a sense of unreality. The village where everyone indulged old Willie was the same village where men who looked like terrorists marched on another man's house to scare him into good behaviour. She believed Edward when he said there would be no violence, but the distant, sinister beating still made her shiver as she went upstairs.

Wrapped in a hazy cloud of well-being, Neville was enjoying his evening. Lilian appeared to have retired to her bedroom to brood on cost-effective revenge, while he lolled before the television in his study at the side of the house with a whisky decanter at his elbow, watching, with satisfied contempt, a rival drama series.

Lilian's sudden reappearance did not startle him. 'Look at this – the man's hopeless!' he crowed, without turning as his wife entered the room.

She went over and snapped off the set, ignoring his indignant protests. 'Shut up, Neville. Something's going on – saw it from the bedroom window. You'd better come.'

Her heels skittering on the tiled floor, Lilian hurried to the dining-room, on the right of the front door, and did not switch on the lights. The noise was loud now, loud and menacing.

'What in hell –'

Neville crossed to the window, shouldering Lilian aside, and thought for a confused moment that he had strayed on to a film set, with extras playing *sans culottes* demanding aristo blood.

Men were marching towards him – an indeterminate, but alarming number. They were hooded and faceless shapes, like Irish terrorists, and they howled a voiceless, bloodcurdling paean of hate. The drumming of wood on metal, which had been keeping march time, mounted to an erratic crescendo, until his head throbbed with the din. Lilian crouched in the opposite corner, hands over her ears.

The brandished flares formed an aisle, and down it, from the back, moved a procession, carrying high the figure lashed to its chair which they set down in full view of the window.

Neville drew back into the shadows, but the surge of sound from the mob told him they had seen him. He was sweating now, afraid to stay, afraid to move.

One of the figures, bearing a torch, moved to the front, and at a violent gesture from him a hush fell, shocking after the din.

'You'll be next, Fielding!' His yell broke the silence, then he thrust the torch to the scarecrow figure which the cowering victim inside recognized as a caricature of himself.

In a shower of sparks, the guy, composed mainly of dry hay, flared spectacularly, to renewed cheers from the crowd and even more frenzied drumming, as they advanced to circle it triumphantly.

'Oh god!' Lilian whimpered. 'What are they going to do now? Do something, Neville! Stop them!'

Fear was almost expelled by rage at her stupidity. 'What the hell do you expect me to do?' he snarled in a savage undertone. 'Reason with them, or attack them single-handed?'

But even as they spoke, abruptly it was over. The noise died. The torches were extinguished. The black figures faded into the darkness. Within seconds, no sign of their ordeal remained except the collapsed, smouldering embers of the effigy, and the remnants of a tweed jacket and a trilby hat beside a scorched and broken chair.

With the removal of immediate danger, he turned on Lilian, incandescent with rage. 'Well, phone the sodding police, woman, why don't you? Do they have to burn the house down first?'

Without argument, Lilian fled.

The interview with the police did nothing to calm Neville's rage. Having assured themselves that, despite Lilian's incoherent distress, the mob had in fact dispersed, they took almost an hour to come from Limber, and then were less than sanguine.

'Not a lot we can do about it till morning, sir, when we can go round and ask some questions. Though we're not likely to get much out of them – close-mouthed in Radnesfield, they are. Famous for it.'

Fielding was starting to go white about the mouth. 'Don't you think you might just possibly try for a few arrests tonight? There were dozens of them involved, after all.'

The sergeant, with a disapproving intake of breath, shook his head. 'Not tonight, no, sir. We'd have them complaining about midnight raids and Gestapo tactics and such over what is just really a nasty prank, when all's said and done. Unless you can think of anyone who might be harbouring a particular grudge?'

Lilian, sipping a brandy, sneered. 'Apart from the whole village, you mean, sergeant? He's planning to turn it into Welwyn Garden City, and for some funny reason they're not very pleased.'

'That's still not exactly a lead, madam. If you were in a position to be more specific, now –'

She shot a sidelong, vindictive look at her husband. 'Oh, try Jack Daley,' she said. 'The bungalow up towards the Home Farm. He's got such a common little slag for a wife; just Neville's mark.'

'Bitch!' The venomous exclamation was surprised out of him; the policemen exchanged significant glances.

'Perhaps we'll pop round there before we go,' the sergeant said pacifically. 'Gives us something to go on. We'll show ourselves out and take a look at the remains of the fire round the front.'

Fielding followed them to lock up. When he returned, he poured himself another whisky, his hands shaking with fury. He had been made to look an impotent fool, and the world was going to pay for it. Lilian being the most immediate target, he turned on her.

But bullying her was unrewarding, now she had nothing to lose. He discovered that, possibly to her surprise as much as his, she had lost none of her one-time command of pungent invective, and retired to the spare room, still raging. Smashing a pretty Chinese bowl afforded him only limited satisfaction.

When Jack Daley came to the door, he was in short sleeves and slippers. He looked relaxed, and artistically surprised to see the representatives of the law on his doorstep.

'Stone the crows, if it isn't the Fuzz,' he said humorously. 'What can I do for you? Surely you're not chasing stolen cars at this time of night?'

'Er – no. Sorry to trouble you so late, sir, but we saw your lights were on. Just a routine enquiry, really. Can you give me some idea of your movements this evening? There's been a bit of a disturbance in the village, see, and we're trying to find out if anyone saw anything unusual.'

'Disturbance? In Radnesfield? That's a bit funky, isn't it, lads?' He was laughing at them, and the sergeant, who was not a stupid man, eyed him narrowly as he went on.

'Well, being a public-spirited citizen, I'd have loved to be able to help you, but I've been at home, haven't I, having a quiet evening with the old trouble and strife. So I'm not going to be much use to you, am I?' The light brown eyes were hard and bright. 'But of course, you don't like taking anybody's word, do you? Sandra!' he called over his shoulder, 'Come here, will you?'

Sandra Daley, looking sullen, appeared from the lounge, and Daley put his arm round her.

'Oh there you are, pet. Tell the nice gentlemen where I was this evening. They're afraid I might be telling naughty porkies when I say I didn't go out.'

She hesitated, but only for a second. 'That's right,' she said tonelessly. 'He was here with me all evening.'

'Very good, madam.' The sergeant's voice was expressionless, but he gave his subordinate a speaking look. 'We may need a full statement later, but we won't disturb you any more tonight.'

Daley was still smiling as they drove away, but as he closed the door his smile faded.

'You didn't need to hurt me.' She was resentful. 'I'll have bruises on my arm tomorrow.'

'So?' He swung away from her, back to the lounge and the late-night film.

'Where – where were you, anyway?'

Without replying, he shut the door. She was left standing alone in the hall, rubbing her painful arm with a nervous movement.

Lilian stayed in bed on Saturday morning. Sharon, looking scared, had given Neville breakfast with the air of one putting meat into a lion's cage, then scuttled about to light a fire in the study before withdrawing to the comparative safety of the kitchen.

Neville, suffering the after-effects of whisky and bad-temper, settled himself once more in the study with the newspapers. He flicked through impatiently, scanning them for any mention of the Bradman furore; finding none, he threw them crumpled to the floor in annoyance, and went back to his unrewarding thoughts.

Exhilaration, that was what he was entitled to feel. Freedom was so nearly within his grasp, freedom from those pettifogging restrictions that little men kept trying to impose on Harry.

It almost made him laugh. Restrict Harry? Tie down a hurricane! Harry had grown too big for them, and Harry was taking Neville with him. In fact, these days it was pretty hard to be sure where he stopped and Harry began.

He frowned thoughtfully. There had been differences, at one time, but when he looked back, all he could envisage was a blank canvas, waiting for Harry's bold brushstrokes to give him identity.

He had no doubt of his power now. He could do as he chose, and he had noticed that as his personal behaviour became more and more confidently outrageous, his victims became less and less able to use the polite barricade of assumed indifference.

It was hugely pleasing. Sometimes he felt like one of the great film directors – Buñuel, perhaps, or Godard – but greater than any, of course, since they dealt in celluloid and he in people's lives. Helena, Jack Daley, Sandra, Lilian, George Wagstaff, Chris, even the vicar's unspeakable wife – he had them all helplessly dancing to the tune he piped.

Last night's episode, however, was not part of his composition. He had pencilled in orchestration for opposition and hostility, and it had all been quite clear in his head. The angry peasantry, lumpish and inarticulate: he, suave, Olympian, turning them aside with mocking superiority.

But that! He could blot out the memory of his private fear, but not of his public humiliation. He suspected mockery even in Sharon's timid servility, and down in the village they would be sniggering. It was intolerable.

He would have the last word, of course, when Harry's hurricane of change blew their village apart, and there would be plenty who would come to beg him to alter his course. He would enjoy that, especially when he could tell them he didn't give a monkey's. That was another of Harry's gifts.

So it was the least he could do, to repay Harry, so to speak; take him away from the limitations imposed by small screens, small budgets, small minds.

Really, they should all be grateful for the chance to lay their sacrifices on so glorious an altar. Instead, they made him their victim.

The cloud descended on his brow again.

Dora Wagstaff, her arms full of dirty clothes, whisked down the kitchen passage to the utility room. She was keeping herself very busy this morning; it was the only response to trouble that she knew. If you were scrubbing collars caked with farm grime, you didn't have a hand free for wiping away tears.

It just wasn't fair. After all, she'd never wanted much. There were so many discontented people in the world; you'd only to put on the telly to see them moaning about all the things they wanted that they hadn't got.

She'd always been a contented woman – and grateful, too. She'd never forgotten to say thank-you, in the prayers she said every night, kneeling like a child at the end of her bed; thank-you for George and the kids and this place where she'd lived all her married life. Oh, there had been day-to-day problems, of course, like Sally kicking up her heels a bit, and the longer-term worry about Jim, who was a born farmer if ever there was one, with no promise of a farm he could call his own.

But she'd never expected life to be plain sailing. You couldn't be married to a farmer for twenty-five years without getting used to ups and downs. What she'd never expected was this – this sudden catastrophe that had overtaken them.

They weren't the sort of people dramatic things happened to. They were ordinary folk; illness and sudden death were the only catastrophes they knew. They had no way of dealing with this, no words for talking about what it was doing to them. You couldn't say, 'My heart is breaking,' even if that was true. It wasn't the sort of thing they said.

She and George had never really needed to talk much, except about the comfortable, everyday things. They had understood each other wordlessly for years, and now, when he had closed his mind against her, shut in with his own misery, there were no familiar habits of speech to provide a bridge. They were each alone with their demons, and she felt separate from him in a way she had never been since the day the vicar had pronounced them man and wife, one flesh.

There was fear about the future, of course, but she was almost more frightened about what was going on in his darkened mind, fearful what unknown monsters might lurk in the depths she had never considered him to possess.

She thought she had the house to herself, and the figure, dark against the light from the window and seated by the old wooden work-table, gave her such a fright that she jumped and gasped aloud.

'Oh! George Wagstaff, what a start you gave me, sitting there! I thought you'd gone out.'

He was busy at something; she came round behind him and saw what he was doing. Meticulously, with oil, a rag and a rod, he was cleaning a shotgun.

'George!' She had not meant that her alarm should show in her voice, but she was no actress. 'What are you doing with that?'

'What does it look as if I'm doing?' His reply was brusque, but he looked up and read the consternation in her face. 'I've been out shooting rabbits, you stupid woman,' he said, with exasperated affection. 'They're hanging in the larder, if you don't believe me. You didn't think I'd be puddinghead enough to go out after Fielding with my own gun?'

' 'Course I didn't. Don't be daft,' she said, but her voice wobbled, and dumping the pile of laundry in her arms on to the table, she sat down beside him. 'Oh my dear, what are we going to do?' Her voice was thick with tears.

He set down the little oil bottle carefully and stretched out his hard, cracked farmer's hand to cover hers, attempting comfort where there was none.

'I don't know, lass.'

'Surely he can't do this to us – surely we must have some rights –'

He shook his grizzled pate. 'I always knew we hadn't much safeguard. Maybe I should have taken it up with Radley, but it didn't matter then. Oh, he's got his faults, same as everyone, but he'd never have let us down this way.'

She tried not to cry, but the tears would come, and she tried to wipe them away with the back of her hand, like a child.

'Here,' he said gruffly, taking a red spotted handkerchief out of his back pocket.

It must be, she knew, a particular agony for a man as old-fashioned as George to watch helplessly while his woman suffered, and all the talking in the world wasn't going to change anything. She mopped her eyes briskly, then viewed the handkerchief with distaste. 'Just look at this! It's filthy, George. With a pile of clean ones in your chest of drawers, how you can't remember to change them . . .'

Fussing, she got to her feet, and, adding the handkerchief to the pile, picked up the laundry and the reins of her household once more.

In a voice that shook with intensity of feeling, he promised, 'I'll – I'll think of something, Dora. Don't you worry. I'll sort it out somehow.'

The smile she gave him was one of perfect trust, because she knew that was what he needed just then. Perhaps she wouldn't make such a bad actress after all.

It was the first time Helena had been to Radnesfield House since the day she left it, in such high emotion, almost a year ago.

Nothing had changed. Only a broken and scorched kitchen chair, and some charred remnants of cloth on the lawn at the front suggested that anything at all had taken place in the intervening time.

It was Sharon who answered when she rang the bell, Sharon looking awkward at seeing her one-time mistress on the doorstep.

Helena was brisk. 'Good morning, Sharon. I've come to see Mr Fielding.' She stepped inside as she spoke.

The girl looked flustered. 'Yes – yes, of course, Mrs Field – er – Mrs Radley. I'll tell him you want to see him, like, shall I?'

'Don't bother, Sharon. Is he in the study? I'll go myself.'

She walked swiftly across to the door, tapped on it, and without waiting for an answer, walked in.

Slumped in his chair, Neville was looking black, but when he saw Helena in the doorway, a slow and unpleasant smile crossed his face.

'Well, if it isn't Nella!' he drawled. 'And how's the radiant bride?'

He got to his feet, and she submitted to his impudent kiss on the cheek without comment.

'Do you know,' he went on jovially, 'I had a presentiment that I might be having a visit from you today? I don't know what it is about the country air. Somehow it seems to sharpen my intuition.'

Helena sat down. She had known Neville would try to provoke her, and she was determined not to give him the satisfaction of knowing that he had succeeded.

'I should think you'll be having a steady stream of visitors this weekend, Neville. You've managed to upset an awful lot of people.'

It was clear this cheered him up enormously. His eyes were sparkling as he said, with mock seriousness, 'I know. Isn't it dreadful? The phone is positively red-hot this morning. Even the vicar seems awfully cross with me for some reason. But you would understand, Nella darling. We must all make sacrifices for the sake of Art.'

She drew a steadying breath. 'As you no doubt realize, after the blunt message you got last night, feeling is running high. There will be organized opposition, objections made to the planning authorities . . .'

A slow, mournful shake of the head. 'How sad for them! The planners have been itching to get their hands on Radnesfield for years. Edward is an economic moron; if he'd played his cards right, he could have got twenty times the figure he got from me.'

'Don't be rude about Edward to me, please. He cares about the local community, which you plainly don't. Be careful, Neville, I warn you. There are people out there who really hate you.'

'Oh, I know! Isn't it stimulating? Whoever would have dreamed these bucolic sons of toil could be stirred to such frenzied emotion? George Wagstaff, even –' He held up his hands in a Harry gesture.

Well, she had done her best for Radnesfield, and it had proved, as she had thought, useless. With a mental shrug, she moved on.

'Neville, you know that I have a maintenance order against you for Stephanie.'

'Yes, of course I do.' The reply was tetchy, but at least more sober.

'I know what you'll say about schooling – all the old "never-did-me-any-harm" arguments –'

'I certainly don't want a daughter who's a silly little rich bitch.'

She forced herself to reply calmly. 'Neither do I, but I don't think that's a problem. Of course Darnley Hall is expensive, but you were all in favour of it, remember? I'm not bothered about the frills, I'm talking about her friends and above all her security. She had an appalling time last summer; I don't suppose you noticed, but she lost almost a stone in weight, and I thought that anorexia would be the next thing. But she's happy and confident at Darnley Hall, and that's what allows her to cope with the sort of mess we've inflicted on her. Take it away from her now, and you could produce lifelong damage.'

Neville scowled. 'Well, that's a bit of a problem. Quite frankly, Helena, it's a hell of a lot of money, and I need every penny to put into this new project. It's a fantastic opportunity – to take Harry on to the broad screen, where he can become a world star. I've got a Hollywood producer right on the line, provided I can raise enough capital to put up my share. And I will raise it, if it's the last thing I do.'

He had forgotten grievance in his enthusiasm. 'It will be a bit tight for the first bit, Nella, but after that – well, Harry Bradman will be up there with the greats, and the sky's the limit.'

'Don't you mean Neville Fielding?' she could not resist interjecting.

He checked his flow, shaking his head as if irritated by some small insect. 'Harry, Neville, same thing,' he said impatiently. 'But when I make it, I promise you that you and Stephie won't be forgotten in the pay-off.'

'When you make it? In – what? Two, three years? We have Stephanie's school career to think of. In two years, she has major exams. We can't muck about with her education. I'm sorry, but if you won't do it willingly, I'm going to get Henry Stanton to invoke the law. I've got that maintenance order, and you'll be forced to pay it.'

His face grew dark once more. 'Same old thing – you always let me down when it came to the point, didn't you? Thank god I'm free of you – I can't think why I didn't break up that dismal farce of a marriage years ago.

'You could never understand Harry's stature, could you? I really think you were jealous of him, in some extraordinary, perverted way. And now you're trying to contain a character that's bigger than you, bigger than me, bigger than petty little Chris Dyer, who's started taking refuge in standards of bourgeois morality which he simply cannot see don't apply.

'But I've taken care of you all. I've found the smartest lawyer in the business, and stuffy Stanton can do his worst. I'm about to sign a deed creating the Harry Bradman Trust, and I won't even own the suit I stand up in. But Harry will lend it to me – he always was generous to his friends.'

Helena stood up, feeling sick at heart. 'Neville, I think you've gone mad.'

That was the trigger. 'Mad?' he yelled suddenly. 'How dare you, you stupid, superficial woman, with your small-town husband and your small-town mind!'

Her resolve crumbled. At last, she felt herself emotionally confident enough to shout back.

'Don't dare talk to me like that! Small-town mind? That's better than no mind at all. You're nothing but a vacuum, and Harry Bradman moved in to take over the empty space inside.

'I will fight you, not because I want anything for myself – I never have, as you know – but for Stephanie. She loves her pony, that you bought her. She loves her expensive school, where you sent her. You bought her off, because she wasn't a toy you cared to play with any more. I won't stand by and see her sacrificed to your monumental selfishness.'

For a moment he looked dangerous, then broke, instead, into ironic applause. 'Oh bravo, Nella! Perhaps you should have done that more often. Such wonderful, crashing emotions! You almost make me regret that I let you go. There is something so awfully trivial about Lilian.'

'Given the banality of your own mind, I don't know how you can tell. You seem to me perfectly matched – a case of shallow calling to shallow. Oh, and one other point. You didn't let me go. I went.

'Just let me say this finally, Neville. If there is anything I can do to ensure my daughter's security, I shan't scruple to do it – up to and including murdering you with my own bare hands!'

She flung open the door as she spoke, theatrical instinct telling her that she could hope for no better exit line. Neville, well pleased with the effect of his provocation, threw back his head and laughed, as she slammed the door on the maddening sound.

The movement at the back of the hall caught her eye: Sharon, whisking out of sight below stairs.

With her temper cooling as rapidly as it had flared up, Helena sighed ruefully. That would be all round the village by nightfall, without a doubt.

8

'He can't do that – he can't!' Stephanie was a child again, tears pouring down her cheeks in a tempest of reaction to the unfairness of life. 'Mummy, you've got to stop him! I'll die if he sells Angel and makes me leave Darnley Hall.'

She cast herself on to the sofa. Helena, grim-faced, went to put her arm round her.

'We'll certainly do everything we can. I'll phone the lawyer first thing on Monday, but according to your father that won't do any good. He may be bluffing, but I'm afraid you may just have to be brave, Stephanie. Worse things happen to lots of people.'

Stephanie sat up, her face blotchy and her lips quivering. 'For heavens' sake, I realize that! And if things had gone really wrong and there wasn't any money, I wouldn't moan. But he's doing this deliberately. He doesn't care about me one little bit.'

'Don't be melodramatic, dear. Of course he does,' Helena said mechanically. Stephanie was a child of the theatre, and at the dramatic age anyway, but she was right. Neville didn't care about her, or about anyone except himself.

Edward's voice was purposely matter-of-fact. 'I don't think we should get too worked up about it at the moment. I can't believe the law is as powerless as Neville thinks, and anyway, Hollywood producers can change their minds; someone could make Neville a better offer next week, and he'll be off on a different enthusiasm. Dyer is certainly trying everything he can do to stop him, so who knows?'

Stephanie was silent all through lunch, and only picked at her food; Helena wasn't hungry either. It seemed a long time until Edward finished and suggested they take coffee through to the sitting-room.

Stephanie disappeared, and as they sat over their coffee, they heard her running downstairs. 'Just going to borrow Jim Wagstaff's horse and go for a ride,' she shouted, and then the front door slammed in a way which suggested reflection had not softened her mood.

'She's sure to go and see Neville,' Helena said apprehensively. 'Oh Edward, I do hope he's kind to her, at least. She's at such a vulnerable age.'

She realized how much upset he too had been when he replied curtly, 'I should think it very unlikely. I don't think Neville knows the meaning of the word kindness – or honour, or decency, come to that.'

Edward went out at just after two, to take Helena's watch to Willie Comberton before he met the vicar at quarter to three.

'It gives me an excuse to have a chat – though no doubt I'll have to listen again to the story about his grandfather's grandfather clock. Still, he doesn't get about much these days, poor old boy.'

Helena made a reply which was purely mechanical. She found it hard to settle to anything, and as much by way of therapy for herself as anything else, decided Stephanie might be just young enough to be cheered by a cake for tea. She was still in the kitchen some time later when she heard the front door slam once more, and footsteps pound up the stairs to Stephanie's attic bedroom.

She went into the hall. 'Stephanie,' she called, but the distant crash of the bedroom door was the only answer. She hesitated, then climbed the stairs and tapped softly.

'Stephie, are you all right?'

There was no reply, and hearing the sound of muffled weeping, she turned the handle, but the door was locked.

'Oh, go away, Mum, leave me alone!' Stephanie's cry was despairing, and Helena felt her pain like a knife in her own heart. If Neville had been brutal to the child there was nothing she could do.

But as she went slowly back downstairs, the anger that had seized her this morning rose once more, in a primitive response to this attack on her young.

She had once been able to influence Neville; now, if he were hiding behind the great, ugly, looming figure of Harry Bradman, then he must be dragged out. And she, according to Chris Dyer, was the only person who had even the slightest chance of doing it.

On this surge of determination, she hurried to the cloakroom, grabbing a light raincoat but not pausing to cover her head. It was raining lightly, as she took the short-cut path that led up across the little rise, past the Daleys' house and below the Home Farm, up to the garden of Radnesfield House itself.

She attempted, as she set out, to plan tactics, but half-way there, in a flash of clarity, realized her self-delusion. She was no knight-errant, setting out to slay a dragon; she was a woman spoiling for a fight, and when he proved obdurate (as of course he would) she would relish venting her fury directly upon its object.

Approaching the house, she hesitated. Lilian, by Stephanie's account, spent her country afternoons closeted with beauty aids and exercise machines, so it should prove simple enough to find Neville on his own, if he was in the house at all. But she certainly did not want to ring the bell again, to have to face Sharon after the last embarrassing encounter.

To her satisfaction, as she reached the side lawn through the wicket gate, she noticed the French window into Neville's study was ajar. Perhaps he had gone out that way; if so, she would be waiting for him when he returned.

Daffodils were blooming damply along the border beneath the windows, and a cherry tree had begun to shake its snow in a browning carpet on the pathway as she crossed it. A thrush, undaunted by the rain, was singing somewhere deep in the shrubbery, and glistening gossamer had been stretched across a budding fuchsia. She hardly noticed; yet every detail etched itself on her mind so sharply that sometimes, later, she thought she could count every strand in the spider's web.

She pushed open the door. 'Neville?' she said questioningly. 'Neville? Are you there?'

Helena had chosen the furnishings for his study herself, in rich, rather sombre shades, to complement the colours in the stained glass panels of the French windows, and the dull reds, blues and burnt oranges made the room dark. For a second she blinked, adjusting to the dimmer light.

Neville was there, certainly. At least, what had been Neville Fielding remained, slumped across a low, figured walnut desk, hands splayed across it as if trying to support the weight of his body as he had fallen forward in the swivel chair. His right cheek rested on papers spread out on the gilded leather of the desk top, his visible eye wide open, glazed in surprise, though his mouth seemed to have been denied the opportunity to take on any expression at all. The back of his head showed the gleam of bone in the pulpy, gaping wound responsible for the trickle of blood that marked the checked collar of his Tattersall shirt. There was not much blood: it had been a heavy blow, instantly fatal, and the weapon lay, as if thrown down in temper, on the rug at his feet – the long, heavy-knobbed brass poker from the set of fire-dogs.

At first sight she could not comprehend what she was seeing. She had seen it all too many times: the elaborate stage-set, the carefully-structured wounds, the professional immobility of the actor. At any moment a voice off would say, 'OK, Neville, that's great,' and he would get up, rubbing his back and complaining of stiffness.

But he didn't. She found she was holding her breath, and the room swung crazily round her. She steadied herself on the back of a chair, shutting her eyes briefly as if she could blot it all out, start again.

And still he lay there. She felt, ludicrously, at a loss. Perhaps one should scream – But she had not screamed, and now, though she opened her mouth, no sound came. She could rouse the others in this silent house, fetch help ... But it was all too hideously clear that Neville was far beyond human assistance.

The police. Here, at last, was firm ground. Middle-class conditioning: dial 999 and ask for service required. There was a phone on the fireside table, and she turned to cross the room.

She did not register it at first, stepping over it carefully with some dim recollection that nothing must be touched at the scene of the crime. Indeed, her hand was already on the telephone when the significance struck her, with a force which dropped her into a chair as neatly as if she had been hit across the back of the knees.

Stephanie's riding-crop. She recognized it, because she had bought it herself as a Christmas present; besides, there were the initials, SF, burnt for identification along the wood.

In her horrified mind, the scene took shape in graphic detail: Stephanie goaded beyond endurance by her father; he, turning his back on her in arrogant dismissal; she, throwing down her riding-crop to seize the poker –

She buried her face in her hands. Oh Stephie, Stephie! Why had she not come to her mother, instead of locking herself in her room with this nightmare? Perhaps, between them, they could have concocted an alibi ...

Perhaps they still could. On the thought, she leaped to her feet. No one knew she was here. She could be down the hill in five minutes, and tell the police, when they inevitably came, that she and Stephanie had been in the house together all afternoon. She grabbed the tell-tale crop, then forced herself to pause and think.

Stephanie might have been wearing her riding-gloves. But if not . . . Feverishly, she rummaged in her pockets for a handkerchief, suddenly afraid that the door might at any moment open to admit Sharon or Lilian.

There was no place for squeamishness. She grasped the poker in the handkerchief, rubbing fiercely up and down the length of its shaft, trying not to see the ugly detritus on the knob.

Her instinct was the oldest of all; to protect her child. She felt nothing for Neville. If he had driven their loving, normal Stephanie to the point where she could do this, he was not fit to live, still less to exact vengeance. She had no time to contemplate the wider problems.

Yet, despite her haste, she paused in the window aperture, under some elegiac compulsion to look once more.

It still bore the appearance of theatrical unreality, with a whiff of Bradman in the air. It was as if he had staged it all, as if death were merely the inevitable denouement. In another moment, if she lingered, she would hear Harry's ghostly laughter in the wings.

Clasping her hands to her ears, she fled, plunging down the pathway as if shadowy terrors snapped at her heels.

It was almost four o'clock when, breathless, she slipped in through the back door. Stephanie – she must tell her that she knew, coach her in her answers –

The sound of Edward's voice, calling hopefully, 'Helena? Are you there?' presented a more immediate problem. She could not tell him; the only people in the secret must be Stephanie and herself. She could not ask Edward to perjure himself for her child, could not, in truth, be sure he would not insist on honesty as the only way, and she was not sure she could withstand him.

Dabbing frantically at the dampness clinging to her hair, and schooling her voice, she called, 'In the kitchen,' and turned to resume her interrupted baking, thankful that shock left fewer identifiable marks upon the face than grief.

She even managed a sort of smile as Edward came in. 'How was the vicar?'

Edward, preoccupied and distressed, barely noticed her. 'In a bad way,' he said heavily. 'To tell you the truth, I don't know how he's going to take a service tomorrow. Marcia's walked out – left him with the children, and I don't think he has an idea what to do. He was late for our meeting, then came along wringing his hands and saying he couldn't cope without her. I really wonder if, as church-warden, I should ring the Bishop.'

She heard her own voice saying, quite calmly, 'I would leave things over the weekend, if I were you. She may come back of her own accord.' And anyway, she thought with detachment, no one will be noticing the quality of the sermon.

'Shall I make some tea?'

'Yes please.' She abandoned all pretence of baking, and went to fetch cups and saucers. She discovered her hands were shaking in delayed shock, shaking so that she had to lift each one separately to stop them clattering like castanets.

'What about Stephanie?' Edward asked, as he carried through the tray. 'Shall I call her?'

'She's up in her room. Just leave her.' Keeping her voice level took all the control she had.

But the tea, and the quiet sitting-room, steadied her. There was no reason why the police should even question Stephanie, now that the crucial evidence was safely in the cupboard under the kitchen sink. After the events of last night, surely they would assume that this was connected, and Edward had been confident that they would get no information from the village.

She was just considering making an excuse to go up and see Stephanie, when Edward lowered his newspaper to say in tones of mild surprise, 'Good gracious, isn't that a police car? Oh, last night, of course. I suppose they'll be talking to everyone.'

It was a man and a woman who came in, both in plain clothes. The man, Inspector Coppins, big and bulky in a dark raincoat, did most of the talking while the girl, Frances Howarth, his sergeant, made discreet jottings in a black notebook.

As an actress, Helena was almost sure her reaction was convincing. She sketched in disbelief, shock and distress – though not too much distress, since her relationship with her former husband was well documented.

Once the news had been broken, the questioning, studiedly unemphatic, began.

'Your movements, sir? Oh, just a matter of routine, of course. And yours, Mrs Radley?'

Edward, at least, could refer him to Willie Comberton and his grandfather clock – Willie was always very definite on questions of time – which left only about five minutes unaccounted for while he waited for the vicar. Helena said she had been at home.

'My daughter was here, so we can vouch for each other.' There, she had said it, and a thunderbolt hadn't struck her dead.

'She wasn't out at all then, either?'

'Yes –'

'No –'

She and Edward spoke simultaneously, and glanced towards each other, Edward with a look of surprise on his face. She corrected herself.

'Oh, sorry – yes, she was out, of course, but only for a very short time. She came back minutes after you left, Edward.'

'Oh, I see.' Perhaps he saw too much; certainly he said nothing more.

'Perhaps we could have a word with your daughter,' the policewoman suggested delicately. It was the first time she had spoken, and even in her anxiety Helena noticed that she had a particularly pleasant voice.

'I think that must be later. She's very devoted to her father – it will come as a terrible shock.'

Sure of her ground, Helena's tone made it clear that this was final.

'Naturally,' the other woman was saying, when without warning the door opened and Stephanie came in. Her hair was dishevelled and she had clearly been crying.

'I – I saw the car. What's – what's happening?' she stammered.

'I think we should go upstairs –' Helena got to her feet, but with fatal stubbornness Stephanie held her ground.

'No. Whatever it is, tell me now. Is it – is it Daddy?'

Inwardly, Helena groaned. Why did she have to draw suspicion on herself in that way? She put an arm round her.

113

'I'm afraid it's very dreadful, darling. Daddy's been killed – you know there was that trouble last night –'

It sounded bald, but somehow she must prevent the child from giving herself away.

'Daddy –' She went white to the lips, and the chief inspector rose.

'I think we should leave you for the moment. We can get detailed statements at a more suitable time,' he said, and Helena could have embraced him.

But the quiet sergeant with the watchful eyes paused over her notebook, as if checking what she had written.

'Now, have I got that right? You and your daughter – you were in together virtually all afternoon?'

Stephanie, though she still looked dazed, turned at that. 'I wasn't in,' she said flatly. 'Not for the first half of the afternoon.'

The policeman, on his way to the door, checked. The policewoman had not removed her eyes from the girl's face. 'Not in, Stephanie?'

'Well, of course you were out, just for a little while. I mentioned that. But you were in all the rest of the afternoon, remember? We were in together.'

Helena was talking too fast, unconvincingly; she knew that, but she had to signal to Stephanie somehow, tell her she had her mother protecting her, no matter what she had done.

But Stephanie's brow was creasing in bewilderment. 'I went up to Radnesfield House,' she said slowly. 'I saw Dad, and I had a blazing row with him.' She bit her lip, holding back tears, then steadfastly went on, 'In fact, I threw my whip at him, I was so angry. Then I rushed out through the French windows across to the Home Farm and rode Jim's horse for a bit, but that didn't make me feel any better, so I came back here.'

To Helena, the silence seemed interminable. Then, 'So you went out, leaving the window open? That would be – what time, Stephanie?' The policewoman's low voice again.

She frowned, steadied by the effort of having to consider details. 'About two o'clock, probably, when I left. It must have been about quarter to two when I went from here.'

Two or three pages were neatly flipped back in the notebook. 'Ah, yes, that would be when Sharon Thomas heard Mr Fielding shouting. She went in after that to collect the coffee cups.'

Helena was finding it hard to assimilate. 'And – and he was alive at that time?'

'Oh, yes, last seen at about 2.10. So death took place between then and four o'clock when the girl – what's-her-name – took in the tea-tray, just before Mrs Fielding came downstairs.' That was the inspector.

The relief was dizzying. She managed to say nothing, but her heart was singing hallelujahs.

It was Stephanie, now beginning to shiver with shock, who said slowly, 'So we weren't really together all afternoon, Mummy....'

The realization hit Helena like a douche of icy water, and she noticed, for the first time, the eyes of the younger detective. They were a light hazel in colour, and they were fixed upon her with a sharpness of gaze that would have transfixed a butterfly to a board.

It was an open-and-shut case, apparently. Sharon had described, with dramatic relish, Helena's parting with Neville in the morning. She had been spotted by Sandra Daley as she went up to the house at 3.45; Tamara Farrell, engaged in robbing nests in the little wood, had seen her run back, in obvious distress, ten minutes later. Her fingerprints were on the French window, a nearby chairback, and the telephone, while a search-warrant allowed the police to find the riding-crop and the incriminating handkerchief. Most damning of all, on her own admission she had told a string of lies and attempted to use her daughter to provide a false alibi.

Edward believed her, of course. At least, he said he did, though she was sure that, whatever his private thoughts might be, that was what he would say.

She had tried to explain to Stephanie, wary and hurt at being used in a lie, that she had been trying to protect her. The child's response, an incredulous, shrinking, 'You thought I could do that? To *Daddy*?' left her with the feeling that she had only made bad worse. Oh, how could she tell? Perhaps Stephanie believed her – but by now, things like that were ceasing to have any importance.

Henry Stanton certainly didn't believe her. 'Of course I believe you, dear lady,' he purred, with that unctuousness which she loathed. 'But alas, it is not I whom you must convince, and I'm afraid we must accept that a jury, not knowing you as well as I am privileged to do, may be a trifle swayed by the evidence.'

The police, it appeared, were satisfied; they had checked other people's movements, but in a perfunctory way, and Helena was charged.

With some skill, Stanton managed to achieve bail for her, and she was allowed home, into a limbo where she became daily more detached from everyday life.

So it was, when Stanton, seconded by an anxious Edward, pointed out yet again that in the circumstances, with no fresh evidence, pleading guilty to manslaughter would be, if the prosecution accepted it, the tactic most likely to result in a suspended sentence, she agreed, feeling drearily that her life was meaningless, anyway.

Elated, Stanton expanded his point. 'Provocation, my dear lady, extreme provocation, and motherly instincts for the protection of the interests of your only child. That, coupled with the evidence we have traced of physical brutality and mental cruelty over a period of years, should make even the most case-hardened judge favour a suspended sentence. And we will of course put you up to give evidence in mitigation –'

'No.' So there was, after all, something she still cared about. 'You can make whatever submissions you like on my behalf, but I will not give evidence, except to assert my innocence.'

He was appalled. 'Mrs Radley, that will ruin everything! The assumption will be that you have something to hide. Say you have forgotten – blotted it out, a sort of brainstorm –'

Edward too tried persuasion, even anger, but she was, for once, adamant. 'You may do what you like,' she said. 'I accept all you say, but I will not commit perjury.'

Stanton sighed heavily. She was proving ludicrously stubborn; perhaps she had really managed to convince herself that she was innocent, even if she couldn't convince anyone else. 'We will do our best. The Counsel we have retained is an excellent pleader, but you are tying his hands.'

Ignoring Edward's agonized face, Helena said flatly, 'So be it.'

She only knew that Stephanie had believed her the night they took her in to await sentencing. Summoned downstairs to say goodbye, Stephanie came slowly, her face ravaged and her eyes puffy with tears.

Helena held her for a moment in a short, fierce hug. 'Oh, Stephanie!'

The girl stepped out of her embrace. 'Mum,' she said with difficulty, 'they say in the paper you're pleading guilty. They've got it wrong as usual, haven't they?' Her voice was beseeching.

Helena swallowed hard. They had tried to shield Stephanie from discussion and distress; now she knew with terrible, icy clarity, how wrong this decision had been.

'I have to plead guilty, my darling, but –'

She had no chance to finish. Stephanie drew back, her eyes widening in horror. 'You didn't –' she got out, and then she began to scream, scream upon scream, till Edward slapped her. But as Helena was driven away, the voice echoed in her ears, 'I never want to see you again!'

Henry Stanton was right. The judge, sympathetic initially, was clearly suspicious of her failure to give her version of events.

She had been well warned; she had gone through all the motions of intellectual acceptance, but it was only now she understood her true mental attitude over these months.

At heart, she had classified this as something too bad to happen, and was still, psychologically, no better prepared than she had been on the day of Neville's death. She had not looked ahead, and now she dare not. The present moment was as much as she could bear, and she went below, under escort, with a white, blind look on her face.

She did not see the policewoman with hazel eyes watching her leave the dock with bewilderment and not a little concern.

PART THREE

9

Frances Howarth had always hated to apologize. A certain stubborn arrogance made it difficult to surmount the molehill of saying, 'I was wrong'; now, when the result of error was the imprisonment of a vicar's daughter, almost certainly innocent of the crime which Frances, virtually single-handed, had pinned on her, that difficulty assumed mountainous proportions.

Why, then, against the dictates of common sense as well as self-preservation, had she got herself into this hideous situation? Duty, she supposed grimly. It wasn't a jazzy virtue, and ever since Wordsworth it had received a bad press, but on the quiet days when the tempests of events didn't roar too loudly, she could still hear that stern voice, even if the early idealism that had taken her into the police force in the first place had become tempered by pragmatism.

Helena's telephone response to her letter had at least been prompt. Now, that same afternoon, Frances found herself sitting opposite a woman outwardly calm but bearing all the stigmata of the ordeal to which she had been, as Frances now believed, so unjustly subjected.

There is only the finest dividing line between explanation and excuse, as Frances was uneasily aware. She was seeking expiation, yes, though her motivation was not merely to set her own moral record straight.

But talking was not the least of her skills. As she explained her reasoning, she saw the woman's wariness give way to reluctant attention and felt almost ashamed, as if some sort of chicanery were involved. Yet now she was coming to the hardest part of all. She could still see the woman in the dock, her head bowed. It was an image she had lived with ever since.

'When you refused to give evidence, that – that threw me. I had seen you lying, remember, and you did it consummately. I could not understand why you should object to turning in a performance in the dock which might have let you walk out, a free woman.

'So you must have balked at taking the oath. And it seemed quaint, to say the least, that a woman who had involved her teenage daughter in a false alibi should turn scrupulous over a little thing like perjury.

'I even discussed it with my boss, but he laughed at me.' ('Evidence?' Coppins had demanded, then, when she tried to explain, 'Woman's intuition,' he had mocked. 'Don't come to me with woman's bloody intuition.') 'He said you were probably afraid they'd dig up a lover or a scandalous past. But we hadn't found anything like that, and believe me, we had your life under a microscope.

'Then I turned it on its head. If I accepted that you lied initially to protect your child, and otherwise told the truth, a different picture began to emerge.

'There was plenty of time, between Sharon taking away the coffee tray, and your arrival, for someone else to have been in. The list of people with a motive was extensive, but after your arrest enquiries stopped. A few sketchy statements had been taken, two or three alibis checked out, that was all: a nice, straightforward case, with no further need to squander manpower.

'I've tried to get the case re-opened, but they think I'm mad, and my boss would be furious if he knew I was here. So . . .'

She came to a halt, her throat dry from so much talking. There was a long, long silence. Then Helena gave a deep, shivering sigh and spoke.

'Oh, I didn't kill him. But I've known that all along, so it doesn't make any difference, does it?' A little shakily, she got to her feet and spoke with awful politeness. 'I hope you feel better for having told me. And now, perhaps, you might be kind enough to leave.'

Frances stared at her blankly. 'But I want to fight for you – clear your name –'

Helena's smile was bitter. 'Clear my name? Rake everything up again, for the press to have another Roman holiday, do you mean?' Her tone was one of detached contempt. 'Don't be a fool. I've served my time, I've survived, more or less. Debt to society paid, case closed. Let's leave it that way.'

'Mrs Radley, if you didn't do it, someone else did.'

The huge, haunted blue-grey eyes turned on her, almost showing the animation of impatience. 'Well, of course they did. I'm not stupid. But then, Neville deserved it. I didn't kill him, but I can't condemn whoever did. He probably tortured them into it.

'You seem to think you're offering me something worth having. Can you remove my grey hairs, and the lines on my face? Can you give me back my daughter's love?' Her voice cracked, but she carried on fiercely, 'I mustn't think about it. I've closed that door, and Edward says I need never talk about it again.'

She was a remarkably disciplined woman, Frances thought, a remarkably tough woman. But she still hadn't understood.

'You know you didn't do it. Everyone else thinks you did, with one exception. There is one person who knows you didn't, and who knows that you know.'

'Well, obviously.' Her reply was almost snappish.

'It doesn't occur to you that it's a very dangerous thing to be the only person who knows for certain that there is an unconvicted murderer at large?'

It was clear that it had not. The realization shattered her artificial composure like a brick thrown through a plate-glass window, and she put both hands up to her cheeks. 'Oh my god!' she whispered, and began to cry.

After that, Helena talked and talked. She fetched some brandy, which she drank and Frances sipped at; she spoke of Neville, and of Harry's influence, and of Neville's sense of destiny at the Radnesfield crossroads. She looked, eventually, as if her soul had once more made connection with her body, and though the pain might be sharp, it seemed to have lanced that festering repression.

About Radnesfield, she was virulent, and Frances said at last, 'Are you really saying that someone in the village was responsible for Neville's death?'

Helena paused, frowning. 'I can't say that. But I believe that if Radnesfield had been different, none of this would have happened.'

'Hmm.' Frances digested this. Was it merely dislike of being an outcast – natural enough, but unhelpful – or was there somewhere hard, if unrecognized evidence?

'Could you give me a concrete example of what you mean?'

Helena retreated. 'Oh, I'm probably being silly. Neville and Edward both thought I was unbalanced on the subject. But I'll tell you who you should talk to – Mr Tiggywinkle.'

'Mr Tiggywinkle?'

'Neville's name for him.' Helena bit her lip. 'He was good fun, Neville, good company, and very acute. If you remember Mr Tilson you'll understand. He's old and harmless-looking, but he has penetrating eyes that see through you and out the other side. He's not local, but he's made a hobby of this village, studying it, almost. You know, the way some small boys keep a colony of slugs in a jamjar.'

Frances laughed. 'You're feeling better.'

Her companion stared at her. 'You know, I am,' she said, wonderingly. 'Nothing's changed – in fact you've given me something new to worry about – but you've believed I'm innocent. And I knew that, yet suddenly I don't feel guilty any more. Perhaps it's the brandy.'

She was laughing, almost naturally, when she heard the front door opening. 'Half-past four – it's probably Edward. Hello!' she called. 'In here!'

Stephanie, in the hall, heard the voices with relief. At least she wouldn't be alone with her mother. She opened the door and hesitated on the threshold.

Her mother must have had her hair done. It wasn't the way it used to be, but it was elegant, not weird like it was yesterday. And she was smiling, and when she spoke it wasn't in that funny artificial voice. It was a bit high-pitched, perhaps, but it sounded warm and natural again.

'Oh, it's you, Stephanie. Darling, do you remember Detective-Sergeant Howarth? She's realized I was innocent all along, and she's going to do what she can to convince everyone else.'

For a moment Stephanie could not take it in; the miracle she hadn't even dared to pray for.

'Oh Mum,' she said, and as her mother held out her arms, she hurled herself into that safe haven, sobbing her relief.

Feeling an intruder, Frances rose quietly. Over her daughter's head, Helena met her eyes. 'Thank you.'

Frances paused. 'It won't all be this easy,' she cautioned, but Helena smiled, though the corners of her mouth were quivering.

'Worth it for this alone,' she said, and Frances's last glimpse, as she left a card with her phone number on a table, was of the two heads, the blonde and the dark, pressed together in the big arm-chair.

She was closing the gate as Edward Radley's car drew up. Seeing her, he leaped out, advancing on her with bristling courtesy.

'Can I help you?'

'Mr Radley – you may remember me. I'm Frances Howarth.'

She saw an expression she recognized appear on his face. It was a look compounded of uneasiness, suspicion and distaste, and she knew it from a thousand other encounters with those who had reason to be wary of the law.

'What do you want?' he demanded roughly.

'I've just been to see your wife –'

A less controlled man, she thought, would have struck her. 'Dear god!' he said. 'Haven't you done enough to her already? You've seen her – isn't she broken enough for you?'

'I appreciate your feelings. But I felt I must come to tell your wife that I now believe her to be innocent and want to do what I can to put the record straight.'

He did not unbend. 'It would certainly have been welcome if you had experienced this Pauline conversion at the time. Now, when my wife is trying to put it all behind her, I cannot see that disinter-ring the past will serve any useful purpose.'

She looked at him thoughtfully. 'Mr Radley, do you believe your wife is innocent?'

He squared his shoulders. 'My wife told me that at the time when you, Sergeant Howarth, so unfortunately refused to accept her word.'

She was not in the habit of quoting Shakespeare on investigations, but now she heard herself saying, ' "When my love swears that she is made of truth, I do believe her, though I know she lies." '

His face flamed. 'How dare you!' he snarled, and turned on his heel.

Not clever. She turned, and wearily crossed the square to Tyler's Barn and Mr Tilson.

She had time to regret her decision as she waited on the doorstep. She could claim no official standing; she was arriving, unannounced, with little purpose other than to persuade him to gossip about his neighbours. She could have been on her way home to Limber by now; she wished she had spent more time on reflection before she had rung the bell.

But to her surprise, Maxwell Tilson recognized her, and was refreshingly pleased to see her. 'Miss Howarth – or should I call you Sergeant? What an agreeable surprise!' He twinkled sharp brown eyes at her, and reminded of his nickname, Frances almost expected to see his nose twitch interrogatively as he ushered her in.

'How clever of you to remember me. Frances will do – this is a very unofficial visit.'

'How exciting.' The room into which he led her was lit by lamps and untidy with papers and books. The chairs were huge, shabby and comfortable, and on the table beside his leather wing-chair sat what appeared to be a fairly ambitious Scotch.

Mindful of her drive home, Frances requested a tonic, and, reassured as to his willingness to help, went on to explain her mission.

He heard her out in attentive silence, and did not speak for a few moments after she had finished.

'Yes,' he said at last. 'The more I think about it, the more I think your reasoning is probably correct. Though it didn't surprise me much at the time, I have to admit.'

Frances was taken aback. 'Didn't surprise you? Helena Radley's arrest? Oh, you mean Fielding's murder.'

'No, I don't in fact. That did surprise me, because in my experience of life it is, don't you find, never the things one would say were totally predictable that actually happen?'

She was surprised into laughter, and, satisfied, he went on.

'There was enormous tension building up, with Fielding at its centre. He was provoking it, of course, but others were colluding, or it could never have happened. He was staging real-life melodrama, using this place as a setting for the grand illusion which became tragic reality.'

'Helena felt that. She talked of his becoming Harry – his television character – when they moved down here.'

'Precisely. I even took to watching the programme, you know, and it was quite obvious. But then, she was in the illusion business too. That's a powerful force; act it out, become it . . . Aristotle knew all about it, as he did about so many things.'

She refused the sidetrack. 'Are you saying she helped set up the situation? According to her, she hated it –'

'Oh no, by no means. Grand Guignol would never be to her taste. Her creation was completely different, and ultimately came into conflict with his when he landed a role that suited him better than being cast as *enfant terrible*. When he found he could actually manipulate real people . . . infinitely more satisfying.'

'I accept what you say about his scenario. Several people spoke in precisely those terms at the time of his death – Dyer, the producer, for one. But I'm intrigued – why do you say Helena was trying to create a fantasy?'

His look expressed pity at her poverty of observation. 'That girl lives a fantasy. She's probably done it all her life – I would guess at an unhappy childhood, wouldn't you? She's afraid of being less than perfect in case no one loves her any more, and she has created this elegant carapace of the perfect wife and mother. Virtuous, long-suffering, beautiful, talented but self-sacrificing; the modern Patient Griselda. Nobody is that good, my dear, nobody, and if you force yourself to tolerate your husband's infidelities, brutalities and total lack of consideration without complaint or even acknow-ledgement, something has to give. I thought she murdered him; perhaps she simply murdered her selfhood.'

Frances remained sceptical. 'It's a pretty theory. But she did di-vorce him, after all.'

'Ah yes! But that fascinated me almost more than anything else. She found a replacement, virtually overnight, who let her carry on the illusion.

'Edward, you see, is an incurable idealist; the role of perfect wife, once more, was just waiting for her. I often wondered if there was more to their relationship, if they ever came off stage, as it were – and, recently, how it would survive the revelation that she was imperfect enough to take a poker to someone's head.'

'I think he has simply blotted out what he doesn't want to see.'

'That would be typical, I surmise, though I have never got to know him well. But as for her – well, deep and troubled waters lie beneath the serenity.

'But as I said, you've made out a good case. And there have been one or two things – oh, no more than straws in the wind . . .'

She had been listening, fascinated, to this fluent and persuasive analysis, but at these words her professional ears pricked up.

'Straws in the wind?'

He hesitated, weighing his words. 'I must be at some pains not to overstate this. But – the village is unsettled. They know something, I think, or at least believe they do. They're uneasy.'

'Well, a murder in a village – they would be, wouldn't they?'

'Not if they felt it had nothing to do with them, no. Perhaps not even if they felt it met the standards of natural justice. And Neville, don't forget, brought his play-acting headlong into conflict with their precious world-in-amber. George Wagstaff was going to lose his farm, the village was about to be overrun by foreigners, and don't think it wasn't resented quite as much as Dyer resented the loss of his golden egg-laying goose.'

'You're not suggesting they would deliberately connive at murder?'

The reply shot back. 'Yes, without a doubt.'

At her shocked expression, he paused. 'Now I've horrified you. It's not quite as bald as that. If they had seen someone bringing the poker down on Fielding's head, they wouldn't lie to the police about it – oh, unless it were a brother, a son, a lover, something like that, but that obtains the world over.

'It's probably merely that they think they know something that might shed a light on whatever took place. They wouldn't feel it their business to report what may be only opinion or gossip. Particularly in a situation where, in a most satisfactorily primitive sense, someone got their just deserts.'

Frances still found it hard to accept. 'Even if it resulted in the wrong person being convicted?'

'Ah. Now, you see, this is where my observation begins to tie in with your theory. As I said, they are uneasy. Something is wrong, and perhaps if your policemen had gone and talked to them at the time, they'd have let something slip, more or less deliberately. Especially if you found one with local connections.'

'Mmmm.' Frances considered that one uncomfortably. 'So you think, if I went and chatted to them now, told them what I think . . .'

He looked at her under his heavy brows. 'You do have a need to put it right, don't you? Now, is that an abstract passion for justice, or merely sinful personal pride?'

She sat up, stung, but before she could defend herself he laughed wheezily, and went on. 'I doubt if you would get anywhere. Unless they could see some future reason, one which they would accept, I think you would meet with a stone wall of the type they are so good at erecting.'

All at once Frances felt sickened, and very, very tired. 'Do you suppose it would weigh at all with the Radnesfield moralists that Mrs Radley might be at risk of meeting with a very nasty accident?'

He looked startled, then pursed his lips in a soundless whistle, making him look oddly like a schoolboy, got up, for reasons which remained obscure, in an old man's white wig.

'You're right, of course. It might be in someone's interests to – er, dispose of her, I suppose –'

'Discreetly, naturally. Yes, I'm very much afraid it might.' She got to her feet. 'I must go – I've taken up far too much of your time, but it has been most illuminating. Thank you, Mr Tilson.'

He blinked at her reproachfully. 'My dear, Maxwell, please. I am not so old that I like to think that the uppermost emotion a pretty girl has towards me is respect. *Eheu fugaces!*'

She laughed. 'I'm happy to call you Maxwell, and I don't think respect is the right word. I think it's terror. Helena Radley warned me you were dangerously perceptive, and I'm going before you discover all my secrets too.'

He smiled. 'Come and talk to me again. I collect people, you know.'

' "Like slugs in a jamjar," ' Frances quoted, and had the satisfaction of leaving him looking puzzled.

She slumped exhausted in her seat when she reached her car.

Maxwell Tilson! What a murderer he would make, and he might have constructed their hour together as an exercise in misdirection. His alibi certainly warranted checking.

How unpleasant it was to have a detective's suspicious mind. She smiled ruefully, and pushed in a cassette as she drove off. The healing, ordered sounds of Bach's Goldberg Variations flooded the car, and she could feel tension beginning to seep from her as she drove, her fingers picking out imaginary notes on the steering wheel.

She would play one of them when she got home, as a soothing mental discipline, then have a Scotch, an omelette and a deep bath, and she would allow herself the indulgence of a late start tomorrow. Surely, with this week off, she could unearth enough to persuade them to re-open the case, at least.

At last she swung the car into the drive of a neat, smug, suburban villa. Its one virtue was that she had her flat upstairs, while her mother lived a life of semi-independence below. The wheelchair to which Poppy Howarth's failed hip replacement had confined her limited her sphere of operations to downstairs, without which barrier Frances thought she would surely have gone mad.

A strange car sat in the driveway, and Frances sighed heavily. Mrs Clarke, the home help, went at five, and someone else always came to help her mother to bed. This must be a new one, and Poppy would have trapped her, talking. They would have to go through the usual charade, and tonight she wasn't sure that she could bear it.

She turned the key delicately in the lock, closing the door quietly, but Poppy despite her seventy-two years had ears like a bat, registering the slightest vibration of movement in her environment.

'Hello? Is that you, dear? Come along in, I have a visitor.'

Frances, pulling a childish face, entered the hub of her mother's universe. The room was furnished in pinks and greens, with frilled lampshades and pleated velvet cushions.

'You have to say this for Mrs Howarth, she's never given in,' Mrs Clarke was frequently heard to say, wryly.

And she hadn't. Courtesy of a beautician sent by the social services, Poppy's crowning glory retained its hennaed red, and her nails were shining scarlet talons. Her mouth was a vivid, if haphazard, gash of colour, and the high-arched brows, such a feature in her youth, were still marked, even if improbably black and slightly askew.

The helper, a pleasant-faced woman in a blue nylon overall, was sitting holding a cup of tea as if she weren't sure how it got there. She looked round with evident relief when Frances entered.

'Ah, there you are,' said Poppy majestically. 'Mrs Christie, my daughter Rose.'

Frances forced a polite smile. Her mother had started using her hated second name, as a controlling mechanism, when her daughter had taken the deplorable and unfeminine step of joining the police force. Protest was vain, and frequently embarrassing.

'That must have been a *very* late meeting! What sort of a day have you had, Rose dear?'

It was coming, inexorably. None the less, having shaken hands with Mrs Christie, she attempted escape.

'Terribly busy, I'm afraid. In fact, I'm not fit company for anyone until I've had a bath and something to eat. If you wouldn't think me rude, Mrs Christie –'

'Poor sweetie!' Poppy's laugh tinkled out. 'What was it today – personality conflicts in the staff-room, or the girls being difficult? Schoolgirls, even in the most *select* girls' schools, do seem so different today from the way we all were, don't they, Mrs Christie? I always think teachers like Rose do such a wonderful job.'

Mrs Christie thought Mrs Howarth's daughter a strange, awkward sort of girl; with her mother beaming upon her encouragingly, she had made a funny sound and left the room. And she had been no help at all in persuading her mother to settle down for the night.

Minutes later she heard a piano upstairs being played loudly, with lots of crashing chords – something Russian, perhaps, though she was no expert.

'Rachmaninov,' Mrs Howarth supplied. 'So talented – she teaches music, of course. And just the teensiest bit temperamental, I have to confess, as all musicians are!'

10

Sharon Thomas was looking even more oppressed than usual as she scurried to her work on Saturday morning. It was through no wish of hers that she found herself knowing what no one else knew, and if Martha discovered her concealing something, something like this – Sharon was a timid creature, and she shuddered.

Her feet, she found, had made the decision for her, and she was standing on Martha's doorstep, raising her hand to the dazzling brass of the knocker. She tapped gingerly, once.

The door seemed to open at her touch and Martha stood on the threshold, like the trap-door spider waiting for her victim. She was wearing her working coat, ready to leave for the Red House.

'Oh, it's you, Sharon Thomas, is it? And what's brought you round, looking as if someone's stolen your tuppenny bun? Come to tell me the sky's falling, have you?'

Sharon, with a gulp, blurted out what she knew, and had the doubtful satisfaction of seeing Martha Bateman's face take on a grimmer expression than she had ever seen before.

Frances was still in her dressing-gown when Helena phoned; she had forgotten to mention the party the day before, but now it had occurred to her that this was an ideal observation opportunity.

'It won't do any harm, either, if lots of people know that you're not alone in the knowledge that Neville's murderer is still at large,' Frances said, and knew by the pause before her agreement that Helena had thought of that too.

She made herself a pot of coffee while she planned her day. Saturday: unless some emergency had come up, Coppins would be off. She could sneak into headquarters and take a quiet look at the file, unquestioned, before she went off to Radnesfield.

She dressed, then went to the piano, as she still did every morning, heaven knew why. She had been just not good enough to be a concert pianist, and wounded pride prevented her from teaching instead, but unless she spent ten minutes wrestling with the more awkward scales (D Minor Melodic today), she felt dissatisfied and out of sorts, the way other people did if they were prevented from working out.

When she went downstairs, there were the sounds of Blessed Mrs Clarke working in the kitchen, and her mother was sitting at a low table with a tray of tea and toast. She had not put on her make-up: her face was sleep-wrinkled and sallow, and her hair still a bird's nest.

'Morning, Mrs Clarke!' Frances called. 'Morning, Mother.' She went across to peck her on the cheek.

Disapproval pervaded the air like a miasma as Poppy noticed her coat. 'Going out, I see.' The statement was an accusation.

'I'm sorry, Mother, but –'

'Now, why should you feel you have to apologize? You know I don't expect you to limit your social life, just because I'm a lonely old woman. I may be a burden to myself, but heaven forbid that I should be a burden to you.'

The brave smile was one of Poppy's better effects, but today Frances would not indulge her by taking notice. 'I'm working this morning, but I should be back sometime in the afternoon, and then –'

A gesture of one imperious, red-nailed hand stopped her. 'No, no. There's no need to make excuses. It's your job, no doubt – though, with your responsibilities, one might have thought . . .' She trailed into provocative silence.

'I should have taken a job like teaching, instead of so recklessly going into the police force, you mean. Mother, I was really angry last night. You put me in an impossible position.'

The faded blue eyes drifted off into the middle distance, vague and unfocused. 'I don't know what you mean – I get confused . . .'

'Of course you don't. You know perfectly well – oh, what's the use? I've got to go now. Mrs Clarke will see that you're all right, and I'll phone you if by any chance I'm delayed.'

Poppy didn't reply, only directing a baleful stare at her daughter's departing back. Impatiently, she tinkled a brass bell on the table at her side, and Mrs Clarke appeared, a dish-towel in her hands.

'You won't forget the sandwiches for my bridge game this afternoon, Mrs Clarke, will you?'

'No, dear, I won't,' the other woman said patiently, only adding, 'Not now you've reminded me four times, no,' once she was safely out of earshot.

Outside in the car, Frances hesitated. It could be a long day when you were all on your own. Perhaps she should have stayed at home. But she had promised Helena, and in addition, a certain unease was festering – that strange little village!

She sighed as she started the engine. Guilt! If it didn't exist, mothers would invent it. It seemed to be the inevitable lot of any woman in a family situation, and it was enough to put you off the whole idea. Which was, perhaps, fortunate, since the world seemed

133

conspicuously lacking in young men prepared to adapt to the working schedules of female detective-sergeants.

'Thought you were off this week,' the uniformed file clerk said to her when she requested 5337/JC/FH.

That was all she needed – questions about why she wanted to waste her precious leave on a file for a case that was closed.

'I wasn't sure I could survive a week without seeing you, Ron, and it's the best excuse I could come up with.'

She winked, and the man, grinning, went off to fetch it. She took it back to the CID office, empty this morning, and settled down.

The interviewing had been, as she suspected, perfunctory. There were preliminary statements from those who would have been principal suspects initially – Helena, Edward, Lilian, Chris Dyer, George Wagstaff, Jack Daley – and mainly carried out before forensic had come up with all the damning evidence. At that point, the investigation had been scaled down; police forces didn't have the manpower to waste on unnecessary enquiries.

Then there were the more detailed statements, concentrating on the case against Helena, from Sharon Thomas, Tamara Farrell and Sandra Daley.

She flipped through them. Most, as one would imagine, were unsupported accounts, though a few, like Wagstaff, Radley and Daley had alibis of a sort, more or less confirmed. Radley's seemed pretty solid – they had actually moved fast enough to have checked the clockmaker's timepiece and got the vicar's confirmation on Monday, before Helena was arrested. Similarly, Wagstaff's wife and son had claimed he was in view of one or other all afternoon, if you found that convincing. Daley had a gap or two in the course of the afternoon, but no more than quarter of an hour here or there unverified. In a place the size of Radnesfield, that could be significant. Or not.

Frowning, she moved on to Sandra Daley's statement and studied it. Now, that was interesting. She had a large window in her kitchen; if she had been working there all afternoon, as she claimed, she was almost bound to notice anyone going up to Radnesfield House from the village. She had mentioned only Stephanie and Helena, yet Tamara Farrell, by her own admission, had been in the little wood below the house for at least the latter part of the afternoon. Had she another way of getting there, or was Sandra's statement, for some reason, incomplete? Come to that, no one was nearer to the scene of the crime than Sandra herself, with no one to watch her mount the path; Tamara had seen Helena but not Stephanie, so, according to Helena's evidence, the murderer had been and gone by that time.

Sandra certainly had reason enough to hate Fielding, once she found out that he had been two-timing her. That, of course, went for the other women he was laying as well, and their husbands, though they did not seem to feature anywhere in the profile of the crime. She scribbled a note on the pad at her side.

She looked in vain for any record of interviews carried out in the village. There had, after all, been the burning in effigy and the death threat, but thanks to her over-slick detective work, no one had considered questioning any of the locals except Sharon Thomas, and she certainly wouldn't volunteer anything they hadn't quarried out with a chisel. Maxwell Tilson had not been interviewed. She couldn't quite see what his motive might be, and murder as an intellectual exercise would be unusual, to say the least.

Leaning back in her chair, she shut her eyes in concentration, trying to tease out the strands that were so messily interwoven. Sometimes – though heaven help her if Joe Coppins ever found out – characters emerged in her mind like themes in a piece of music, and she could already hear the shrill, titupping strings that indicated Sandra Daley, and the ponderous bassoon notes of Edward Radley. But beneath it all, she could feel a ground bass, swelling and insistent, marked by a harsh discordancy – the theme of Radnesfield itself.

She opened her eyes, shaking her head to clear it. This was self-indulgence. 'Don't waste your time with bloody nonsense!' She could almost hear Coppin's diapason roar.

The next step was to record, as best she could, her recollection of the interview with Helena. She typed for half an hour, then sat back to analyse what she had written, and the notes she had made from the file.

The evidence was still an amorphous mass. The statements, as they stood, were rambling and incoherent, full of inconsistencies and gaps you could drive a bus through. Yet some sort of shape was starting to emerge.

135

With a certain amount of overlap, Fielding's enemies fell into three definite categories. There were the village people – the largest body, this – resentful of the changes he was about to impose on their way of life, and, according to Maxwell Tilson, amoral at the very least.

Next, there were those with some deep-seated and personal reason for hatred. That could mean Jack Daley, and the other husbands like him – the cuckolds, their sexual shame exposed – or even Helena herself, who could not be scientifically eliminated from the enquiry.

Finally – and this was the group which must come most heavily under suspicion if contiguity of time were significant – there were those for whom Neville's decision would mean a serious change of circumstances. Wagstaff, for instance; Chris Dyer, of course; even the vicar, dismayed and helpless without his wife; Lilian.

Here she paused. That had, after all, been her first instinct. Was it really in any sense likely that the languid, posing Lilian had wielded a poker to such deadly purpose?

Motive, means and opportunity: these were the textbook cornerstones of any murder enquiry, and instinctively she reverted to them as an aid to structured thought.

The mainsprings of motive were, by convention, gain, revenge, blood-lust and principle. Well, score two out of four for Lilian on that; blood-lust seemed improbable, and gain covered the only principle Lilian Sheldon Fielding was likely to cherish.

Opportunity wasn't lacking. With Sharon in the kitchen, who was to see Lilian tiptoe downstairs to the study? Neville, trusting, his back turned; the means, which she knew to be to hand . . .

She added her own personal fifth indicator. Character? A moody drift of saxophone suggested itself, but that could become strident. Yes, on reflection, there might well be steel beneath the candy-floss. Lilian could repay investigation.

But then, on this basis, Helena would score high as well. She wasn't going to build any satisfactory case on such shifting sands as these.

She looked at her watch, then hastily shuffled the papers back into their file. It was time she was heading for Radnesfield, and once more she was aware of the faint, uneasy tingle of concern.

Edward was fussing; there was no more charitable way to describe it.

'Well, at least we've got a glorious day,' he said for the fourth time. 'You know, I do believe it's mild enough to open the doors into the garden, so that people can spill out and it won't be such a crush.'

'Why not?' Helena agreed. 'But not your office, Edward, with all your papers littered around.'

'No, I suppose not.' He contemplated traffic flow moodily. 'It's a pity, though – they could have got out into the garden that way. Still, I suppose they can use the door at the back of the hall, and –'

He was interrupted by the telephone, and came back looking gloomy. 'That was Annabel Gray. She and James have this wretched 'flu that's going about. The Stanningtons called off last night too, did I tell you? Simon's gone down with it.'

'Yes, you did. But does it really matter? Dozens of people are coming anyway. Oh, and I phoned Frances Howarth. She's going to look in.'

Edward did not look overjoyed at the news. He was still clearly uneasy about what had happened, but this was hardly the moment to try to convince him of the detective's good faith.

Stephanie appeared from the back of the hall.

'The buffet's absolutely brilliant – if you want me, I'll be looking after the meringues to see that no one disturbs them. The caterers seem fine, and Ma Bateman's there too, buttering things in a corner with a face like fizz.'

'Oh dear,' Helena said feebly. You did have to feel so strong to cope with Mrs Bateman in one of her sourer moods. 'Edward, could you possibly –?'

'Yes, of course. She's probably upset at having all these people in her kitchen. I'll go and smooth the ruffled feathers.' He bustled out.

'Thank heavens for that! I'm just going upstairs to change – they'll be here in half an hour.'

When she came hurrying back down again, fixing her earrings, Edward, trim as always in blazer and regimental tie, was hovering in the hall, fidgeting with his cuffs as if he were as much on edge as she was. He looked up as he heard her coming.

'Darling, you look quite lovely.' He came to take her hands.

She had put on a silk dress with a screen print of blues and greens, then, finding herself shivering, though more with nerves than cold, added a jade-green, loose jacket in mohair. Her hair lay smooth and shiny in its curved bob, and the excitement of performance had brought hectic spots of colour to her cheeks, making her eyes seem brighter than usual.

For the first time, she did not shrink from his kiss. Indeed, the feel of his cheek, well-shaven and leathery, smelling of Floris soap, was satisfying, and she rubbed her own against it, like a kitten, in sensual enjoyment. His grasp on her hand tightened, but he said only, 'Better not spoil the effect, I suppose,' and with a final squeeze of her fingers let her go as the bell rang to announce the first arrivals.

It was a relief to find that it was Charles and Jennifer Morley who stood on the doorstep.

Jennifer swept in, mistress of every situation. 'Helena, how gorgeous –' and then she stopped. 'Oh, my dear, you've had to cut your lovely hair!' Her eyes brimmed with tears, and Helena, touched, held out her arms to be hugged with Jennifer's usual whole-hearted enthusiasm.

Sniffing, Jennifer emerged from the embrace. 'I don't know why I should be crying about your hair. It looks absolutely stunning. Sheer jealousy, probably. Anyway, I'm so pleased to see you.'

'It's good to see you too,' Helena was able to reply with unfeigned sincerity.

To Helena's astonished relief, it wasn't embarrassing, much. She was moved by the number of people who seemed genuinely happy to welcome her home, and if there was a slight constraint with one or two of those who, like Edward's colleagues from work, had known her less well, there was certainly no one who had made her feel like a freak in a sideshow.

Chris made his usual stage entrance, side-stepping the rigidly-disapproving Edward to sweep her into a bearhug.

'Now, let me look at you,' he said with enthusiasm that was only slightly forced. 'Oh yes, I like the hair. I definitely like the hair – a bit more of a come-on, isn't it? But the figure – no. You're much sexier carrying a bit more in the strategic places, so hit the cream buns, sweetheart. You wouldn't want to disappoint me, now would you?'

'Oh, for heaven's sake, Chris,' she said, freeing herself with all the old exasperation.

'That's my girl,' he said, giving her another playful squeeze before going off in search of a drink.

Helena looked anxiously at her watch. It would have been reassuring to have Frances Howarth there before Lilian made her usual entrance, late by calculation rather than chance. The Daleys were apparently bringing her, which would have the merit of getting two very trying encounters over at once. Her stomach still churned at the prospect, but otherwise she was almost ready to be convinced that Edward's high-risk strategy of brazening it out was a triumph.

She was engaged in anodyne conversation with Edward's partner's wife, whose flow of small talk was so well-bred that no topic of any interest, let alone embarrassment, was ever permitted to arise, when she heard the stir of Lilian's arrival. Her nails bit into her palms in tension as she excused herself.

As she went towards the front door, Edward materialized at her side. How like him, she thought gratefully, to understand her nervousness, and be there in support.

Lilian, however, seemed oblivious to any awkwardness. 'Helena, darling!' she trilled. 'So sorry we're so awfully late – don't blame Jack, will you? Poor sweetie, he's been hanging about for half an hour while I changed my mind about what to wear.'

The turquoise sleeveless dress with plunging back which had been the final selection was too summery for the weak spring sunshine, but distinctly becoming.

Halfway to an embrace, Lilian checked, as she took in Helena's appearance. 'Oh, my dear, twinnies,' she said, patting her own sleek head, and Helena realized, with a jolt, that her new hairstyle had, indeed, unconsciously echoed Lilian's. Once more, she felt at a disadvantage.

'It – it just seemed a good idea to have a change,' she blurted, then Edward was drawing Lilian off, leaving her face to face with Jack Daley and, a few paces behind like some unwelcome encumbrance, Sandra.

Jack, certainly, was ill at ease. He said, 'Hello, Helena,' abruptly, and plunged into the crowd without a pause. Sandra, making to follow him, was thwarted by a group movement, and turned her eyes on Helena.

They seemed almost unfocused, and Helena, seeing the woman for the first time in eighteen months, found it hard not to recoil in shock.

At Jack's command, his wife had visited the hairdresser, but from the disorder of the hard curls, it seemed unlikely that she had combed them this morning. Make-up had been applied, but so indiscriminately that one cheek was noticeably redder than the other, and bright blue eye-shadow had been smeared unevenly on her lids. When she put up a trembling hand to her mouth, the nails were broken and dirty.

'Sandra!' Helena said, in horrified compassion, putting out a hand towards her, but the other woman backed away.

'No,' she whispered fiercely. 'Leave me alone – I don't want anyone – anyone – to touch me.' She backed, like some frightened wild creature, into a dark corner of the hall, and Helena, recognizing that she was doing more harm than good, left her, forgetting her own awkwardness in concern. Perhaps Chris might be able to talk to the woman.

When she went through to the sitting-room, Lilian was already the centre of a group of people. Surely she, too, was a little on edge, after all; her colour was high, and her voice seemed louder than usual, her laughter forced. Looking for Chris, Helena skirted the group, but Lilian's words brought her up short.

'Yes, it's all decided,' she was saying. 'I'm afraid you're just going to have to get along without me. Radnesfield will never be the same again, will it?'

The hubbub of voices still rose from the hall, but from the sudden silence it was evident that she had struck dumb her audience in the sitting-room. Daley, whose hand was resting possessively on her haunch, was staring at her now with his mouth unbecomingly open; George Wagstaff, in another group, had stopped pretending that he wasn't eavesdropping; Chris, standing detached on the fringe of the circle, was studying the tableau with the sardonic amusement of the only person unsurprised.

It was Helena who first found her voice. 'Are you really planning to leave, Lilian? Sell Radnesfield House?' She would need permission from the trustees, if she wanted to do that; she had only a life-interest, before Neville's estate reverted to Stephanie.

Lilian turned to her, as if almost relieved at the chance to make her statement. 'Well, naturally, I simply *adore* the place – such an amusing little village, and poor darling Neville absolutely loved it, of course – but the dear little man who made Neville that fabulous

140

offer has gone on and on, and it simply got too exhausting to go on saying no. He was so grateful, bless his heart, and I'm sure he'll build simply lovely houses.'

It was Wagstaff's bellow that shattered the silence following on this ingenuous exposition. 'I don't bloody believe it! Not after last time – not all over again! You'd stopped it all, you said, no need for us to do anything else, you said – you lying bitch!' he shouted, his painful sincerity, like a blunt instrument, splintering her artifice.

'George!' Dora, her face white, was tugging at his arm, but he jerked his sleeve free of her plucking fingers.

'It's people's lives you're talking about, do you know that? Look here, I'm willing to offer you a fair price for the farm –'

Lilian's eyes had flashed dangerously for a moment, but she recovered her composure to murmur sweetly, 'I'm awfully sorry, George. I'd love to help you out, of course, but I'm afraid it simply has to be a package deal.'

Wagstaff's round, fleshy face was suffused with purple. 'It's a game to you, isn't it? But don't think you'll walk away from it, just like that. My lawyer was a useless bastard last time, but this time, god help me, I'm going to make you pay.'

'George, you'll do no good that way. Think of your blood pressure. Just come and see Jim, talk it over with him. I think he's out in the garden somewhere with Stephanie.' Dora was shaking, but her voice sounded calmly authoritative, and he allowed himself to be led away.

The groups reformed, uneasily; Lilian and Jack were left standing alone.

'Never lowered yourself to breathe a word of this to me, did you?' Helena heard him say roughly, and was almost knocked off balance as he passed her, dragging Lilian by the wrist. His face was a shade of crimson that conflicted unkindly with his hair, and he, too, was in a towering temper.

Looking for somewhere less public to have a row! That was all she needed. Helena seized a bottle from a side-table and began to circulate. Keeping everyone's glass topped up was the best she could do.

'And *do* tell me, has your experience made you feel you want to work for prisoners' rights in the future?' Marcia Farrell had not improved during Helena's absence. 'There's a wonderful diocesan group that does such marvellous work in the prisons . . .'

Helena looked for help to Peter Farrell, who, as usual, was standing a little behind his wife, but he was uncomfortable, persistently refusing to meet her eye, and perspiring more than the temperature warranted.

'I'm sure they do.' In desperation, she changed the subject. 'I'm sorry if I appear a little inattentive. I'm expecting Frances Howarth – the policewoman, you know.'

'Oh yes, of course.' Marcia's pale, gooseberry eyes studied her, greedy for signs of weakness. 'Is she helping with your rehabilitation?'

Irritation could be useful. 'No,' Helena said crisply. 'She's realized now that I wasn't guilty, and she's helping me establish my innocence.'

Marcia, for once, had no prefabricated response; her husband looked shocked.

'But – but I thought the case had been closed,' he bleated.

'I know. And it does seem awfully unnecessary to open it all up again, doesn't it, even if the wrong person has been found guilty.'

Helena flashed them a brilliant smile, and turned away. The atmosphere of this party, which had started so promisingly, was becoming noticeably strained, and it was beginning to get to her. She had tried to keep her voice down, but she was aware of covert glances in her direction.

She was making her way across the hall, trying to look busy so that no one would accost her, when Lilian came in from the garden. The sun was still bright and warm for the time of year, but in her flimsy frock Lilian looked pale and chilled. Seeing Helena, she came between two groups of people to reach her.

'Look, could I possibly have a couple of aspirins and a lie-down? I'm feeling perfectly foul – I think I must have a touch of this stupid 'flu – and Jack's just been yelling at me in the garden, awful man.'

'Well, there's certainly no problem, but wouldn't you rather go home? I'm sure someone would –'

Lilian shook her head. 'Don't bother. Ten minutes for the aspirin to work, and I'll be fine. Chris is giving me a lift up to London after lunch. He's got a new part for me, and I promised he could try to talk me into it on the way back to town. Anyway, I've suddenly got radically bored with Radnesfield.'

'Whatever you like. Shall I take you upstairs, or do you want just to lie down on the couch in Edward's office? No one will disturb you there.'

'That would be perfect, darling.'

Helena led her along the back corridor to the office. Mrs Bateman, coming out of the kitchen carrying a tray, stood aside to let them pass, but returned Helena's nervous smile with a sullen glare.

'Here you are. It's not very tidy, I'm afraid.' Helena cleared some papers off the elderly chesterfield drawn up in front of the fire-place.

Lilian sank down gratefully. 'Oh, that's better. My head! And Jack would keep shouting! Whatever did he expect? It was a bit of fun, and now it's over. A long-standing affair with a glorified mechanic isn't really part of my career plan – however good he may like to think he is in bed.'

Helena did not comment on this supremely egotistical remark. It was, however, likely to be her last chance to talk face-to-face with Lilian. 'This business of selling the house – have you consulted the trustees?'

Despite her headache, Lilian's expression became alert and busi-ness-like, and she dropped her drawl.

'You think I'm stupid, don't you? That's all been taken care of, and they're delighted. You'll be hearing from them whenever I give the word.'

'Don't you think it was a little unkind and – well, dishonest, not to put too fine a point on it, to lead people like poor George to think you'd dropped the whole idea? It obviously came as a terrible shock to everyone.'

Lilian's eyes narrowed, and she bared her neat white teeth in a mirthless smile.

'Warn them, you mean, and find myself lying there with a poker embedded in the back of my skull? Cheers! No, I wasn't about to announce my plans to blow apart this godawful little place until I knew I wasn't going back to the house to give them a second bite at the cherry.'

There was an underlying assumption here, which made Helena catch her breath. 'You mean – you think someone from the village killed Neville? You knew it wasn't me?'

When she spoke there was more than a hint of scouse in the carefully-cultivated voice. 'Listen, chuck, you weren't there the night they marched on the house. They scared me, you know – really scared me. They hated him enough to do anything, and if we're being frank – we are being frank, aren't we? – I was quite relieved they only killed Neville.

'And as for you,' the narrow smile held contempt, and the drawl had returned. 'Well, face it, darling, I never thought for a moment you had the guts.'

What could you say? You could hardly take offence because someone had said you weren't a murderess, but while Helena was groping for her reply, the other woman shivered. 'God, it's cold in here,' she muttered.

It wasn't cold, but her face was very flushed. She was clearly unwell, and Helena swallowed her irritation. 'Here,' she said briskly. 'Take my jacket. It's very warm, and I really don't need it. I'm sure there's a rug somewhere – yes, here it is. Put your head on this cushion, and you can pull it over you.'

Lilian did as she was told without protest, snuggling into the cushion and shutting her eyes with a sigh of relief while Helena went to fetch the aspirin.

As she returned, she was drawn in to the kitchen by one of the caterers with a query about the coffee. The kitchen helper deputed to take the aspirins in to Mrs Fielding found her asleep, her breathing deep and even as a child's, her hair fallen forward across her face. The woman set bottle and glass quietly down on a side-table, and left without waking her.

In the silence of the room, the old wall-clock ticked slowly, portentously, as if spelling out the ancient motto, '*Ars longa, vita brevis*', which was inscribed on its face in copperplate characters and flaking paint.

11

Outside, on this mild and windless day, the scene was positively arcadian. In the unexpected warmth, knots of people gathered, parted and reformed, as if in some rustic dance. Some of the younger guests, indifferent to the chill of damp stone, were grouped with unconscious grace on the low, lichened wall by the lawn.

Stephanie was sitting there with Jim Wagstaff. They had been friends for a long time; she treated him much like the older brother she had never had. Today, however, their conversation was strained: he, too indignant and upset to talk of anything but the blow which had fallen, and she, feeling somehow responsible, embarrassed. She had said she was sorry, and agreed it was entirely unfair; there wasn't a lot else she could say, but she lacked the social skill to withdraw without unkindness.

'It's such a helluva shame,' Jim was saying, as if voicing an original thought, and not repeating it for the tenth time. 'When the old man's put so much into that place, it's not right. There ought to be some way of putting a stop to it.'

Stephanie, shifting uncomfortably, became aware of the hurried, crab-like approach, from round the side of the house, of Tamara Farrell. She had a strange expression on her face, and in Stephanie seemed to find the person she was looking for.

The older girl watched her advance without enthusiasm. 'What do you want, Tamara?'

Tamara rubbed one grubby leg against the other, and would not meet her eyes.

'Your mum's dead,' she said, in a sort of sullen mutter.

Stephanie stared at her coldly. 'Your stupid jokes are just so childish. Go away and bother someone else. I certainly don't want to hear them.'

The child looked up with a defiant pout. 'She is, too. She's dead in there.' She jerked her head towards the side of the house. 'She's got a cushion over her head, and I tried her hand and it went all like this.' She demonstrated, horribly, a flopping arm.

Stephanie, suddenly white, was on her feet, but Jim moved faster. 'No, Steph, stay here,' he said, setting off across the grass. His longer legs covered the ground faster, but she was close behind him as he wrenched open the garden door into Edward's office.

After a single glance he turned, blocking her view with his body, but not before she had seen the jade-green mohair jacket and the blonde hair, disordered above the smothering tapestry cushion, and the lifeless arm flung out as if in some brief struggle.

145

It was her screams that alerted the rest to tragedy. Those in the garden clustered round first, as the girl, gasping hysterically, and supported by Jim, grim-faced, came staggering round the corner, but then they were hurrying from the house, too; Edward, Charles, Chris.

Tamara had been standing aloof, with her usual watchful detachment, but it was a shrill shriek from her that made the distraught Stephanie look round.

'It's – it's her!' Tamara was pointing. 'But she's dead, she's dead!'

Coming from the house, Helena, her heart pounding, came running towards her daughter, to see her take one incredulous look and crumple, in a dead faint.

At last the lorry-crane had come, and the wreckage was being towed to the side of the road.

Knowing the difficulties under which her colleagues laboured did not lessen Frances's exasperation. She had told Helena she would be there promptly, and, until she came across this accident, had been making good time. Now she would be lucky if she got there before they had all finished their lunch and gone home.

But there was still a fair number of cars standing in the square when she reached her destination. She parked hurriedly and jumped out.

The Red House was looking pretty today in the unseasonal sunshine, pretty and peaceful. Strangely so, she thought, puzzled, glancing through the sitting-room window at the empty room. She rang the bell.

The door was flung open, and Dyer stood there, the hall telephone in his hand.

'Oh well, well, well,' he said, putting it down, 'and to think that they say you can never find one when you want one. You're the lady detective, aren't you? Radley said you were expected. All right then – this will give you something to detect.'

She had dismissed as irrational the uneasiness she had felt. Wordlessly, she followed him through the hall and along the back corridor to where Radley, looking shaken, stood as if on guard outside a closed door.

'In here,' Dyer said brusquely, and Radley stood mutely aside.

It was dark inside the little stuffy office, and it was a moment before Frances's eyes adjusted to the light. Then she saw the figure on the couch, and caught her breath.

'Helena?' Her lips were almost too rigid to form the word.

'That's what they thought at first. But it's Lilian.'

'Lilian?' Her astonishment was patent, and to Radley at least, offensive.

'Were you expecting someone to kill my wife, Sergeant Howarth?' he asked stiffly.

'Not expecting, no.' She left the subject there. 'Has anything been touched?'

'I lifted the cushion,' Dyer said. 'The vicar's brat found her, and in her usual spirit of helpfulness went and told Stephanie her mother was dead. Stephanie and young Wagstaff came in and saw the body. Then Helena appeared, and Stephie fainted, and a few people screamed, then Helena got hysterical ... Well, you get the picture. I came in and there was poor bloody Lilian. She'd borrowed Helena's jacket, apparently, and with the blonde hair ...'

He paused for a moment. For all his air of sang-froid, Frances noticed that he had positioned himself where he could not see the body; now he glanced quickly at it, then looked away. 'Well, like I said, I lifted the cushion, thought maybe we could still do something. But it's – well, you could say it was unmistakable.'

She was, indeed, in her limpness, unmistakably dead. The tumbled hair was across the face, and the head was still turned to one side, the body twisted; she had fought hard against her unseen assailant, and the travelling rug was wound about her legs as if she had lashed out, in vain. It had not been a peaceful death, and the face, mercifully obscured for the moment, would tell its own tale of agony and terror.

Radley had not come right into the room; he stood, hesitating, in the doorway.

Frances turned from her scrutiny. 'Mr Radley, would you please go and tell your guests that no one may leave, and keep them away from this part of the house and garden. Mr Dyer, perhaps you would now make that phone call? Ask them to get in touch with Inspector Coppins, and tell them I shall need a Criminal Investigation Unit and a police surgeon.'

The matter-of-fact authority in her tone sent them on their way without discussion, leaving Frances alone with all that remained of Lilian Sheldon Fielding.

She had never found herself in this position before. Usually, she came upon the results of violent crime as one of a team; this strange tryst was a much more intimate relationship.

What did she know about Lilian? She was, by reputation, selfish and greatly disliked. Frances herself had observed no signs of real grief over her husband's murder, though much paraded emotion, and there appeared to be no close friends or family. There had been no hint of an interest or objective beyond the enjoyment of the lotos-fruits of media success; Lilian, as far as she could tell, had led a purposeless existence which amounted to little more than the exploitation of a slim, sensuous body and an ephemeral commercial prettiness.

She sighed. What would remain? Only 'a rag, a bone, and a hank of hair', a fast-fading memory, and not one person who would sincerely mourn her.

It seemed a squandered life, and in some ways, this death was the more pitiable for that very reason. She had left so little behind, it was as if her killer had condemned her to extinction, like stamping on a butterfly. Poor pretty, shallow Lilian.

Pity was all very well. But it was by the exercise of her professional skills that she could best discharge this oddly personal sense of responsibility.

While her eyes automatically carried out the procedure that had been dinned into her – look, look, and then look some more – her mind began to race.

Could this disaster, too, be laid at her door, or was she exaggerating the importance of the part she had played? Mentally, she fingered the notion of guilt, like some brilliantly-coloured toadstool, attractive and poisonous. Joe Coppins had accused her of arrogance in her assumptions about this case, and he was frequently right.

More practically, then, could she, somehow, have stopped this, if the accident had not delayed her? Probably not; her attention would have been misdirected, guarding Helena rather than Lilian, who had, after the morning's deliberations, been high on the list of suspects for Fielding's murder. Well, this had certainly cleared her. The drastic method of eliminating suspects.

148

She bent over the chesterfield, frowning in concentration, the body before her a problem now rather than a human tragedy. She dared not touch it until Forensic arrived, but studied its tortured position, knelt down to check the fingernails. Lilian could have raked her assailant with those long, manicured talons, and scratches on hands or face would be hard to disguise. But there was no sign of blood or tissue under the nails, as far as she could see, only a thread which looked as if it might have come from one of the cushions. There was another cushion on the floor; might her killer have used it to shield his hands from her desperate clawing?

She got up and crossed to the garden door. Not much hope of fingerprints there, or from the door to the hall. Too many people would have grabbed the handles, without a thought for the sanctity of evidence, though the experts would try. You never knew when a print in context might be useful. The cushion – she glanced at it, where Dyer had thrown it down – was rough tapestry, and would do them no good.

She dropped to her knees again, feeling across the carpet on the direct route between door and couch, looking for any unusual indication, but there was only the slightly sticky dampness of earth from the feet of those who had come in, the faint smell of garden loam. They would check thoroughly when the Unit arrived.

Time was passing. She was still seeing the room as the killer had left it; what could it tell her?

He had taken quite a risk, coming in here, whether by house or garden door, and then committing a murder in full view of anyone who happened to be passing. Most people, of course, were on the lawn at the back, and by standing to one side of the chesterfield – she took up the position experimentally – you could be in shadow, with only the cushion in full view, and even then, considering the darkness of the room, only if someone stood close to the window and peered in, as Tamara Farrell must have done.

A gambler, then; he would have had to take his risks coming in and going out as well. And people took risks because the stakes were high.

But she did not, as yet, know what had been at stake. She needed to talk to people, get out and ask the questions they had failed to ask before. She sighed again.

Without equipment, there was nothing further she could do here. Shortly, the team would arrive, and the last trace of atmosphere would vanish in a chaos of arc lights and plastic sheeting. She had only a few more minutes alone with the dead woman who knew no more than she did who her murderer had been.

Someone had found a sleeping woman, and held that cushion ruthlessly over her face until her breathing stopped. The woman had displayed blonde hair, like Helena's, and Helena's distinctive green jacket. Had her killer actually murdered the shadow or the substance?

But when Joe Coppins arrived, shouldering his way through the door, she knew he was in no mood to indulge her with the discussion of such theories. He had been dragged away from some domestic Saturday-fest, and finding his sergeant at the scene of the crime in a social capacity was another grievance. And he was not a stupid man; she read in the gathering blackness of his brow his immediate understanding of the reason for her presence, as she tried to explain what she believed to have happened before he erupted.

It was his worst sort of rage. It was ostensibly over her disobedience, arrogance and criminal stupidity, but she knew him well enough to appreciate that what gave it force was the need to banish a darkling suspicion that the horrifying mistake might turn out, after all, to have been his. She hung her head and waited silently until the attack became less violent and more specific.

'That's women for you,' he said with rancour, at last. 'Don't like anything to be straightforward – everything's got to be complicated, hasn't it? Seems to me as plain as the nose on your face – woman's a convicted murderer; only just out of prison, and she's turned into a homicidal maniac. I suppose you've got her under close guard, before she decides to run amok with a carving knife?'

'Well, sir, she's heavily sedated.' Frances was ready to defend her, but for once it transpired that fortune favoured Helena. From the time she had left Lilian (alive, as the waitress who had taken in the aspirin could testify) to the moment, half-an-hour later, when Stephanie's screams summoned her from the house, she had been in the presence of one or more of the catering team, and guests as well.

Marshalling the evidence, Frances tried not to sound triumphant. 'It does tend to suggest she might be in the clear for her husband's murder too – unless you think there are two homicidal maniacs at large?'

'Say "sir" when you're being insubordinate.' Deflated, Coppins groaned. 'It's not evidence, but you could be right, I'll give you that, and if you are it'll be an expensive business for Her Majesty's Government. And we won't come up smelling of roses, whatever we do.'

By Sunday morning an incident room had been set up in a porta-kabin in the forecourt of the Four Feathers, and representatives from most of the larger newspapers were encamped around the square. Coppins, a veteran of Press skirmishes, had opened the campaign with a warning that he was prepared to act on any complaint about harassment or trespass, and they were, for the moment at least, being fairly circumspect.

At the church, there was once more an unnaturally swollen con-gregation. Leaving after the service, the groups of worshippers, mainly women, found cause to cross the street and hold murmured discussions near the cabin, where they could watch the Press and the police who came and went, and ensure that their fellow-villagers could not so far forget themselves as to gossip to foreigners.

From inside, the low buzz of conversation had the threatening note of wasps disturbed in their nest, and a WPC looked up unhap-pily from her keyboard.

'There's a nasty atmosphere here, have you noticed? And we've been here all morning without a soul coming in. It's not natural, that. Usually you have to beat them off with a stick.'

'Got the Thought Police out, haven't they?' One of the uniformed sergeants jerked his head significantly towards the women. 'We're all going to have to get out there and knock on doors. Cosy up to them, a bit.'

The woman shuddered. 'Well, all I can say is, I want someone with me when I do.'

'Ready when you are, darling!' The youngest PC was grinning cheekily, but she did not smile back, and he wandered across to the window. 'That's Fancy Fanny now,' he said, and returned hastily to writing up his notes.

Frances parked her car, grabbed shoulder-bag and notebook and climbed out, directing a death-stare at a nearby journalist, who suddenly changed his mind about trying to chat her up.

Her eyes were gritty after only four hours' sleep, and she was bad-tempered after an early-morning exchange with Poppy, who could not decide whether outraged respectability or morbid fascination were her uppermost emotion. It was going to be a hard day.

The church doors, Frances noticed, still stood open. The vicar was probably in the vestry, disrobing. This might be a good moment to speak to him; in her experience, the vicar was often the person most sensitive to the emotional temperature in a small community.

She pushed open the inside door and went in, pausing for a moment to allow her eyes to adjust to the darkness inside.

The interior was small, very old and very plain, with Norman arches and panes of clear glass. The flagstones were worn in a pathway from the door down the central aisle; small, overhead radiators still bravely burning did little to dispel the airless chill.

It should have been peaceful, but Frances sensed disharmony, even before she identified the sound – a whispered, sobbing gabbling which came from the figure in a white robe kneeling at the altar rail, clutching at it and swaying, the head flung back as if the eyes were raised in frantic supplication to the ornate silver cross on the altar.

She checked, unwilling to intrude. She had no business here, where a man in agony reached out so desperately to his God. He seemed oblivious, but she retreated as silently as she could. She had almost reached the door when the thready, half-heard words began to take a remembered pattern.

'Lord . . . thy people . . . most precious blood . . . be not angry with us for ever.'

Her own lips soundlessly shaped the response, 'Spare us, good Lord.' She had heard the words a hundred times, in the years before the ancient litany with its uncomfortable spiritual power had fallen to modern embarrassment. As the frenzied muttering continued, she found herself supplying those words she could not hear.

'From all evil and mischief; from sin, from the crafts and assaults of the devil; from Thy wrath and from everlasting damnation – Good Lord, deliver us!'

A fit of shivering took her, and forgetting caution, she plunged out. It was familiar, yes, but never before had she heard it spoken by a man who sounded in mortal fear that the devil he named stood at his very shoulder.

Reaching daylight and fresh air, she gasped, bracing herself and clenching her chattering teeth.

The journalist, still lingering like a jackal circling the lion's kill, noticed her rub her hands together.

'Cold in there, is it?' he called cheerfully.

'Cold,' Frances agreed, tersely, as she side-stepped his approach, but she was talking about a chill more ancient than that of old grey stones.

Ten minutes later, juggling a file of statements, Frances let herself into Radley's office at the Red House where Joe Coppins had established himself, as was his custom, at the scene of the crime. It was a habit which Frances found invariably embarrassing and frequently macabre. She had to force herself not to show her distaste as she entered.

The corpse, of course, had gone, but the dent in the cushion into which the head had been forced, was still there, along with a few blonde hairs. The travelling rug lay in a tangle, half-on, half-off the chesterfield, and the windows, the door-handles and the table beside the sofa displayed the greasy traces of aluminium powder.

For a second, he was unaware of her presence, and she thought he looked discouraged and depressed, seated slumped in Radley's old wooden revolving chair. He was always hard on his own mistakes, and this one was serious.

But noticing her, he sat up at once, shooting her a shrewd look from under furrowed brows.

'Shrinking violet today, are we, sergeant? Wishing it was time to take the Lower Third for music instead?'

She had told him, in an unguarded moment, of her mother's determined fantasy, and had since regretted the confidence. He used it like a blunt instrument whenever he felt her reaction was feminine, or middle-class, or over-educated, or in any other sense undesirable.

She said coolly, 'No, sir,' and went to sit on a library stool.

'Right,' he said crisply, 'let's face it and get it over with. We made a total balls-up. Somebody died because we didn't get it right. You figured out we were wrong before I did, but it's still something we're both going to have to live with. Then there's wrongful arrest, the lot. God knows what they'll have in store for us. But that's for later.

'This is now. New day, new problem, and the best we can hope for is to get this wrapped up as quickly as the last one. Only this time – just for variety – we end up with the right person behind bars. OK? So – tell me a story, Frances.'

This was how she earned her keep: the neat, rapid pulling together of strands. Once or twice she had been able to pluck them out of the air, like floating spider threads, and had woven them into a noose strong enough to snare a villain. But she was too close to this one. She needed an objective overview, but here she was down groping in the mud.

His flair, however, was for taking out of her synopsis more than she knew she had put in, so she began, hesitantly.

'The first problem, as I see it, is the confusion of identity. Helena's jacket, same haircut, face buried in the pillow. So did he think he was killing Helena, or Lilian? Lilian had just upset a large number of people, but then, I was worried about Helena because she knew she wasn't guilty.

'In practical terms, given the darkness inside and the element of risk in every second it took – it could easily be mistaken identity. On the other hand, wouldn't you check, before you actually killed someone?'

He pounced. 'An opportunist, you think? No plan of any kind?'

'Could be. Or else, someone knew Lilian was going to lie down – overheard Helena and Lilian talking in the hall –'

'Proof?'

She riffled through her files to Helena's statement, pulled a face.

'Possible, even probable, but hopeless to substantiate. People were going to and fro in the hall all the time. We can question them specifically on that point, but even if they all remembered who was behind them, they won't know for sure what they heard, or if they noticed Helena taking Lilian through.'

'So – it's Lilian he wants to kill. Who is he? Quick, off the top of your head, Frances.'

'Jack Daley.'

She surprised a laugh out of him with the promptness of her reply. 'Got the handcuffs ready, have you? Are you going to pamper me with some proof, or is this just more woman's intuition?'

She bristled. 'If I were a man, you'd call it subconscious logic. He's the obvious candidate – impulsive nature, blistering row with her beforehand. And just for the sake of argument, if he did kill Fielding, he's got the same motive this time round. Public humiliation is nasty enough, but when it's sexual as well . . . He was implicated in that weird business the night before Fielding's death, wasn't he?'

'The burning in effigy? Barely credible, that, in the twentieth century. I seem to remember they questioned him, but I'm not sure they got a lot of joy. We let it go at the time, but maybe we shouldn't have. Though I daresay we have to keep in mind the wide range of Fielding's unpopular activities.'

'In any case, I would suggest that Daley has a high profile on all counts.'

'OK, OK, we'll put your inspiration down as a triumph of subliminal analysis – isn't that what they like to call it these days? Right. Now it's Helena – do it again.'

'That's much harder. Since Lilian was my hot tip as murderer until yesterday, nothing comes to mind. It could be someone like Dyer – clever enough to calculate that the best time to dispose of Helena would be when all the other suspects were around.'

'But of course, you're looking for the same person in either case.'

'Sorry?' She was puzzled; there were, in her mind, two conflicting perceptions of what had taken place, with separate solutions, depending on whether the murder had been done to preserve the status quo, or change it.

'Doesn't actually matter, does it? Come on, Frances! Unless you're suggesting a second "homicidal maniac" – and you were a bit sharp about that yesterday – Neville Fielding's killer has killed again, and who he thought the lady was is one of your fancy academic points.'

He was looking smug. She recognized the force of his argument, only adding carpingly, 'Or she. Sir.'

'Fine, we can be feminist about this. Or she. Only snag about this brilliant piece of deduction is, we've already investigated Fielding's murder and come up with the wrong answer.'

Frances muttered something about processes of elimination, but lapsed into silence at a glare from her chief.

'This one's fresher, at least. So let's go through the practicalities. Alibis?'

155

Frances laughed shortly. 'That's a joke, at a drinks party – groups forming and breaking up all the time, nobody in one place for more than ten minutes.'

'And no forensic wizardry to get us off the hook. Fingerprints a mass of smudges, and we know the rest of what they can tell us already. Time of death: only half an hour between the waitress leaving her asleep and the kid finding her dead. Now you see her, now you don't. Means of death: a cushion left helpfully in place in case we weren't bright enough to figure it out.'

'Every contact leaves a trace. That's what they always said at forensic lectures.'

'I could generalize too, if someone paid me a fat bloody salary to sit in a lab all day. I'll show you how many traces you need to leave. On to the sofa, Frances.'

'Oh, you're not really going to do this, sir –' He had gone to a talk on empathy, once, which in her opinion had done considerably more harm than good, putting into his head the idea that if he played murderer and she victim he could get inside the villain's head. She hadn't liked it before, and she wasn't going to like it now.

'Read my lips, sergeant. On the sofa. I'm going to take it as if I came in from the garden. And time me from when I open the door.'

She had no alternative. With a shudder of distaste, she laid herself gingerly on her side on the chesterfield, her head in the depression where Lilian's head had lain, her hair falling forward to half-cover her face. She pulled the rug up to her shoulders, and out of the corner of her eye she could see the cushion, coarse and dusty-looking. She cringed at the thought of its coming down on her face. Coppins would not shrink from realism.

She could hear him outside the garden door. 'I'm passing, and I look in the window. See Lilian, and quick as lightning, make my plan.

'Start timing. I take out my pocket-handkerchief to turn the handle. Now I step inside, shut it quickly. I hurry over to grab a cushion. Damn!'

She heard the thud as he blundered into a chair. 'I can't see a blind bloody thing. You could be anyone, I'll tell you that.'

For a big man, he was light on his feet. She sensed him moving round the back of the chesterfield, and through the strands of her hair glimpsed the cushion coming down.

Behind him, the door swung open, and after a timid knock the figure of a uniformed constable appeared in the doorway, to gape in horror at the spectacle of a senior officer engaged, apparently, in a copycat killing.

'S – sir!' he stammered.

Coppins swung round, and Frances, glad of the reprieve, sat up, finding it hard not to laugh at the expression on the young man's face.

'Twenty-five seconds, sir,' she said, with offensive efficiency. 'Plus time for any struggle, and getting back out again.'

Ignoring her, Coppins snapped, 'Better shut your mouth, constable, or you'll catch flies. Got some objection to the theory of reconstructing the crime, have you?'

'Yes sir, I mean, no sir.' His accent was broad; he was a bulky, fresh-faced youth, pink to the ears at the moment, whose stability of temperament and sturdiness of physique were more obvious assets than his mental agility.

'Well, get on with it, man. What do you want?'

'They sent me to report to you, sir. Put me on to local interviews, thinking I might get more out of people, seeing as I come from Swaylings. Well, I told them – they wouldn't count me as local, stands to reason.'

'But that's – what? Three miles away?'

'All of that, sir. So you can see why not.'

Coppins and Frances exchanged glances, and Frances cleared her throat.

'Er – even so, constable, you found out something useful, despite the difficulties? I presume they had some reason for sending you up.'

'Didn't tell me a thing, did they? That's what they sent me up here to tell you.'

Coppins's colour was starting to look unhealthy. Frances intervened hastily. 'And what did you make of that?'

He beamed, relieved to find at last some sign of intelligence in his betters. 'Well, it's funny, isn't it? Something like a murder, they'd be full of it, you'd expect. They'd come out with all sorts, what the victim said to them last week, who'd had a barney recently, all that stuff. But they all closed up, close as oysters, didn't they? Didn't know nothing, weren't saying nothing. So there you are.'

157

'Where, exactly, am I?' Coppins's bellow was only just muted, but the constable stood his ground.

'Think it's one of their own, don't they. Shielding someone,' he pointed out, with some pride in his own sagacity.

When he had gone, they looked at each other. 'He's got a point,' Coppins said heavily. 'Scrub Jack Daley.'

' "The dog that didn't bark." I'd better go and talk to Tilson again. He's my best hope of an inside track.'

'Mmmmm.' Coppins was frowning, and she looked at him enquiringly.

'Had a thought, before young Sherlock blundered in. I was the killer; I looked through the window; I saw Lilian. But I was behaving oddly. At a party in someone's house, you don't go shading your eyes and peering into the windows of the other rooms. It's rude.'

'Tamara Farrell did.'

'So maybe she's our killer.'

'I could think of things that would surprise me more. But otherwise –'

'Otherwise, if he came in, he must have known already that Lilian was in here. And that it wasn't Helena. So he – or she, since you insist – could have come in from either the garden or the hall. And if he came from the hall, he had the advantage that he wouldn't bark his shins on the bloody furniture.'

So, at least in theory, they had the answer to the question that she had defined as central, but they were no further forward. She wondered if Coppins felt as helpless as she did, and had her answer when he burst out, 'Give me a nice messy knifing in a disco, every time. Can't stand this fairying about with methods and motives.' He glanced up at the old wall clock, now showing almost twelve o'clock. 'For god's sake, Frances, let's go and see if that miserable bloody pub serves anything resembling a decent pint.'

Tilson was at his desk this time, frowning over balance sheets, when she was ushered in by Mrs Thomas in her Sunday purple-flowered crimplene with an apron on top. He pushed the papers aside with alacrity, coming to greet her with hands outstretched.

158

'My dear Frances! You have no idea how much I have been hoping that you would pop in to see me again. After yesterday's tragic events –'

'I'm here officially, Mr Tilson,' she warned, sitting down on the hard chair opposite his desk and forming with her notebook and pen a barricade against informality.

He sighed theatrically. 'Oh dear, that presumably means that I have to talk while you listen, whereas for me it would be so much more interesting the other way round. I find, the older I get, the less that anything I say myself possesses the charm of novelty.'

She smiled at that, but was not to be diverted. 'The party yesterday – I have your statement of course, but –'

He made a deprecating gesture. 'I know. Dispiriting, isn't it? But even excellent Homer nods. Lilian, in the sitting-room, announces to a stunned audience that she is selling Radnesfield House; I am in the hall discussing house prices with an estate agent – it is, don't you find, always a mistake to talk to an estate agent? It only encourages them. However, there it was. Lilian has a violent altercation with Jack in the garden; I am in the sitting-room. When the deed itself takes place, I am eating a blameless salad in the garden. I couldn't have avoided the action more comprehensively if I tried, and with your knowledge of my temperament you will recognize that avoiding the action would be sadly out of character.'

'What about the reaction to her announcement?'

'Oh, waves of shock and lowered voices and tittle-tattle. George Wagstaff beside himself. Edward grim, Dyer amused. Helena – weighed down by the cares of a hostess when I saw her; Sandra Daley disintegrating visibly; the vicar's wife exuding poison like a tree-frog; Mrs Bateman slicing tomatoes as if she were operating a guillotine . . .'

She jotted down his observations with amused appreciation, but said only, 'You told me, the other day, that you sensed an atmosphere in Radnesfield. In the light of events, is there anything you can add to that?'

'Merely intensification of the impression. Today, for instance – well, you've probably noticed yourself.'

Thinking of the vicar, she nodded, managing to suppress a shudder, and he went on, 'And my dear Jane Thomas for example – well, I would do nothing so crude as to pry, but I know her well enough to see that she is deeply troubled.'

'You can't be more specific? We have a report from a constable who knows this area, saying he thinks they're shielding someone.'

'Actually shielding someone?' Tilson was startled. 'Then that would definitely have to be one of their own. They might choose not to become involved, but they wouldn't protect a stranger.

'Perhaps – perhaps it might be useful to talk to Jane. She pops in on Sunday, you know, just to see that I have a proper lunch, but I suppose you could catch her before she went home.'

He made the suggestion in the tones of one forced, by the laws of hospitality, to offer a gift, while hoping still that it may be refused.

'Thank you, that would be most helpful.'

When Jane Thomas appeared, she looked, indeed, ill at ease. She was a big, sturdy woman with a milkmaid's complexion and an honest blue gaze. But after one startled glance at Frances, she would not meet her eyes, fidgeting with her apron with large, work-roughened hands. She took the chair brought forward by her employer, but sat on its edge, the picture of discomfort.

'Jane, my dear, the sergeant has some questions she would like to ask you, and I think, I really do think, that you should be as helpful to her as possible.'

Still she did not look up, her head bent over the twisted corner of her apron.

'I will, of course, leave if you should wish me to.' Tilson made the honourable offer without real enthusiasm, and looked gratified by the frantic shaking of her head. He sat down, and a little silence fell.

With a sense of walking on eggshells, Frances began, her low voice warm and persuasive. 'Mrs Thomas, it's very hard for you, isn't it? Strangers moved into your village, and there has been violence and ugliness. No wonder you resent that, as well as the fact that I'm here asking you questions you probably don't want to answer.

'But the problem won't go away. Mrs Radley went to prison for something we now believe she didn't do; perhaps if people in the village had come forward to tell us what they knew, that wouldn't have happened.

'Oh, I know there was a lot of hostility to Neville and Lilian Fielding – and I can understand why – but someone has killed twice, and there's no reason why they should stop there. No one's safe – yourself, your family – Mr Tilson –'

She paused, hopefully, but only the twisting went on, more savagely.

She changed the line of questioning as smoothly as she would have modulated into a different key, shading her intonation to make her voice lower, more intimate. 'It may be there is someone who needs help. Perhaps it's not doing them a favour, keeping quiet – perhaps?'

Mrs Thomas's shoulders jerked convulsively and Frances broke off, instantly.

The woman looked up at last, made to speak, then faltered. Neither Frances nor Tilson spoke, and flustered by the lengthening pause, she burst at last into speech.

"Tisn't right, it isn't, and so I've said. But it's not up to me to mess after it, that's the truth, and there's them as should have spoken up long ago. Things have changed, I said to them, it's not the same as when Council used to decide right and wrong – and that was before all we was born, mostly. The dead past's gone, and plenty of it not so good, neither. Maybe we should have them new houses, at that. I never thought to say it, but things has gone wrong about here, things that should have been told have been hid.'

She was wringing the whole apron in her hands now, and close to tears. Tilson was shifting uneasily in his chair, but Frances hardly noticed him. 'Mrs Thomas, you can tell me, can't you?' She was cajoling, coaxing now. 'There's been too much darkness and deceit. Good, honest, plain words – tell me what you know.'

'Know?' she raised her head, and her expression was fierce. 'I don't know nothing. But there's them as do, and it's up to them to tell you.'

'Them?' The detective's voice was as caressing as a mother soothing her child. 'You can tell me who you mean, can't you?'

For just a second it seemed that the siren voice might seduce her; she looked at Frances almost with longing, but then the tears came.

'You're asking me to name names, you are. And I can't do that – not to *you*.'

She jumped to her feet and fled from the room, and Frances made no effort to stop her.

'Not to me, because I'm a foreigner.' Her voice was harsh and ragged with impatience. 'Old loyalties, of course – and who can blame her? But what do I have to do to get through to these people?' She brought her linked fingers down hard on the desk in front of her in a painful expression of exasperation.

Tilson, his chin propped on his hands, was studying her narrowly. 'That was quite a performance,' he said at last. 'What they used to call glamourie, I fancy, and you could get yourself burned at the stake. Are you a musician?'

'Oh, that – yes.' She brushed the query aside, frowning.

Neither spoke for a moment. Then Tilson reached across the desk to pat her hand. 'Don't despair, my child. *Rebus in arduis*, remember.'

Frustration made her tart. 'Not my strongest point, classical quotations.'

' "When the going gets tough, stay cool." A free translation. And Jane won't leave it at that, you know. She's upset, and she'll put the pressure on somewhere else. I'll puzzle over what she said – something may come to me.'

Rising, Frances laughed shortly. 'I have every confidence that it will. I'm only relieved you're on the side of the angels. Probably.'

He pretended shock. 'Definitely, my dear, when they are such very attractive angels. I'll show you out.'

She had been professionally reticent; now, as she was leaving, her guard slipped.

'Well, I suppose this has shed a little light, even if the results are negative. There seemed to be a lot of pointers to Jack Daley, but if there's one thing sure, it's that Radnesfield won't exert itself for a Brummie garage owner who only came here a couple of years ago.'

She was on her way out of the door when she realized that Maxwell Tilson had stopped, and was looking at her strangely.

'Oh dear, dear,' he said gently. 'The police really do know astonishingly little, don't they? Why do you suppose he bought the garage in the first place? Jack Daley's mother was an Ede: he's related to fully half the village.'

12

The neat bungalow belonging to the Daleys looked, as Frances waited on the doorstep, subtly uncared-for. It had been well maintained and the paintwork was fresh, but the window-panes did not shine, and at the window by the front door the hem of a curtain was sagging.

Frances rang the bell, but the sound of the chimes died away without producing a response. Her hand was on the button to press again, when she heard an inside door open, and Daley's voice shout, 'Sandra! Where the hell are you? Can't you even answer the bloody door?'

There was another pause, then the door opened, grudgingly, and Sandra Daley's ravaged face appeared round it. 'Yes?'

Like Helena, Frances was shocked. Today there was not even a pretence at make-up, and her face was blotchy with recently-shed tears. She did not seem entirely sober, and though it was half-past one, Sunday lunch-time, no comfortable smell of cooking came from the kitchen.

'Mrs Daley, I wonder if I might speak to your husband? I'm Sergeant Howarth – you may remember – '

Sandra's jaw sagged, and her eyes, heavy under swollen lids, widened as she retreated a step into the hall.

'Oh my god, my god!' she said, almost in a whisper. 'It's come then, it's come – '

'May I come in?' The request was perfunctory, and Frances pushed the door wider and stepped inside. 'Mrs Daley, you're clearly distressed –'

Alerted by her voice, Daley himself appeared from a room where a television set was relaying the sounds of Sunday sport.

His reaction was swift, his glance at Frances nakedly hostile. Putting a hand on his wife's shoulder, he turned her roughly to face him, making no effort to hide his disgust.

'You're drunk again, Sandra. Do me a favour; make yourself a cup of coffee and sober up.'

He swung her in the direction of the kitchen; she took two un-steady paces, then turned. 'Jack, oh Jack . . .' Tears were pouring, unchecked, down her face.

'Just get hold of yourself, all right? Now, if you'd like to come this way . . .' As he addressed Frances, his tone was frigidly polite.

She hung back. 'I think I might have a word with Mrs Daley.'

'I should have thought it was pretty obvious that she's not in a fit condition to talk to anyone. OK?'

His voice had risen, and it seemed unwise to try to insist. 'Very well. But do you think your wife should be left alone? She seems very – disturbed.'

The kitchen door shut. He sighed heavily, and said, like one explaining to an idiot, 'She's on a drinking jag at the moment. She does that when she's upset, so, even though I'm not a detective, I can work out that something must have upset her. Could it possibly be Lilian getting murdered, do you reckon? For some reason, she seems to be just a little touchy about her friends being rubbed out.

'Still, you won't be keeping me long, will you? Just "one or two routine questions"?'

He was trying to sound cool, off-hand. Clinically, she observed the fine dew of sweat on his upper lip.

'Just one or two questions, as you say, sir.'

The lounge was dusty and untidy. She followed him in, taking her seat on the edge of a deep mock-leather settee. He snapped off the set and threw himself into the chair opposite, one leg over the arm in a pantomime of ease.

'I suppose you're going to tell me I had a quarrel with Lilian yesterday.' It was an aggressive opening; he waited for her response, but she said nothing, and he went on, 'Well, why not? She just throws this at me, OK? Thought we were mates, and she makes a decision like that without a word to me – well, stands to reason anyone would be hurt.'

'Hurt?'

'OK, well, angry, then. But you'd spend your life stepping over bodies if every time someone had a tiff with one of their friends they did them in.'

He showed no grief for the death of the woman whose lover he had been, not even the most formal expression of regret. Had she been no more than a means to some dark revenge, his affair with her only a punishment for his erring wife? Or had he killed Neville, to find that even murder was not enough to obliterate his shame?

'You described Lilian Fielding as a friend of your wife's. Were she and Mrs Daley close friends?'

'Yeah, well, women, you know – always a bit of rivalry –' He faltered under her steady regard, then scowled. 'Oh, don't tell me. The gossips have all crawled out from under the flat stones. OK, so Lilian and I had a bit of a thing going. But it was only a bit of fun – didn't mean anything – and Sandra and me, well, we've got a modern marriage. Got to be a bit broad-minded these days.'

'Mrs Daley doesn't give me the impression at the moment of being a happily broad-minded wife.'

There was no mistaking his unease. 'She's got a bit of a problem with the bottle, like I told you . . .'

'And of course, she was very close to Mr Fielding as well, wasn't she?'

His face flamed with temper. 'God, you make me sick, with your piddling little mealy-mouthed hints. Why can't you come right out and say she was one of his bits on the side? No doubt all the old cats have been happy enough to tell you that as well.'

'What can you tell me about the burning in effigy, the night before Neville Fielding's death?'

The change of tack threw him off balance, and he stammered, 'Wh – what do you mean? If anyone's said anything, said I did anything, they're a liar, that's all.'

Frances made a pretence of consulting the notebook at her side. 'You were seen in the village that night, weren't you?'

He stared at her for a moment, his face scarlet, then, with a short laugh, said, 'Oh well, if they're starting to name names, I can give you a list. Vic Ede, Dave Bateman, George Wagstaff – and plenty of others just along for the ride. But that was just a bit of fun, see if we could scare him, give him a little hint about how we felt about him.'

'And how was that? Violent?'

He shrugged, and fell silent. She had a useful admission there, something to work on later. She tried a new line.

'Your wife – she can't have been too pleased when Fielding married again after his divorce?'

She sensed his rigidity. 'Why should it bother her? Like I said, we're not old-fashioned in our ideas.'

'So she didn't mind too much?'

'No, not too much.'

'And you? Mr Daley, just how much did you really mind all this very *modern* behaviour on the part of your wife?'

The question had been intended as a knife thrust, slipping in under his guard. So why should his fingers, previously digging into the arm of his chair, now have unclenched?

'Well, I suppose you could say it was a bit of a dent to the image – the old lady fancying another guy.' His grin was almost jaunty; she had missed something there. But relief made him incautious, and he added, 'Oh, I might have a bit of a blow-up with him, shout a bit, maybe, but I'll be honest with you – we didn't have such a good marriage it was worth killing for.'

165

That confession held a depressing ring of truth, but she pounced on the indiscretion.

'A blow-up with Neville Fielding? When, exactly, was this?'

She had the satisfaction of seeing uneasiness return. He was licking his lips nervously when they heard the crash and the cry.

He was on his feet at the same instant as she. 'Sandra!' he yelled, wrenching open the door and crossing the narrow hall in three strides. He threw open the door to the kitchen.

Behind him, Frances could hear a hideous, bubbling, gasping groan; over his shoulder, saw the figure that was blotting out the light.

Sandra Daley, a fine rope about her neck and her head lolling horribly sideways, was hanging from the old-fashioned pulley from which, incongruously, some airing clothes still hung. The kitchen stool kicked over on the floor told its own story.

But the pulley had never been intended to take such sudden weight. It had dipped to that side, so that instead of dangling, her toes touched the brightly-patterned vinyl of the kitchen floor, and scrabbled for a firm foothold in an instinctive fight for the life she had tried to squander.

Daley grabbed his wife in his arms, lifting her to take the tension off the rope. Frances, looking swiftly about, saw a block of knives on the kitchen surface and seizing the most dangerous-looking, slashed through the strands of what appeared to be a length of clothes-line.

It was only seconds before they had her flat on the floor, her bruised throat labouring to snatch the precious air back into her lungs. Her face was bluish-purple, and she was semi-conscious, though breathing of her own accord.

Frances knelt down beside her, removing the rope and loosening the collar of her blouse, checking her mouth to make sure the air passage was clear. 'Doctor,' she snapped, and Daley disappeared.

With returning consciousness, Sandra's head began to move restlessly; her eyes flickered open, focused on the other woman's face briefly, then closed again.

But she was coming round. Frances spoke reassuringly. 'Everything's all right, Mrs Daley. You're quite safe.'

Tears began to seep from under the closed eyelids. 'Useless,' she muttered. 'Useless.'

Frances had to bend close to hear. 'Useless?' she said softly, slipping a thin foam cushion from a nearby chair under her head. 'Why useless?'

'Useless, he said – right, wasn't he?' The voice was thready, the words incoherent and punctuated by long, painful breaths. 'Couldn't even – kill myself. Got that wrong, too.' Her eyes opened again, and her hand groped at Frances, who took it in a firm clasp. 'Please – take me – take me instead. Worthless, not like him. Started it all.' She coughed, painfully.

Medically, perhaps, she should be stopped, but Frances was not a doctor. 'Take your time,' she said, patting her hand.

'Flattered, you see, him being a big star. All my fault. All my fault.' She was crying again, drearily and hopelessly. 'Not Jack, you can't blame Jack, you can't! Any man would – all my fault! And now – turned him into a monster.'

The harsh, raw whisper changed to aching sobs, and Frances said slowly, 'You mean, your husband –'

A sound made her turn her head. Jack Daley had come back and was standing behind her, his face a mask of pity and horror.

'Sandra, you silly cow, you don't think I killed them, do you?'

He pushed Frances out of the way, kneeling down by his wife and taking her hand. She gazed up at him, her face still tortured.

'No good, Jack. Saw you – going up the hill –'

He was taken aback. 'Oh god, you saw me, did you? And you never said. Maybe we should talk to each other occasionally. Well, listen to me now, and let's get this straight, OK?

'Sure, I went up the hill. I got there just after the daughter left – saw her crossing to Wagstaff's farm. I'd had it up to here with big-shot Fielding. Our marriage was falling apart because of him, and somehow it was worse when there were all those others too. We'd given him a nasty turn the night before, but I still wanted to look the bastard straight in the face and spit in it. I did, too; he couldn't stop me, and I told him the only reason I didn't hit him was because I didn't want to dirty my hands. He was scared, right enough, but he was certainly alive when I left.'

He took a deep breath. 'But then, you see, when they arrested Helena, I didn't reckon she'd done it either. I thought it would have taken a woman with a lot more nerve –'

Her eyes widened, and she tried to lift her head; the movement gave her acute pain, and he gently restrained her.

'You thought it was me – oh Jack Daley, you stupid sod,' she croaked, and then there was a strange, rasping sound that was Sandra Daley trying to laugh.

Frances met the doctor at the front door. 'She's perfectly all right,' she assured him, 'but it's pure luck she didn't manage to kill herself.'

'I've got an ambulance coming anyway. We can refer her for psychiatric treatment.'

'That may be a wise precaution, but I suspect you'll find it's unnecessary.'

In the kitchen, Sandra was sitting up, propped against her husband's shoulder with her hand clasped firmly in his. They were both looking sheepish, and Frances told them crisply that she would send someone tomorrow to take their statements, then left them with the doctor.

Perhaps being a detective did destroy your sensibilities. She felt no warm rosy glow at the happy ending, no satisfaction at having played the part of a rather macabre cupid.

Detective-Sergeant Howarth, love-knots untied a speciality. She groaned as she went towards her car, planning a speedy getaway before the arrival of the ambulance drew the vultures of the Press.

She had just got in when she noticed a girl coming down the road towards her, glancing curiously at the two cars outside the bungalow, and then, as she noticed Frances, hesitating.

She had come along from the farm, and Frances was vaguely aware that she had seen her before. She was in no mood for idle chit-chat, but in this place you couldn't afford to ignore someone who looked as if she might be prepared to communicate. Even 'Good afternoon' would be hard evidence in comparison to what they'd extracted so far. She rolled down her window as the girl approached.

'Er – excuse me! You're the detective, aren't you? I'm Sally Wagstaff – from the farm, you know. Look – could I possibly talk to you about something?'

'What beautiful words!' Frances smiled at her. 'Why don't you hop in, and we'll find somewhere quiet.'

Sally was the archetypal farmer's daughter, favouring her father in looks. However, along the side of the Wagstaff jaw, Frances's quick eye noticed a faint tell-tale shading of bruise. Perhaps George Wagstaff bit as well as barking, after all.

Finding a lay-by, Frances drew in and turned to her passenger.

'Now, how can I help you?'

'It's – it's a bit difficult. I don't really know where to begin . . .'

She was very young. 'Is it about this?' Frances said gently, pointing to her cheek.

Sally jumped, guiltily. 'Oh damn! Is it as obvious as that? I thought I'd managed to cover it up.'

'But who did it? You needn't be afraid to tell me, you know. We can see he doesn't do it again.'

At that, Sally grinned. It was clear that the assault itself was not what was worrying her.

'Oh, he won't do it again, I promise you that. I may look bad, but you should see what I did to the other fellow.'

Looking at her powerful shoulders, Frances could believe it. 'You're clearly well able to look after yourself,' she said, amused. 'Are you going to tell me who it was, or do I just look for the guy with two broken arms?'

Sally giggled. 'A black eye and a cut on his nose, actually.' Then she sobered. 'But look – if I tell you who it was, do you promise not to tell my dad? If he found out, he'd kill him!'

The cliché had slipped out, and she gasped. 'Oh – I didn't mean it like that, you know. Dad may bluster, but he really wouldn't hurt a fly.'

Frances nodded. 'Go on. They certainly won't find out from me.'

'Well – it was Len Whitton. Do you know him?'

Frances shook her head. 'I've heard his name mentioned once or twice.'

'He's bad news, actually. I knew that, really, and Mum and Dad told me off because I went out with him once or twice. He'd made the odd pass at me before, but it's my car and usually I just laugh and drive off when I've had enough. But this time, he got really serious about it, you know, and wouldn't stop. So then I shoved him off, and he really lost his temper, and hit me across the face. Well, no one ever did that to me before in the whole of my life, and I just saw red and slugged him one, and then his nose was bleeding, so I said sorry and gave him my hanky to mop up.'

'How very charitable of you. Didn't you push him out of the car, and leave him?'

'Well, it would have been quite a walk back. But this is the bit I wanted to tell you about. There's something about the village – something just – not quite right, I've never known what it is . . .'

Frances, who had been listening with some enjoyment to this artless recital, suddenly sat up. 'Go on.'

'Mum and Dad have never liked us to have much to do with the village families. And it's funny, because they're not snobs, not really. And when I was driving him back, Len Whitton said this really strange thing.

'He was furious, sitting there sort of hissing, and then he said, "You should be proud of that mark, you should. That's a badge, that is, and plenty girls in the village wear it and don't complain. Shows what we come from, doesn't it?" ' Her voice had taken on the flat village drawl, and it was clear the words had made a deep impression.

'What did you say then?'

'I told him I didn't know what he was talking about, and he sneered at me. Said, if you really want to know, that I wasn't worth his effing time, along with one or two other choice phrases that I won't repeat. Then he didn't say another word till he got out. He's been avoiding me ever since, and I don't suppose I'll ever speak to him again. But with all that's been going on, it kept coming back to me, and when I saw you . . .' She trailed into silence.

'Well, I'm glad I was here. Thank you, Sally – you're the first person who's actually volunteered something that may give us an inside line.'

'Do you know what he meant?'

'No, I'm afraid I don't, not yet. But I have a feeling that it's a piece of the jigsaw that may fit with some other odd-shaped pieces once I get a chance to think about it. Now, where can I drop you off?'

It was no good. Frances was deathly tired, but she had lain awake for an hour. It was only a job, she told herself, as she thumped her pillows again. If you took it personally every time you couldn't solve a crime, they'd have to retire you on compassionate grounds.

She wasn't even in charge; it was Coppins's case. But she had stuck her neck out, and if Coppins was left to take the blame, it would only make it worse.

She had not felt so vulnerable for a very long time. Pride was the deadliest of her sins, and it had shaped her attitudes for its protection. Professional detachment was a good shield when there was egg flying.

This time it could land all over her face, and maybe it would be good for her. But the prospect didn't make it any easier to get to sleep.

She could hear from downstairs the muffled sound of her mother's rhythmic snoring, and pulled the pillow over her ears with a groan of fury. She was almost tempted to go down and find the sleeping pills which knocked Poppy out so effectively, but she could not risk a valium hangover in the morning.

Then there was the music, weaving in and out of her hectic thoughts in a way which made sleep entirely impossible. There was something there – something that her tired brain couldn't quite grasp. The Radnesfield theme – it was stronger and clearer than ever . . .

At last, in a fury of irritation, she flung back the covers. It was cold now, with the heating off for the night; she thrust her feet into slippers and pulled on her pink woolly dressing-gown as she padded through to the living-room where she had her treasured Bechstein baby grand.

There wasn't a chance Poppy would wake, but even so she pressed down the soft pedal as she felt her way to the chords and patterns that approximated to the mind music that would not leave her alone. There were the themes she had identified before – Neville and Lilian, Helena and Edward, Sandra Daley, even a chirruping flute for Sally Wagstaff. But as she played and replayed the ever more intricate figures, it emerged more and more strongly – errant, illogical, picking up and weaving lesser strands into one powerful statement – the sound of Radnesfield.

At last she was satisfied that she had caught it, set it down in the black and white of sharps and flats. She had been concentrating on the technicalities; now she could play it, and listen.

It was a strange composition, a fantasia obeying none of the musical rules, harsh and primitive. But it was compelling, and as she played, and thought, she realized that it held more than she had been aware of putting in. There were suggestions of other people, people she did not know, as well as those she did. They formed, yet

171

were subordinate to the main theme, their own development restricted in the final exposition.

As the last, harsh chord died into silence, she sat on the piano stool unmoving, her head bowed. At last she could begin to understand.

13

Saturday, and much of Sunday, had passed for Helena and Stephanie in sedated sleep, but in the long, slow hours of Sunday evening, they sat with Edward in the silent sitting-room of the Red House.

He was frowning over some papers. Stephanie was aimlessly flipping over the pages of a pile of magazines and Helena held a book, though she had not turned a page in the last half-hour.

No one had spoken for a long time. Helena would have been grateful for conversation, for anything that would anchor her more firmly in the real world. It was tempting her again, that state of denial in which she could live only in the present moment where there was animal contentment in not being cold or hungry or in pain. There were so many questions she dare not consider, so much that she must, for her own sanity, shut out.

The sedatives seemed to be lingering, a muzzy fog which made other people seem insubstantial, wraiths in a distant world. She had only to let go, and blessed oblivion would be hers once more.

But then there was Stephanie, Stephanie looking drawn and shadowed today, shivery as if she were coming down with flu. Helena had no right to retreat, leaving Stephanie with cold, ugly reality, unprotected against the confusion and pain and horror that her mother was too cowardly to face. At whatever cost to herself, she must shield Stephanie.

Speaking was an effort of will, to banish a little further off the mists of withdrawal.

'I wonder if you shouldn't just go back to school tomorrow, Stephie. You've given your statement to the police, and they know where to find you. Another day like this won't do you any good.'

Stephanie's face perceptibly brightened, but she said loyally, 'I couldn't do that. I'd feel such a rat, leaving you with all this hanging over –'

'I've got Edward to look after me. I'd be happier, truly, knowing that you had your friends to take your mind off things. And you've got your work to think about too.'

'We-ell –' Her relief was transparent.

Somehow, Helena contrived to sound brisk. 'Fine. I'll take you over in the morning, then. But I do think you should get off to bed now, and have a good rest.'

'I won't sleep!' Stephanie's eyes, which had been drooping, widened with alarm. 'I'll just lie awake, going over it all again.'

'Darling, just try. I don't want to give you anything – you shouldn't get into the habit of taking pills at your age – but you'll probably find you're much sleepier than you think.'

Normally, the issue of going to bed early would have set off an argument, but the girl, it seemed, lacked energy even for that. 'Can I come down if I can't sleep?' was all she said, as she drifted to the door.

'Of course. Have a bath, and see if that helps. Goodnight, love.'

It had cost her to sound bright and purposeful. Helena sank back in her chair, allowing her eyes to close for a moment. The silence, now Stephanie had gone, seemed to be closing about her; she realized she was taking short, anxious breaths, as if struggling for air.

She opened her eyes. Edward was still studying his papers with apparent concentration. She wondered if he had any more idea what he was reading than she did of the contents of the book on her knee. Would it help to drop this façade, find words for whatever mental agonies were thickening the silence in this peaceful room?

But they had never had that sort of relationship. They had come to this marriage two intensely private people; tacitly they had agreed to build a marriage of grace and order and tranquillity – and yes, she supposed, a certain superficiality – and the sun was always going to shine.

But life had been cruel to their pretty little summerhouse. And when the rain descended, and the floods came and the winds blew and beat upon it, there was no rock foundation. They could only patch and patch, and Edward, she suspected, would prefer that she should withdraw tidily to her haven of denial until the storms had passed rather than inflict on him the messiness of emotions she had difficulty in defining, even to herself. She wouldn't know how to begin.

So there was no option but to keep the act going, and give normality her best shot. If there was nothing beyond the illusion, then the show had to go on. She must ignore the foreboding (drug-induced, surely) that they were rolling up the backdrop and starting to run the curtains down.

Her voice sounded quite level as she laid down her book and said, 'I think I might take my own advice and have a leisurely bath. Are you able to have an early night too, Edward? I think you should – it's going to be a difficult week ahead.'

'Yes, I think it is, in every possible way.' He put the cap on his pen with his usual deliberation, laying aside the papers. Under the light cast by the reading-lamp at his side, his deep-set eyes were shadowy. 'You know, I hate to say this, but one of the first things we're going to have to tackle is the business of Stephanie's inheritance.'

She shrank, like a snail with salt burning its tender flesh. 'Oh, Edward! It seems – well, ghoulish even to talk about it, with poor Lilian's body in some police mortuary, and your office still –' She broke off, shuddering.

He was quick to sympathize. 'My darling, I know. It seems the worst sort of insensitivity. But a lifetime's experience of dealing with speculators tells me the vultures will be gathering. If we don't get a phone call from that man tomorrow I'll be astonished. And we should be prepared.'

'Oh, the developer. Of course, he's bound to be anxious.'

'We'll have to be ready to tell him the deal's off. He may turn nasty – after all, it's the second time the thing's fallen through. But Lilian can't have had the trustees' formal consent to the sale, or Stephanie would surely have been informed. So we shouldn't have any technical problem about backing out.'

The light-headed feeling was returning. She wasn't strong enough to cope with this yet, though if she had been feeling less woolly-minded, she should have foreseen it. Edward was bound to see this as the silver lining to the whole grim affair, and she was tempted to give way, weakly, as she had done so many times in the past.

174

But this was for Stephanie. She had no right to indulge her cowardice at Stephanie's expense, even though what she must say would cause the sort of trouble she had spent a lifetime avoiding.

As if from a long way off, she heard her own voice saying, 'Edward, I don't think the trustees will advise Stephanie to withdraw.'

'Well no, they probably won't. You can't expect accountants to appreciate anything but the money side. But you're her mother and sole guardian, so if you and she take a stand, say you definitely don't want it to be sold –'

'No.'

She had said it, and he was gaping at her blankly. However, with the flat negative, it seemed the fog in her brain began to lift.

'Edward, I'm sorry. I know this means a lot to you, but I can't stand in the way of this sale. The trustees will point out that it's a splendid deal because it will be easy to get planning permission. If we turn it down they'll find somewhere else, and Stephanie won't be able to sell at all.'

He got to his feet in some agitation. 'Why should she want to sell? It's a home for her; we could even move back in, if she wanted to –'

Helena stared at him. 'You're not really suggesting, are you, that Stephanie and I move back into the house where Neville was murdered?'

He paused. 'Well no, perhaps not. It's such an ugly house, anyway. But she could let it, I'm sure. It doesn't really matter, as long as this appalling business doesn't go ahead.'

'Edward, why is it so appalling? Oh, I'm sorry for the Wagstaffs, of course, but Stephanie could find them another farm nearby – give them a proper tenancy agreement, so that Jim would have a secure future – but otherwise –'

'Oh, never mind the Wagstaffs. They've been here for barely twenty-five years. I'm talking about the destruction of a unique society, a society that has survived centuries of so-called progress without losing its character.'

She had no strength left for self-control. 'Oh, for goodness' sake!' she snapped. 'You're – you're fossilized! Can't you see that this is a disgusting little place? You love beauty – can't you see how ugly it is, morally as well as physically? As a matter of fact, I think it would be wonderful if all those poisonous, interbred "old families" were swamped by an influx of new people. It's a horrible, diseased sort of atmosphere, where you sense that everyone is guarding secrets that should have had light shone on them years ago. It needs fresh people, and fresh attitudes, and fresh air. So I'm not going to recommend to Stephanie that she back out. I don't even want her to.'

In other circumstances, she would have found Edward's exaggerated dismay comical.

'You mean – you can't mean you wouldn't do this for me? Helena, I beg you to change your mind!'

'How can I? If it were only for me, things would be different. I'd do my best to see your point of view, and yes, if it meant so much to you I might agree, even against my better judgement. But how can I ignore my daughter's interests?

'In any case, Edward, it's not for you. It's for this unspeakable village, and its immediate past record says nothing for the merits of its unique society. All it has ever done for me is to shelter a murderer and let me go to prison instead.'

'And if I assure you, most earnestly, that it would be for me, for both of us –'

Riding the tide of her emotion, she did not listen. 'Then I would assure you that you are over-dramatizing. Don't put me in the position where I must choose between you and Stephanie, because my first loyalty is to my child.'

For a second she thought, with astonished alarm, that he might hit her. She had never before seen a hint that he was capable of a passion so intense; the man who stood before her was a man she did not know. But with a visible effort, he controlled himself.

Uncannily, he said, 'Helena, I hardly recognize you. Let's try to be calm and sensible, and I'll ask you once more. Will you, for my sake, stop this sale?'

There was a part of her which longed to back down, to avoid confrontation. The pliant, passive Helena, so carefully constructed over the years, would submit, then adeptly find cogent, imaginative reasons to justify the decision.

But she was no longer Helena, the Perfect Wife. Too much had happened. Perfect wives did not find themselves in gaol. They did not throw parties where one of the guests ended up dead. They did not look at their husbands, as Helena did now, wondering with

176

detachment how she had ever come to marry him in the first place – this strange, too rigid man with his unhealthy obsession with a community she found repellent.

'No,' said Helena once more.

'And that is positively your last word?'

'It is.'

A muscle in his jaw tightened. 'You – disappoint me, Helena,' was all he said, and walked stiffly from the room.

Slowly the fight drained out of her, and shivering reaction took its place. It had all flared up so unexpectedly, summer lightning from a clear sky. She had had no time to work out a less confrontational response.

But perhaps, in this situation, there was no such thing. In the final analysis, their reactions were visceral, not cerebral. If it broke their marriage, so be it; a marriage which foundered so readily was a charade. Again, the image returned: not only were they bringing down the curtains, but the scenery was starting to fall, with the flames of destruction licking round them in the twilight.

She felt icy cold, her limbs leaden and unresponsive. Slowly, she dragged herself upstairs and ran a hot bath.

The figure waiting on the landing when she came out of the bathroom startled her momentarily, but it was Edward, holding out his hands in smiling reconciliation.

'My darling, I'm sorry I lost my temper. It was inexcusable, when you're so strained and worn out. I suppose I must be upset too. Forgive me?'

It was the plea she could never resist. 'Oh, Edward,' she said, and walked into his arms to be kissed and soothed.

'I'm sorry too,' she said, her voice muffled in his shoulder. 'But Edward, you know –'

'Ssh, ssh,' he scolded her gently. 'We're not going to talk any more tonight. I'm going to tuck you into bed, you're going to take the pills Dr Shepherd left for you, and we'll sort everything out in the morning.'

She allowed herself to be led to bed, sinking gratefully on to the cool softness of the pillows.

'Here you are.' He was holding a glass of water, and two of the brightly-coloured capsules.

'I'm sure one would do, she remonstrated feebly, but smiling he said only, 'Doctor's orders. He said you needed all the rest you can get over the next few days, and I promised to see to it. Don't get up in the morning until you feel ready for it.'

He kissed her forehead, and her eyes shut automatically, like a china doll's when it is laid down.

She had no idea how much later it was when the door opened again, but her head was feeling huge and light, an enormous balloon floating away, and she had to struggle to open her eyes at the sound of Edward's voice, close to her ear.

'Helena, can you hear me? It's Stephanie – she hasn't gone to sleep, and she's getting herself into a bit of a state.'

She tried to raise herself, saying, 'I mustn – musht go to her.' But her lips were flaccid, and her doll's eyes were closing again.

'Stay where you are.' His hands on her shoulders were gentle, but firm. 'I'll give her one of your pills, shall I, and make her some hot chocolate. She'll feel better in the morning after a good night's sleep.'

Reassured, she smiled vaguely. Already the thick, cobwebby curtains of sleep were closing about her.

Once more, Detective-Inspector Coppins was not pleased with his subordinate. He was, in fact, outraged.

A fruitless visit to Lilian Sheldon's agent had kept him in London until late the night before: over his early-morning tea, he had read the newspaper he was now brandishing under Detective- Sergeant Howarth's nose.

'Suicide bid during police grilling,' ran the headline, and she groaned. 'It – it wasn't quite like that, sir,' she offered, not very hopefully.

'I'm hardly daft enough to have supposed it was. You can't get thumbscrews without a magistrate's warrant these days, can you? But it isn't clever. The Chief Constable will get to that rubbish whenever he finishes his mail, and then that phone's going to ring. And when it does, I want to hit him with something positive. We're on borrowed time already. So where do we go from here?'

Frances felt her cheeks start to burn. She could hardly hum him a tune, and the three o'clock theory that had looked so good had fizzled out in an 8 a.m. check.

'What did you get out of them, then?' he prompted. 'I mean, before they started trying to kill themselves?'

'Well, I'm afraid it looks very much as if they're both in the clear.'

'In the clear?' Coppins's bellow was given resonance by a mixture of rage and anguish. 'After all that, they're both *in the clear*?'

'They didn't realize – they each thought the other had done it, so inevitably they reacted oddly. We'll have to check it through, of course, but unless they're both astonishing actors . . .'

She ran down. Coppins, pursing his lips, was absorbing the bad news.

'OK, OK. But I wasted a day checking out the London end, which is stone dead. So you're in the driving seat – what's our lead?'

'Well – more statements, sir. The new information from the Daleys may turn up something fresh. Then question people more thoroughly, concentrating on the village families this time . . .'

His second bellow was even louder than the first. 'That's not a *lead*, sergeant! That's a –'

He was cut short by the ringing of the telephone on his desk. 'Coppins,' he said, still looking daggers at her, then, 'For you.'

Frances took it, with a silent prayer that at this crucial juncture in her police career, Poppy had not been inspired to call her with some domestic complaint. But it was Maxwell Tilson's voice that spoke in her ear.

'Martha Bateman,' he said, without preamble.

'Martha Bateman?' Out of the corner of her eye, she could see Coppins's face brighten.

'Everything points to Martha. She's cock of the walk in the village, and she and Jane are old enemies, which in many ways makes them closer than friends. Reading between the lines, I would lay you a tidy wager that she knows what's going on.'

'She's high on my list of people to see today anyway, so I'll move on that at once. But are you saying she would be capable of actual murder?'

'Capable? Oh, most certainly. I can see Martha with the cushion in her hand and not a moment's compunction. On the other hand, too many people know something, and Martha, I assure you, would never give anything away.'

'Might they merely suspect, and be shielding her?'

'The suggestion, I suppose, is possible. Talk to her anyway, and see what comes of it.'

'I'll do that. Thanks. You've been more than helpful.'

'*Rebus in arduis*, my dear, remember. Good luck.'

'Well?' Coppins pounced hopefully.

'Maxwell Tilson thinks Mrs Bateman might know something she's not telling.'

'Bateman? She's that hatchet-faced cleaning-woman, yes? Looks at us as if we were the sort of thing you find in the bottom of a water-barrel. Now, her I like. Just the type to be obsessional – sees the village as her patch, takes out anyone who threatens it –'

'Tilson seems doubtful.'

'They all want it to be the tramp in the bushes. But let's keep in mind, Frances, that it has to be someone. Soon would be nice. Soon would be very nice. So get to it, will you? I'll be down later in the day, but I've got a meeting here first, if you need to make contact. To tell me you've made an arrest, or anything like that.'

'Yes, sir.' At least she was Frances again, but his determined optimism depressed her even more than she was depressed already.

The phone rang again as she left the room. As she shut the door, she could hear him saying earnestly, 'Well sir, I'm not denying we've had a few problems, and it would certainly be premature to say more at this stage, but we have developed an active and promising line of enquiry. . .'

Frances always thought better in the car, where there were no interruptions and the actions required were purely mechanical. She followed the now-familiar road to Radnesfield without conscious thought.

The original list of suspects was looking increasingly ragged. Jack and Sandra: theoretically, they might have staged the whole thing, but in fact, she believed them. Edward: well-alibied for Neville's death at least by a watchmaker, then a vicar, so try arguing that one in court. George Wagstaff: more likely, in her estimation, to settle the matter with his fists, like his daughter, but no hard alibi for either murder, so he had to be considered along with Chris Dyer and Peter Farrell – haunted by who knew what demons . . . Well, perhaps it was time to widen the net.

She had noted the people Daley had fingered as being involved in the demonstration against Fielding, and they too were on her list of interviews today. Though none of them had been invited to the fatal party, it was no secret that it was taking place. Perhaps Neville's murderer had, after all, thought he had the chance to silence Helena. Or had he known earlier about Lilian's new threat to Radnesfield?

Could it even be a conspiracy? It was hard to imagine, unless it were the tacit conspiracy of silence. Yet even in the cold light of day she could not shake her conviction that the heart of this community was the core of evil.

Martha Bateman, now. She was as near to being that heart as anyone, and within it a powerful and ruthless woman . . .

Martha, the crazed killer. But as she played with the idea, the image that came to mind, more chillingly, was of an executioner, inexorable but just.

Just! That was it. There was a sort of cold, puritanical rectitude about the woman, an adherence to rigid principle, which was not normally characteristic of a killer. The snag was that here they had a different vernacular of morality, and Martha's ideas of justice might be rooted in tenth- rather than twentieth-century principles.

Reaching Radnesfield, she turned the car once more into the Four Feathers forecourt to check in at the trailer before she went across to the Red House to see Mrs Bateman.

The young WPC was alone, sorting out files. She had a round pleasant face, but today she was looking subdued.

'Anything come in, Sue?'

'Chance would be a fine thing. They're all out there asking questions, but you'd need lighted matches under the fingernails here to get an answer to "What's the time?" It's getting to me, I can tell you.'

Frances laughed. 'You're not taken with Radnesfield, then?'

The girl shuddered. 'They don't live in this century, this lot. Andy Smith saw one garden with beehives, all hung round with black streamers. They told him it was because the bees knew there was death about – gives you the shivers, doesn't it?'

'It does, a bit. Well, I'm just on my way to interview another of Radnesfield's attractions – Martha Bateman. Do you know her?'

'Oh, we all know Martha. Three constables have tried asking her questions, and she's chewed them up and spat out the bones. She passed here just a few minutes ago.'

'On her way to the Red House?'

'No, the other direction. Going home, I think.'

'That's lucky. I didn't fancy interviewing her at the Red House with Edward Radley supervising. If I'm not back in an hour, send them with a shovel to scrape me off the carpet.'

It was niggling anxiety which forced its way at last into her drugged state in the morning. It emerged first in convoluted, anxious dreams, where obstacle after crazy obstacle was put in her way. Moaning and muttering, she struggled to break free; several times, the drowsy undertow dragged her back, but at last she forced her eyes open.

The red figures of the digital clock glowed in the darkened room. Nine thirty-four, they said.

Lord, she felt terrible! Her eyes were trying to close again, her head was muzzy, and her tongue seemed thick and swollen. She rolled herself out of bed and groped her way to the bathroom.

Water helped: greedily, she gulped a glassful, then went to stand under a lukewarm shower.

Stephie, that was the thought that had brought her to the surface. Stephanie had been upset last night, but Edward had dealt with it, which was just as well, since she couldn't have moved if the bed had gone on fire. She must sort things out properly before she let her go back to school.

She shied away from the problem of Edward. They had both been overwrought last night; they weren't in the habit of losing their tempers, and they had no practice in coping with the results. She tried to tell herself that perhaps, after all, some sort of compromise would be possible once they talked it through calmly. Things often looked better in the morning.

It was only when she opened her bedroom door that she realized how quiet the house was. Usually by this time Mrs Bateman was pushing a hoover round, clattering plates and slamming doors.

Stephanie would still be asleep, of course, after taking a pill. She wouldn't disturb her, at least until she had had the chance to talk to Edward, who would be downstairs. He never slept late in the morning, however tired he might be.

Sure enough, he was sitting at the breakfast table in the kitchen, presenting a pleasantly domestic picture with a newspaper in his hands. He smiled up at her.

'Now, I thought you might have slept later.' He looked strained and weary still, but sounded determinedly cheerful. 'I even told Martha not to come in, so that she wouldn't wake you – I don't think she knows how to work quietly. Let me make some fresh coffee.'

'Yes, please. It might make me feel rather more as if my head belongs to me. In fact, I woke up worrying about Stephanie. I didn't dream it, did I, that you came in and said she was upset last night?'

A frown crossed his face. 'No, you didn't,' he said slowly. 'Actually, I was sorry you were so dopey – I'd hoped you might still be awake enough to talk some sense into her.'

Helena stiffened. 'What do you mean?'

'Well –' Edward was fiddling with coffee and kettle, as if he found it hard to go on. 'It's awfully stupid, really – you know how irrational they can be at that age, and Stephie's shaken anyway – but she seemed to have gone back to that idiotic notion about Neville, when she was convinced you had done it –'

'Oh, no! Surely she can't – and Lilian? What about Lilian?'

'Yes, Lilian too, that was the thing. She had worked herself up into such a state that she just wasn't prepared to listen to reason. I talked to her, of course – scolded her, really, for being so silly, but in the end the best thing seemed to be just to give her the sedative and leave her till the morning.'

'I must go up to her – explain –' She was on her feet, but Edward gently urged her back into her chair.

'Leave her to have her sleep out. She was wildly over-wrought, and she's much more likely to get things back into perspective once she's properly rested. Drink some coffee at least, and then you'll be better able to cope yourself. There's no point going up in an agitated state and upsetting her all over again.'

It was sensible advice, but twenty minutes later she could bear it no longer.

'I'm going up.' She sprang to her feet, taking Edward by surprise, but as she hurried up the stairs she heard him come out of the kitchen behind her.

There was no answer when she tapped on the door; calling, 'Stephie!' softly, she opened it.

The darkened room was in its usual state of frantic disorder, and Stephanie was only a mass of tangled black hair on the pillow. She did not move as her mother came in, but Helena could no longer contain her anxiety.

'Stephanie,' she said, touching the girl's shoulder, then shaking it a little when there was no response.

It was as she bent towards her sleeping daughter that the small brown bottle, with the rest of the clutter on the table at the bedside, caught her eye. It was her own bottle of sleeping pills, and it was empty.

14

Martha Bateman had never dealt in uncertainties. Through ancestral osmosis, she had always been sure how the Old Ones would have thought, and the principles, until now, had been clear. But her lips were pleated into a thin line as she let herself into her cold, quiet, tidy house.

She went into the sitting-room and hovered, looking about her, but there was not so much as a stray speck of lint to pick up from the carpet. What she needed to take her mind off things was to give something a good turn out, but there was nothing to do.

She lifted a cushion which did not need plumping, and shook it vigorously. She turned to pick up another, and, in turning, her eye fell on the photograph on the mantelpiece.

She picked it up, automatically rubbing the already dazzling brass of the cheap frame on the edge of her sleeve, and looked at the picture of the boy with his too-eager smile and bright, unfocused eyes. She gulped, and her eyes went to the only other photograph in the room; the picture of a woman in late middle age, handsome rather than pretty, with strongly-marked brows and a square, definite chin. Her eyes were clear and commanding.

Martha's gaze dropped. 'I can't,' she muttered. 'You made me promise, but I got to break it – I got to!'

She jumped at the knock on the door, but when she saw Frances Howarth on the doorstep, her shoulders sagged in a movement that almost suggested relief.

'Mrs Bateman, I know you've spoken to the police already, but I think it's time you and I had a talk.'

The woman did not make the sharp rejoinder Frances had expected. She stood aside, saying only, 'You'd best come in then, since you're here.'

Frances followed her through into the neat living-room: her quick eyes noticed the picture of the boy, laid flat on the table as if it had just been set down.

'Your son?' She picked up the photograph.

'He were.' It was almost snatched from her hands, set up again on the mantelpiece in its accustomed place.

'I'm sorry.'

Martha sneered, openly. 'That's the right thing to say, isn't it? Don't mean much.'

'I didn't know your son, obviously, but I'm sorry for anyone who has that particular grief.'

Martha looked away, and the aggression went out of her; she turned, saying, as if to herself, 'Better off where he is,' and Frances, looking again, saw with renewed pity the tell-tale signs of retardation. But she had to go on.

With a confidence she was far from feeling, she perched on the unyielding edge of the moquette sofa: after a moment's pause, Martha sat down on an upright chair as far from her inquisitor as possible.

'Well?' she said provocatively, 'Aren't you going to start asking me them questions?'

'It would probably be better to say I just want you to talk to me. I'm a foreigner here, and it's becoming plain that we need answers to questions we don't know to ask. But you know, Mrs Bateman – you know, but you've chosen not to tell anyone.'

The other woman became visibly agitated. 'I'm – I'm sure I don't know what you mean . . . .'

Frances, though she did not show it, was surprised. She had expected cold hostility; she had found, instead, a troubled woman, and these she had dealt with before.

Her tone had been authoritative. Now she sat back, sounding relaxed, almost casual.

'Oh, I'm not asking you for a statement, or taking notes. It's just an informal chat. And I'm not in a hurry. I can sit here all day, until you feel like talking.'

'You'll do no such thing!' She was definitely shaken.

'No? Are you going out?'

'My husband – comes home for his dinner, he does; won't be best pleased to find you've forced your way in here.'

'Then wouldn't it be better to talk to me now, so that I can leave you with plenty of time to get his meal ready?'

Martha glared at the voice of sweet reason and closed her mouth as if it would never open again. The silence prolonged itself and became oppressive.

Unused to this weapon, Martha's nerve broke. Jumping to her feet, she exclaimed, 'Oh, let's have done with this here nonsense. I don't know what you want, that I don't.'

'Tell me about the woman in the picture.' Using the silence, Frances had noted that this was the only other photograph in the room, and that it had a handsome leather presentation case.

Martha took it up, as if to remove it from the desecration of her gaze. 'Mrs Radley, that is. *My* Mrs Radley – not that other woman.'   'Not Mrs Helena Radley, you mean? You don't approve of her?'

Martha sniffed. 'Nothing special wrong with her, except she were another man's wife, to my way of thinking. Nothing good comes of that sort of thing, and so I told him. Anyway, *she* said he shouldn't marry – that I told him too. But he were beyond all by then, paying no heed –'

'She? The late Mrs Radley?'

'She were a saint, with all she had to put up with, a saint and a wise woman. Owed her everything, I did, would have done anything for her, anything she asked. And now –'

Her voice shook, and she stopped. Resisting the temptation to prompt her to finish the sentence, Frances said gently, 'You must have been very fond of her.'

Martha looked down at the picture. 'She were kind –' She faltered again.

'Tell me what happened, Martha.' The detective's voice was melodious, warm, insistent.

There were tears on the woman's cheeks; she stood silent for a moment, then, pulling out a pristine man's handkerchief, mopped her eyes and blew her nose, savagely. She sat down again on the chair, her spine so erect that it did not touch the chairback.

'All right,' she said harshly. 'Maybe she'd have wanted it, at that.' She sat with the photograph cradled in her roughened hands as if it were a talisman.

'I were fifteen when I went into service up at the House, fifteen and never been a night over the doorstep. But my pa died, and my ma, she had my sister to help her with the young 'uns then, and if the wages wasn't much, I got my keep anyways.

'Hard work, it were, but I never been afraid of hard work, nor never knew anything different. And Mrs Radley, she were a good mistress.'

Frances's quick ear picked up the emphasis, slight but definite. 'And Mr Radley?'

The steely look returned. 'I don't never say that bastard's name. There's nothing too bad for him, not if he fries in hell till Doomsday. I never spoke of it to no one, but you that's so clever, you can guess.'

'He got you pregnant?'

She could hardly bring herself to nod. 'We was a good family, my ma a regular church-goer, and brought me up to respect myself, but I hadn't no say, had I? Then she found me crying one day.'

'Mrs Radley?'

'Blackleading the grate in the drawing-room, I were, worried sick because I were beginning to show – she got me to tell her, had a sort of way with her. You couldn't help it, not when she looked at you with them great grey eyes. And she believed me. Plenty would have turned me off, but she knew what he were like. Not at first she didn't, or she wouldn't never have married him, but by then she did, poor lady. She knew Joe and me had been walking out of a Sunday, and she made it all right with him, gave him the money so he could marry me right away. So if it weren't for her, wouldn't be a respectable married woman, would I? I'd be a tart, and I'd have broke my ma's heart. So there weren't nothing I wouldn't do for her.'

'And then the baby was born.'

Martha met her eyes defiantly. 'That's right. And he were never quite – right, as you might say. But I loved him anyways. He were my boy, and even if he might be – difficult, a bit rough, maybe, he were all I had. Joe took the money, but he never loved me after that – never pretended to –'

'Mrs Radley was sympathetic about your son?'

'Well, she would be, being as she knew –' The woman broke off.

In the corner of the sofa, Frances became very still. They had come, she realized with a prickling of the hairs on the back of her neck, to the dark heart of it.

187

'Knew?'

For a moment she feared Martha would not answer. Then the words came tumbling out, as the last defence was breached.

'All the Radleys. Back as far as we know, they been – strange. Oh, some been all right, mostly. But – violent – anyone could tell you that. Mrs Radley's ma-in-law, the old lady, she left Radnesfield House after her husband tried to kill her. Oh, we all knew that – but nobody never said. There were never what you might call proof, and we didn't want nobody poking their nose in here. We all lived with the Radleys, all these years, they're all right –'

Frances gaped at her. 'You don't mean – there haven't been murders before?'

'No, not murders, exactly. Just – sort of – accidents. Not within the village, mind.' She seemed to be offering this as an excuse. 'Just, maybe, a poacher from Limber, something like that . . .'

The heart of darkness, indeed. And bloodlines running all through the village, presumably, if the recent late Mr Radley was representative of his ancestors. Sickened, Frances challenged her. 'Are you saying there is a homicidal strain in the Radleys?'

'No, no, not that. It's just – there was always these – accidents –' Her voice ran down into silence, and she would not look up.

'And the present generation? Edward? Was that why his mother didn't want him to marry – so the strain would die out?'

'That's right, so they'd be gone, so that was all right.'

She had spoken too eagerly; with professional instinct, Frances pressed the question. 'Edward?'

'I promised her – promised her when she were dying!' The words broke from her like a sob. 'Said I would look after him, like if he were my own boy . . . And he weren't like his brother, no; his brother, he were all bad, like his pa, and going the same way –'

'The brother who was shot?' Frances was upright on the edge of the sofa now, and seeing the other woman turn her head away, grabbed her so that she dropped the photograph. 'Martha, you've got to tell me. How – did – he – die?'

'It were an accident.' She was mumbling, ducking and weaving her head in evasion. 'An accident, that's what it were, that's what we was told. Mrs Radley, she said it were a tragic accident, so we knew. Her sons, they was, and he were a desperate bad lot, deserved all he got, we reckoned –'

Frances dropped her hands as if they had become red-hot. 'Are you saying that you all knew he had killed his brother, and you – *and his mother* – did nothing?'

'Not knew,' she maintained. 'Not knew, exactly.' Her look at Frances was almost sly. 'Police said it were an accident, anyways, didn't they? They should know, they should. And she'd lost one son. Where would be the point, taking away the other one?'

Frances had to turn her head to conceal her revulsion. 'And the murders?'

The woman shifted, uneasily. 'We didn't *know*, rightly . . .'

'Dear god, no wonder Radnesfield has tried to keep strangers out! Heaven knows what may come out in the course of time.'

'Well, he's in a world of his own, we knew that. But he's one of the old families, and foreigners who come here, ruining everything –'

She stopped, suddenly aware of where the sentence was leading her.

Professional detachment had gone. Frances looked at her with open horror. 'I think you're all mad – all quite, quite mad! And the sooner we get Radley restrained, the safer everyone will be –'

And then she stopped. 'His alibi,' she said. 'He's got an alibi for Neville Fielding's murder. It's the only one that holds water.'

Martha stiffened. 'An alibi? Do you mean –?'

Frances could read her face as the emotions swept over it. Relief, first and foremost: then rage, that she had been unnecessarily lured into confession.

Her shoulders straightened. 'Well, that's all right then, isn't it? And the other – well, I daresay it were just a lot of talk, load of old gossips we have down the village, talking a lot of rubbish. You just forget what I said to you now, it'll do nobody no good.'

Frances barely heard her. 'Last night, I thought I had it at last – he just seemed to fit, somehow. But this morning I went right through that evidence, and there isn't a crack. He left the house, walked straight to Willie Comberton's; someone saw him going in there; left at twenty to on the grandfather clock – Comberton's unshake-able on that – then was met by the vicar seven minutes later –'

Martha was staring at her, her shoulders sagging once more. 'Comberton's clock? His alibi?' Her cackle of laughter was humourless. 'Well, you lot don't know nothing around here, do you? Comberton's clock, that's a byword in this village.'

189

'What do you mean? It was checked by a constable on the Monday after Fielding's death, and it was almost exactly right.'

'That were on Monday. Well, Monday it would be right, wouldn't it? He winds it and sets it right Sunday night, but being he's a clockmaker, he won't admit he can't make his own clock run true. By Saturday, it's all of twenty minutes out, though he won't agree to that, will he? Everybody knows that.'

'Oh yes,' Frances said bitterly. 'Everybody who matters doesn't have to be told. And as a result of your selective discretion, two people are dead, and one has been wrongfully imprisoned. What about poor Helena Radley?'

Martha dropped her eyes. 'Nothing we could do – nobody asked us, did they, and Mr Edward, he told me she would get off . . .'

'Oh, what's the use? I'm simply wasting my time. I'd better get round to the Red House before he decides that he really has a taste for it.'

She was on the way to the door when she sensed Martha's unnatural stillness. She turned, to see that the woman's high colour had drained from her cheeks.

'I – I couldn't get in this morning,' she stammered. 'You put it out of my mind. But there were a note on the door, saying they was all sleeping late –'

Frances was out of the house and running along the street towards the Red House before Martha could get to her feet.

Helena's heart seemed to stop. After a second of frozen immobility, she grabbed Stephanie frantically, turning her over, and her body flopped slowly and horribly on to its back. Too horror-stricken to scream, she felt the cheek; it was still warm, though clammy, and the faintest of faint breaths was still moving the dry, parted lips.

'Oh, thank god, thank god,' she sobbed, starting to slap at the girl's cheeks in an attempt to rouse her. 'Edward! Edward!' she screamed, finding her voice, and heard him taking the last flight of stairs two at a time.

'Stephanie – overdose!' she gasped as he came in and stood, looking shocked, on the threshold.

190

'Oh no! the pills?'

She nodded.

'It's my fault – it's all my fault!' He was wringing his hands. 'I must have left them there, after I gave her one. How could I be so criminally careless, when she was so distraught –'

'Never mind that! An ambulance, get an ambulance!'

'My dear,' he said gently, putting an arm round her shoulders, 'perhaps the police. . .'

'She's alive!' she snapped. 'For heaven's sake, hurry!'

'Alive!' he said, and he was very still. 'Are you – are you sure?'

'Yes, yes,' she sobbed. 'Now go!'

She barely registered his footsteps going down the stairs again, slow and heavy, as if he were carrying a great weight. She was concentrating on her child, willing her to take the next breath, calling to her, shaking her, trying to bring her back to the life that was almost visibly ebbing away.

She tried to raise Stephanie, but the girl was as big as her mother, and in her inert state too heavy to lift. Perhaps Edward would manage, get her moving, while she phoned.

She flew downstairs, calling, 'Edward!'

He was standing in the hall, the telephone in his hand, jiggling the rests. 'That's strange,' he said, without turning. 'It seems to be out of order.'

'Then fetch the police! They're only across the square, and they'll know what to do.'

But he didn't move. And at that moment, she saw the trailing flex of the telephone, pulled from its jackpoint.

For a fraction of a second, her brain refused to register the implication of what her eyes had seen. Then she was across the hall, wrestling with the key in the front door.

But it was stiff, her fingers were clumsy, and he was on her, his arms pinning her hands to her sides, dragging her back from the doorway to help, safety and sanity. 'Helena, Helena,' he kept groaning, as if in pain. 'I didn't want this – you made me do it, Helena!'

He was not a great deal taller than she, but his strength seemed to her, in her terror, almost superhuman. But this was her daughter's life as well as her own, and lashing out, biting, scratching, she fought like an alley cat.

191

He seemed impervious to the wounds she was inflicting. She was forced to give ground, until at last he had backed her into the corner of the staircase.

They were face to face now, and she could see that there were tears pouring down his cheeks. 'Edward,' she begged, frantically, 'please – don't do it! Please let me go! I'll help you, do anything –'

Unspeaking, he shook his head. She was totally cornered now. His body weight held her pinned, her left arm immobilized by the angle of the stairs. Slowly, still shaken by sobs, he raised his hands, and now they were beginning to tighten round her throat.

He had left her right arm free. Groping blindly, with nothing left but the instinct for self-preservation, her fingers encountered something – something fine and feathery; the draping fronds of cupressus.

She had set them there herself, a lifetime ago, on Saturday before party guests started arriving. It had been an effective arrangement; daffodils, freesias, cupressus and winter jasmine in a holder set on top of the huge heavy-based pewter candlestick which always stood on the chest at the foot of the stairs.

Her sudden lunge took him by surprise, and then it was in her hand – two pounds of weighted metal. The flowers cascaded to the ground as she brought it up with all her strength, making sharp contact just above his left ear.

His eyes widened in shock, pain, and, it seemed, reproach, before his hands loosened from about her throat and he slumped to the floor to lie, as if laid out already for burial, on a bier of crumpled spring flowers.

'Oh god, oh god, what have I done?' She dropped the candlestick, and with her hands over her mouth as if to stifle a rising scream, backed away from her victim.

In the grip of shock, she knew only that she must open the door, though it needed painful concentration to steady her hands enough to turn the key. At last she wrenched the door wide just as Frances Howarth appeared at the gate, a constable hurrying up in her wake.

At the sight, Helena, dishevelled and frantic, stopped dead, then burst into peal after peal of hysterical laughter.

'Just – just the person I wanted to see! You can tell me. I've killed my husband – do you hear me? I've killed him. And what I want to know – what I want to know is, if I've served my time for killing one husband when I didn't, but I've killed another one instead, is it all square?'

15

It was half-past eight when Frances drove wearily back to Radnesfield. There were files she must collect before she could start making her report, and she preferred to fetch them tonight. Then, with luck, she need never set foot in this evil little place again.

The operation was winding down and the trailer was in darkness, the extra manpower that had been drafted in already deployed elsewhere. She let herself in, snapped on the light and looked round at the piles of papers on the worktop with revulsion.

It had been a long, gruelling day. The lingering pressmen still staked out in the square had found themselves with ringside seats for the dramatic events of the morning, and tomorrow's papers would no doubt feature sensational headlines and a lot of rhetorical questions about police effectiveness. What fun it must be, she thought savagely, as she sorted through a mountain of statements, to be able to ask questions without dealing with the answers people gave you.

There had been television cameras, too, of course, and poor Joe Coppins dragged out of his meeting to explain this mayhem during a police investigation. He had done a sturdy job of stone-walling, but in the context of shots of Stephanie being carried out on a stretcher, and Edward, the square of plaster on his head clearly visible, being marched to a car in handcuffs, it all sounded distinctly lame. They had dragged out all the footage from Helena's trial too, and got one of the more magisterial interviewers to make the point that surely this must raise the question of wrongful imprisonment, to which the answer could only be yes.

It didn't feel quite like that from this side. Helena had pleaded guilty on the expensive advice of a leading barrister, after all, and for the record books, cleaning up Lilian Sheldon's murder in less than forty-eight hours wasn't so bad. But she would have to admit that it didn't look good, and that she felt responsible.

Coppins was in the front line, because it was his case. Technically. But by a conspiracy of events – no, she corrected herself scrupulously, by a conspiracy of events *and* her own determination to fly solo, she had become involved, as bystander, catalyst and even participant. She hadn't taken him into her confidence, exposing her fledgeling theories to his shrewd scrutiny, partly because she didn't like being wrong and partly because she had wanted, childishly, to lay down all the cards and say 'Gin!'

She had gone to him before she left for Radnesfield, and offered to put in her resignation. She had been sincere, but in her current mood of acid self-appraisal she admitted there had also been a touch of secret pride in her own high-mindedness.

Across the desk, he had looked at her sardonically from under heavy brows.

'Nice little spot of drama to round off the day? I should have thought today's events would have satisfied anyone's appetite for histrionics.'

'Sir – ' she protested, but he held up his hand.

'Spare me! I've had a long day. You've still got an awful lot to learn, sergeant, haven't you? If this is the worst you ever have to take in the police force, you can count yourself lucky. And if you offer yourself up as a martyr, you're inviting people to throw stones.

'You didn't point out that I should have listened to you in the first place, and I might even agree with you, if I were into self-flagellation, which I'm not. Take it from me, as a sport, it's over-rated.

'Just use the wits the good lord gave you, Frances, will you? Write it up so it looks as good as you can make it, then we'll keep our heads down for a bit. They'll be so grateful to find we didn't beat anyone up round the back of the station or plant evidence on them that they'll probably give us a citation.'

So she still felt responsible, but now she felt foolish as well. Yes, it had been a very gruelling day. She was tired, and foul-tempered, and when the tap came at the door, even the sight of Mr Tiggywinkle poking his nose round it, almost sniffing the air like his namesake, was not engaging.

'Can I help you?' she said, ice forming on the words as she spoke.

He looked comically crestfallen. 'That's a very forbidding greeting, I always think, don't you? I don't want to disturb you – '

She did not quite say, 'Then go away,' but the thought hung almost audibly on the air between them.

'I'm sorry. I shall, of course, withdraw immediately and leave you to your labours. It was merely that I happened to see your car arrive, and wondered whether you had eaten? Jane has left me a quite enormous beef carbonnade – she has rather a way with it, I fancy – and if I had a guest, it would justify opening a bottle of an interesting Rioja I've been anxious to try.'

Beef carbonnade. She had not eaten since an early breakfast, but she shook her head. 'You're very kind, but I have one or two things to finish here, and then I must get back.'

He nodded, retreating sadly. As he reached the door, she added, with some measure of compunction, 'In any case, I'm not fit company for anyone tonight. I wouldn't like you to think I was ungrateful for all your help, but I'm in a very bad mood, best left to myself.'

He brightened immediately. 'If you change your mind,' he said with a wave, and she saw him scuttle off across the square, as if anxious that his linens might be scorching.

She turned back to her files. Once she had done this, she could go home. But home to what? Another inquisition from Poppy, a solitary Scotch and a TV dinner. Beef carbonnade . . .

'You must have been very sure I would come.' Frances settled back into one of the big leather armchairs with a groan that was half-pain, half-pleasure as she relaxed her aching shoulders.

The bottle had been standing on a side-table, already open, and he was pouring it into two goblets. The beef stew, on a hot-plate beside it with a dish of baked potatoes, was sending out an aroma so exquisitely sensuous that she almost groaned again.

'You would not expect me to be so crude as to suggest that when a lady says no she sometimes means yes. But you had, it seemed to me, the air of one in need of a confidant, and I, as you know, am the very persona of discretion.'

'Even if the *Sun* offered you £100,000?'

'Sadly, my dear Frances, at my advanced age large sums of money cease to have any great attraction. *Tempus edax rerum* – and when time has devoured the appetites which these funds might be expected to feed . . . But talking of appetites, may I help you to some of this?'

'I thought you'd never ask.' Frances eyed the heaping plateful hungrily. 'That's wonderful.'

He served himself, then, sitting down with the air of one accustomed to bringing meetings to order, 'Now, first of all, tell me about that poor child. I've been thinking about her, and about the whole sad situation, all day.'

'Stephanie's remarkable. She's not hard or uncaring, but she's certainly tough. When I called in at the hospital she was eating a hearty meal and inclined to be indignant at her own naïvety.'

'She hadn't suspected Edward?'

'Not for an instant. She had always compared him to her father, I would guess, and had him pegged as a rather wimpish figure. She was even fond of him, in a slightly patronizing way, and of course she had come to depend on him quite a bit when Helena was in prison.

'She drank the hot chocolate he had so thoughtfully brought up for her without a qualm, so it was only luck that saved her. The doctor said that when Edward emptied in the contents of the capsules and stirred it, quite a lot would sink into the sludge at the bottom. In fact it made her so sleepy that she didn't even finish it. But even so, if Helena hadn't found her . . .'

She fell silent, looking into the fire.

'And Helena? How is she?'

'Not too good. They've got her in the private wing under sedation at the moment, but they think she'll need a lot of psychiatric help. With all she's gone through, it's hardly surprising. She seemed almost punch-drunk, when she was trying to explain what had happened.'

He nodded, but did not pursue the subject. 'I think, you know, one tended to think of Edward rather as poor Stephanie did, though I was always aware of quite a formidable determination when there was something he wanted. Would you have got him, do you think, without this last mad effort?'

'We were on our way to take him in, after I'd managed to get Martha Batemen to talk, on your suggestion. That's what makes the whole thing so galling.'

She allowed him to top up her glass, then had the satisfaction of seeing him, for once, totally confounded, as she told him Martha's tale.

'There are the families, now you mention it,' he said slowly. 'The Edes – a couple of them have done time for assault, and there are one or two others where a violent temper runs in the family, like red hair. But I had no idea . . . And to think that I believed I knew something about them.' His tone was vexed. 'Even Jane has never given me the slightest hint of this.'

'You're a foreigner too,' she said brutally. 'They may tolerate you, but you're on the outside, by definition, because you aren't privy to that sort of information. No one needs to be told, because they've always known. And they would view talking about it as breaking a tribal taboo. You almost feel they have different gods – ugly, primitive, powerful ones.'

He was eying her sceptically, and she was defensive. 'Oh, I know it sounds whimsical. But I came on the vicar yesterday, praying after the Sunday service, and it gave me cold shivers. He seemed overwhelmed by a sense of evil gathering about him. If that was a response to a spiritual atmosphere –'

He shook his head. 'They're not as heathen as you think, you know. Some will have suffered very troubled minds in these last few months, and they will have gone to him – told him something, but not enough. He's been under a lot of strain, and that wife of his is more of a hindrance than a help-meet.'

'You're probably right. It's the atmosphere of the place – it makes one fanciful. And I'm feeling upset about the whole thing anyway. Poor Coppins is taking the flak, but I can't help feeling I sparked it all into action when I came to see Helena. Openers for the last act, if you like.'

'Coincidence,' he said crisply. 'Nothing more than a curtain-raiser. It was bound to happen whenever Lilian announced that she was going to sell.'

'Yes, I suppose it was. And I suppose that even if Edward had done nothing further we'd have reached him sooner or later, given enough leg-work. He was always an obvious suspect, but then his alibi seemed rock solid. We questioned Willie Comberton twice, you know, and he was adamant about the time on his clock –'

'Willie Comberton's clock! But everyone knows –'

'Don't you start! *Everyone* has known everything, all along, except the poor benighted fuzz, but no one has thought to mention it. It's been like working in the dark with sheets draped over the furniture.'

'And have you managed to twitch them off now?'

'Oh, Radley's been extremely frank. He's the despair of his lawyers – he's wanted to tell us all about it.'

'Boasting?'

'No, not that, exactly. He just seems to think that once he's explained it properly, no one could possibly blame him for what he did.'

'*Tout comprendre, c'est tout pardonner.*'

'Something like that. Apparently, on the day of Neville's murder, he walked along to Comberton's house with Helena's watch, which had broken. Then at two-forty on Willie's clock he went out through his back garden and up through the wood beyond to Radnesfield House, which explains why Sandra Daley didn't see him from her window. Neville was, as it happened, in his study alone; they argued, then, when Neville turned round to get plans for the new estate out of his desk – simply to gloat, as far as I can make out – Edward seized the poker and struck him down. Then of course, he returned the same way, met the vicar, and there was his alibi, intact. Quite straightforward.'

Tilson stared at her. 'But how could he possibly have set that up – Neville alone, ready to be killed with a handy poker? I can understand the rest of the planning, all quite well thought-out, but –'

Frances smiled wryly. 'There wasn't any planning. That was the irony of the whole thing – it was just the way it happened. Edward, you see, famously loses his temper – it's what the Radleys do from time to time. But it passes quickly, and then he's quite calm and normal and, indeed, detached from what he has done. He went up through Willie's garden, not to escape observation, but because that was the route he had used since he was a child. He didn't reckon on Willie's clock providing an alibi; he hadn't thought about it till we asked him, because he hadn't planned to kill Fielding. He simply lost his temper when the man, as he saw it, refused to see reason. He wasn't even being clever about fingerprints; he just happened to be wearing gloves because it was a cold day.'

'Then how in the world did he expect to get away with it?'

Frances reflected, choosing her words carefully. 'I think, you know, he believed at some level that within the village, no matter what he did, nothing could touch him. His ways were their ways, and as long as no one got in to dig too deeply, they were all able to cover up for each other. It might be quite instructive to analyse any accidental deaths over the last thirty years and see if any of them have the hallmarks of violence. Wife-beating, as far as I can make out, is endemic, and accepted as a normal part of life.

'And then, of course, Radley had killed before, on impulse, when he fell out with his brother, and it had been made all right for him – very much all right, because he got exactly what he wanted. Insofar as he thought about it at all, I think he felt that here, in Radnesfield, the magic would work again. It almost did.'

'But Helena! He seemed quite devoted to her – how could he let her take the blame?'

'Now that is quite a curious piece of double thinking. He believes it to have been entirely her own fault; in fact, I'm not sure he's ever forgiven her. If she had gone into the witness box and admitted guilt and penitence, as her lawyer recommended, it could have been a suspended sentence.'

'*Ergo*, she deserved to go to prison.' Tilson shook his head. 'I hear what you are saying, but I can't quite take it in.'

'You should be used to it. They all behave like that around here, with that sort of Alice in Wonderland moral logic. Martha Bateman – but don't let me get started on her twisted psychology, or we'll be here all night. And I'm exhausted.'

Replete, she yawned and stretched uninhibitedly. Tilson looked alarmed.

'Now, you mustn't go without telling me about Lilian.'

'Lilian? Nothing to tell, there, really. That one, I don't think we could ever have pinned on him, if he weren't behaving as if he thought he should get a medal for doing it. The perfect crime, that was. He saw his chance, when Helena took Lilian to lie down; like another half-dozen people, he heard them talking, and of course he'd been on the look-out for his chance ever since Mrs Bateman had told him about Lilian's plans in the morning. It wasn't murder in a homicidal fit of temper, like Neville's; it was quite cold-blooded. He heard the waitress say she was asleep so, with a quick look round, he slipped in, held the cushion over her face, and went out through the garden door after checking there was no one to see him. He went back in through the kitchen door, which is only a few yards away, and apart from that made no effort to cover his tracks – and basically there weren't any.

'Where he did fall down hopelessly was in the attempt on Stephanie's life. And there, you see, he had tried frantically and quite incompetently to make it look like suicide. He told Helena that Stephanie was in a state the night before, when Helena was too doped to react, in an effort to set the scene. He said he had left the pills accidentally where she had taken them, but the mug on the table was full of powder dregs, while the capsules he had emptied – leaving fingerprint evidence all over them – were in the bin downstairs.

'So he wasn't clever at all, just lucky – if you could call it that. Certainly the devil looked after his own.'

'Will he be fit to plead?'

Frances shrugged. 'His lawyer will strongly deny it, of course, and bring in any number of shrinks to expound in bewildering scientific detail the theory of hereditary insanity. They may be right, at that, but the prosecution can point out that all his efforts had good sound motives – solidly financial, in two cases, after all – and since his conduct is otherwise rational, he may be judged as fit to serve a prison sentence as the next man.'

'Either way, I cherish little hope that he will be incarcerated for any realistic length of time.' Tilson sighed. 'The older I become, the less I understand the judicial system. Do you think he'll kill again?'

'Who knows? I don't believe there will be meaningful rehabilitation, if you want the jargon. Perhaps this whole thing will tip him over the edge into insanity, or perhaps if his ancestral cess pit becomes an ordinary, not-very-attractive small commuter town, the focus of his obsession may be removed. We've played our part, anyway, and tomorrow the show will be somewhere else.

'No, no thank you. I won't have another glass of wine. I'm driving, and it's time I did. I shall go home and have a long, scented bath in an attempt to get the stench of this whole thing out of my nostrils.'

She got to her feet, yawning again. 'Well, I certainly did the talking tonight. I hope you're satisfied.'

'My dear child, I have been honoured by your confidence, and feel positively sated after having the itch of curiosity so royally assuaged.'

Frances sighed. 'At least that's a job finished, even if a botched job.'

'Don't blame yourself. You may have felt involved in events, but in Radnesfield that is a delusion. You are merely watching them take place from the other side of the glass.'

She looked at him curiously. 'Will you go on living here, after all this?'

He did not hesitate. 'Oh yes. You accused me of social voyeurism, once, in a telling image involving slugs. But with the merciless approach of second childishness, one recovers one's boyhood fascination with the most extraordinary pets. I think I shall enjoy watching their adaptation to a new habitat.'

He blinked at her benevolently, but suddenly the sharp bright eyes seemed cold, somehow inhuman, the hedgehog nose almost snuffling already in the anticipation of a succulent reward for this scrabbling in mud and dirt. She grabbed her coat and bag in almost indecent haste, and made for the door.

'I really must go. Tomorrow we have Lilian's inquest, as well as ordeal by Press and television. And tonight I'll have ordeal by mother as well; she hates to see me mixed up in these sordid situations. She can't understand why I don't teach music in a nice girls' school, and to tell you the truth I'm not sure I know why, either.'

She thanked him profusely as she took her leave, but could not quite bring herself to bestow the kiss on the cheek he so obviously expected. None the less, he waved her off with undiminished good humour, the light streaming from the doorway behind him outlining his short, stocky figure and the aureole of fuzzy white hair.

The street was deserted as she drove through Radnesfield for the last time, the lighted windows close-curtained and the pub in darkness.

She groped for a cassette to slot into the player. It didn't matter what; anything to blot out the Radnesfield fantasia which still beat so remorselessly through her brain.

But as she reached the main road, the car's headlights picked up the fingerposts at the staggered crossroads, and she paused for a moment to study them. 'Radnesfield', one said, the other 'Dusebury', pointing over the road in the other direction.

'That was the crossroads in our life', Helena had said once, 'when Neville chose the Radnesfield turning.'

Would it have made any difference, anyway? Perhaps Dusebury was a pretty village, with a green and a duck-pond with white ducks, and an old grey stone pub full of jolly villagers, and the whole thing was just a freakish chance. Fielding had seen it as destiny, but perhaps he was no more than a discarded match tossed into a powder keg.

Or had they brought it upon themselves? Nasty Neville and Helena, victim and martyr – had their sick little dramatic creations taken on an evil life of their own?

There was never going to be an answer to that question. Turning the music up even louder, she drove away.